LATE
CHECKOUT

LATE CHECKOUT

A MESS HOPKINS NOVEL

ALAN ORLOFF

Also by Alan Orloff

Diamonds for the Dead
Killer Routine
Deadly Campaign
The Taste
First Time Killer
Ride-Along
Running From the Past
Pray for the Innocent (ITW Thriller Award Winner)
I Know Where You Sleep (Shamus Award Finalist)
I Play One On TV (Agatha Award Winner, Anthony Award Winner)
Sanctuary Motel

To my fam: Janet, Mark, and Stuart

Praise for Late Checkout

"Mess Hopkins, Alan Orloff's charming and self-deprecating modern-day Robin Hood, gets better with every outing."—Donna Andrews, *New York Times* bestselling author of the Meg Langslow series

Chapter One

They said you could pick your friends, but you couldn't pick your family. I didn't know who *they* were, but—sadly—they had a point. A damn good point. I got along with my parents okay—as long as they were traveling the world and basically incommunicado.

My Uncle Phil, however, was another story. He was a constant pain in my side. My *back*side. I stared at his name on my phone's screen, finger hovering over *Decline*. I wasn't in the mood to hear his monthly lecture, but if I didn't answer, he'd just hound me until I did.

I sighed, hit *Answer*, and flopped on my bed in Room 13 of the Fairfax Manor Inn. I ran the motel, and one of the perks—if you could call it that—was a room to live in. *Home sweet home.*

"Hello, Uncle Phil. How are you?"

"Fine, Benjamin, fine. I'd like to discuss a few things with you."

Phil was the only person who didn't call me by my nickname, Mess. It irked me, not because I didn't like the name, but because he was deliberately trying to antagonize me. Of course, I tried to get his goat whenever I could, too. *Ah, families.*

I supposed I loved him—after all, my parents instilled in me a fierce devotion to family at all costs. *No matter what*, family always comes first. Hell, I'd take a bullet for my sister Izzy or her two daughters. But that didn't mean I had to *like* every member of my family.

"Benjamin? You still there?"

"Yes. I'm listening."

"The motel has lost money nine months in a row. Even you must realize that's not a sustainable business model." As usual, the subject of today's lecture was my poor business acumen.

We usually had these discussions in the wood-paneled den of his mini-mansion in McLean. He nursed a scotch, no matter what time of day, while I drank water. Not because I liked water so much, but because I liked being a contrarian, especially when it came to my uncle.

"Look, I can't be responsible for the entire economy, right?" I said. "When things are tight, people stop traveling. And when they don't travel, they don't need to stay in motels."

"I don't think the economy is the problem here, Benjamin."

"So what *is* the problem?" I braced for the inevitable.

"You could stop giving rooms away, for a start."

Same admonition, every month. I gave him my stock answer. "I'm helping people, Uncle Phil. People who need help. People without a home or who are escaping a bad situation. People who could just use a warm—or cool—place to lay their head and regroup. Don't you have any compassion?"

"There's no need to attack me personally. This is a business. And I'm not against helping the needy. To a point. But I think you've gone overboard. It reflects poorly on our property to have all these vagrants squatting there."

Our property? "My parents put me in charge, and I'm running this place as I see fit. Besides, they're not vagrants. They are my guests."

"Why must we go through this every single time?"

"Surely you don't think helping others in need is a bad thing?"

His voice sharpened. "Why would you say that?"

I hesitated, not wanting to hurt him, but I had a point to make, and I was tired of Phil running me down. "Didn't you ever wish that someone like me stepped up to help Finn along the way?"

My remark was met with complete silence. His son, my cousin Finn, ran away six years ago, never looking back. While Phil and I had many, many discussions about the motel, I'd never once brought up Finn. What Phil didn't know was that Finn's situation was the major reason I did what I did.

I pictured Phil scratching his nose like he did when he was pondering something. He paused so long I thought he might have hung up on me.

Then, "My personal life is not part of this discussion."

In the six years Finn has been gone, I don't recall ever hearing Phil talk about his feelings. Every time the subject got broached, he changed it. Why should now be any different? "I guess we're done then."

"Not quite. Your parents may have put you in charge, but your father asked me to keep an eye on things and report back. And that's exactly what I'm doing. I'm loyal to my family. Why don't you let me ask my questions, and *then* we can be done?" Phil recovered nicely from my emotional dagger.

"Sure."

"What are your plans for increasing revenue? Cutting costs? You must have given some thought to making money. After all, this is what you live on."

My parents—who at the moment were in Nepal on a month-long Qi Xong retreat—had handed me the reins of the motel. Whatever I made, I kept. The Inn had seen better days, but the land it sat upon—along a major thoroughfare in the City of Fairfax—was worth a lot to greedy developers. My parents were simply waiting until they received an offer they couldn't refuse. In the meantime, I could do pretty much what I wanted, as long as I didn't destroy the place.

I cleared my throat. "I'm working on a comprehensive, multi-year revenue enhancement plan, developed with considerable input from Cesar, if you must know."

"And I'm only hearing about this now? I should be in the loop for these things. I should be providing input as well. After all, who knows this business, and the ins and outs of this motel, better than I do?"

"Good one."

"What?"

"You said *ins* and outs. Nice pun."

Phil sighed. "Why can't you be more serious? You're not a teenager anymore. In fact, you're not even a twenty-something anymore. Don't you think it's time to buckle down and try to make a life for yourself? Maybe give up the motel business and work at something you're good at?"

Ouch. I wondered if antagonizing gasbag relatives paid well, because I was damn good at it. "Okay, Uncle Phil, I get your point. Once I finish this plan, I'll run it by you to get your feedback. Then, once it's all finalized, we can get started with implementation. That's when I think your experience will really be valuable. Don't you agree?" I imagined him sitting in his den with his chest all puffed out.

"Happy to help."

"Well, then, I better get busy. Just got some finishing touches to put on the plan, then I'll send it to you."

"I'll look for it."

"Great."

"Okay, gotta run." I disconnected.

You might not be able to choose your family, but you certainly could choose whether to put up with their bullshit.

Chapter Two

After the call with Uncle Phil, I retreated to my workspace in the adjoining Room 14. I tried to keep my personal stuff from overflowing into the office and vice versa. I was successful some of the time.

I replayed the conversation in my head. As much as I hated to admit it, Phil had a point, even if he buried it in manure. I'd be able to do a lot more for a lot more people if the motel actually turned a profit.

I sat at my desk and booted up my laptop. Opened a blank document and named it "Multi-year Revenue Enhancement Plan." Stared at it while my finger loitered near the Enter key. Finally, I erased what I'd typed and renamed it "Try to Make a Buck."

Then, I stared at the blank page for about twenty minutes.

Stymied, I got up, went next door to my room, and watched old episodes of *Seinfeld* for an hour. Uncle Phil said I wasn't serious? Ha!

I returned to my laptop. What could we do to boost revenue? Over the years, my parents had tried all sorts of things to increase the occupancy rate. They'd advertised—in newspapers, on the radio, in magazines. But advertising was expensive, and the results were sometimes nebulous. Besides, did people even read newspapers and magazines or listen to the radio anymore? There were always ads on social media, but did people choose a motel based on those?

Back in the day, my parents were involved in the community. They'd march in the July 4th parade and sponsor Little League baseball teams—complete with *Fairfax Manor Inn* stitched across the back of the uniform.

But those seemed more like goodwill gestures than ways to increase the number of guests.

There was always the elephant in the room—online reviews. Namely, ours sucked. And not unfairly. Our motel was what you might call Economy. Which, in the hospitality business, meant crappy.

Some of the more complimentary reviews used the words classic, retro, quaint, and throwback, which meant old, unappealing, cramped, and dated, respectively. Some referred to it as kitschy, which I could understand, given that the mini-golf course we used to operate next door still stood, abandoned, with its giant fiberglass structures—Eiffel Tower, Dutch windmill, Big Ben replicas—reminding locals of past times. Unfortunately, the segment of the market that placed a premium on kitschy wasn't very large.

Then there were those who cited the "very affordable" rates, which I'm sure most people translated as "cheap and you-get-what-you-paid-for."

Uncle Phil wanted us to upgrade the place, but I didn't think he understood exactly how far we would need to go to become competitive—even at the lowest end of the market—and how much that would all cost.

If you looked at the numbers—and they were indeed trending downward—most people in the industry would say we'd be better off closing our doors than trying to overhaul the place. Unfortunately, I was afraid my parents might agree. To them, it was all about the land.

To me, however, it was all about the chance to help those in need.

Which brought me back full circle. To do that best, I'd have to bring in more paying customers.

My head hurt, and my stomach growled. I'd been spinning my wheels the entire afternoon. Maybe some dinner would fuel my creative juices.

I got very, very tired of eating all my meals out—not very healthy, expensive, time-consuming. But I lived in a motel and, without a kitchen in my room, my decision usually came down to take-out or eat-in. I seemed to spend an inordinate amount of time in restaurants. At least it gave me an excuse to get together with my friends.

I texted Lia Katsaros to see if she'd like to join me. She was a reporter for the Fairfax Observer, and we'd met a few months ago when she included the motel as part of a piece on some of the City of Fairfax's history.

We'd hit it off, and we'd worked together to expose a spate of crime and corruption in our midst. We'd dated since, and I guessed you could say things were definitely trending in the right direction.

She texted back, saying she'd love to, but she'd just gotten an important assignment. I texted back, *rain check?* And she replied quickly, *you know it.*

That's the kind of rejection I could handle.

Next, I texted my buddy, Vell Jackson. *Dinner?*

Three seconds later: *sorry, man. Catch you tomorrow?*

I texted back: *sure.*

I was on my own.

Time for a stroll. I walked east along Route 50 on the sidewalk, past an auto parts shop and a CVS and a bunch of other mundane stores. Traffic was pretty heavy, but traffic was always pretty heavy. It was the DMV, after all.

In a mile and a half, I turned right into a classic—old—strip shopping center where there was an acceptable sandwich place. I ordered a couple of Italian subs, extra banana peppers, and when they were ready, I trekked back. It felt good to stretch my legs. One of these days, I needed to get started on the exercise program I'd been meaning to start for months.

When I got to the motel, I stopped in at the registration office to check with Fareed.

"Hello, Mess," said Cesar, the motel manager, the man responsible for keeping the place running, and a dear family friend.

"I thought Fareed was on tonight."

"He'll be here at eight. You'd know that, if you'd consulted the schedule I sent you. The one I send you every day." He said it without a hint of sarcasm or disdain. Well, maybe there was a hint of disdain.

"Okay then, here." I gave him one of the Italian subs. "Have you had dinner yet?"

"Yes. We ate early tonight. Diego took Abie to watch a soccer game. Fairfax High, I believe." He took the sub. "I'll put this in the fridge for Fareed. I assume you purchased it for him, considering you thought he was working."

"Sure. Fine. How are things going?"

"Ah. You mean with the motel? How nice of you to ask."

Now, that was clearly sarcasm. "Yes. The motel."

"No new guests. On the bright side, no visits from the police. So, on balance, I'd say we were ahead."

"The police don't come that often."

"I suppose that depends on your definition of often. Anyway, there was one small thing. A visitor. For you." Cesar raised an eyebrow.

"Oh? Why didn't you lead with that?"

"I am telling you now."

"Did he give his name?"

"He did not. And I did not ask."

"*Okayyyy*." I drew out the word. Probably someone in need of a little help who wished to remain anonymous. Those were the people who sought me out, and I was getting a lot of homeless people lately, for some reason. I didn't mind a bit. The more people I could help, the better. "Do you know what he wanted?"

"I do not, but—"

"But what?"

"But you can ask him yourself. I believe he is sitting at the picnic table awaiting your return."

"Why didn't you say so?" I took a couple of steps to my right, trying to catch a glimpse of him out the window, but all I could see was one corner of the bench. "Thanks, I'll check him out."

"Shall I find him a room?"

"Give me a few minutes," I said. "But I'd say it's a distinct possibility."

I left the office and scuffed across the cracked asphalt parking lot. We'd brought in a picnic table last year, salvaged from a public park renovation, and it usually remained unoccupied. Which made sense; we didn't get a lot of picnickers at the motel.

A man sat on the bench. Calmly. Staring into space. He must have heard me approach, because he swung his head in my direction.

Something about him seemed familiar, although I couldn't identify it.

He didn't strike me as a typical street person. I'd seen a lot of them over the years, and most of them displayed a certain sameness. Thick layer of grime enveloping them like a wetsuit. Stringy, oily hair, often matted, often housing other living creatures. Sallow complexion or the complete opposite, shoe leather skin from too much sun. Ravages of alcohol and drugs, evidenced by the wrinkles—crevasses, in some cases—lining their skin.

All terrible reminders of what they had to endure, living exposed to the elements. But the most depressing sign of a street survivor was the look of pure defeat in their stone-dead eyes.

Although this man had a lot of hair, it wasn't dirty, and it wasn't tangled. His beard was neatly trimmed. No rips in his clothes and no duct tape holding his shoes together. Seemed like he'd bathed recently. When I got closer, I noticed this man's eyes held something that wasn't defeat. Recognition? Hope? Happiness? He rose to greet me.

"It is so damn good to see you."

Something about his voice was familiar, too. I stared at him, waiting for recognition to dawn.

He smiled, and it came across as sad and old. "I know. I didn't look like this the last time you saw me. A lot less hairy."

I opened my mouth to say something but came up empty.

His smile faltered. "It's me, Mess. Finn. Your cousin Finn."

My knees started to buckle, but I steadied myself on the picnic table. Then, I slowly lowered myself onto the bench seat. "I thought you were dead."

Chapter Three

F inn kept smiling. "Still kicking, although I thought I was dead myself, many times over the years."

I stared at him, trying to remember what Finn had looked like the last time I'd seen him, about six years ago. Upon closer examination, I could spot more signs of wear and tear. He was a year younger than me, but now he looked a few years older. More wrinkles and some distinct lines around the eyes, too many for someone his age. He was still handsome, though. Just not *young* and handsome.

Underneath all the hair and scruff, his piercing baby-blue eyes shone through. Maybe not quite as much sparkle now, though.

We'd been close, very close, and his abrupt disappearance had knocked me for a serious loop. Other family members hadn't taken it well either. I had so many questions, I didn't know where to begin. "Where have you been? Are you okay? Have you spoken to your parents? I'm pretty sure they think you're dead, too. We all do, er, did."

Emotions roared through me. Tears welled in my eyes. I stood and engulfed him in the tightest hug I could, only letting go when I felt him gasp for air. "I could kill you, shithead, for putting us through what you did. Jesus H. Christ."

I began crying, full force, and plopped down on the bench again, unable to think straight. Finn Hopkins, alive. And not in a coma or anything. I stared at him through blurry tears. "Have you been in town the whole time?"

Finn laughed, a thin, sad sound. "Nope. Came back a month, six weeks ago. I've been...around."

A month? Six weeks? "Around where?"

Finn waved his hand. "I'll fill you in on everything. I won't blame you or my parents—who I haven't told just yet—for hating me. Looking back, I regret ninety percent of what I did. But at the time, I felt it was something I had to do."

"What did you have to do?" Anger started to percolate. What kind of selfish person does that to the people he loves? "What was so goddamn important that you put us all through hell?"

Finn sighed. "I'll tell you, and I'm sure you'll think I should have made better decisions. And I probably should have. When I came out to my parents—I'm gay, by the way—I should have eased into it. Told my mother first, and then we could have figured out a way to tell my father. Instead, they exploded. Practically disowned me on the spot." Finn stopped, gauged my expression. "Bet they didn't tell you that, did they?"

I shook my head. I'd had an inkling Finn was gay, but I hadn't known how his parents had acted when he told them. Uncle Phil's reaction didn't really surprise me, but I wondered how much was simply shock. The fact they'd kept all that a secret didn't surprise me either. My family was big on secrets. "He hired a private detective to try to locate you. That went on for a couple of years."

"Really?" Finn seemed taken aback. And a little guilty, too, although that might have just been me imagining how I would have felt in his shoes.

"I have no idea what went on between you and them, but they were royally torn up over it. Still haven't recovered. I'm sure when they see you, they will be incredibly relieved."

Finn's eyes widened. "You can't tell them about me. Not yet."

"Why the hell not?" My anger returned.

"I need to square away some things first."

"It's been *six* years. Don't you think you should tell them, as soon as absolutely possible?"

Finn smiled weakly. "It's been six years. They can wait another coupla days." He exhaled. "Mess, you don't know how many hundreds of times I picked up the phone, wanting to call you. It ate at me that I did what I did. To you. To others. Tore me apart. But I was so…ashamed. So terribly ashamed of what I'd become." He swallowed hard.

"You should have reached out. I could have helped. *We* could have helped. Your family loves you." I felt so bad for him, yet so happy at the same time. A bizarre dichotomy.

"Water under the bridge, I guess," Finn said. "It's so great to see you. Finally, after so many godawful times, I feel like there's some hope for me. A glimmer of light in my future. I've worked hard, very hard, to get myself clean so I could come back here and be proud of myself. Not be some derelict, strung out, looking for my next score. I just need to get a few things settled before I face my parents."

I had no yardstick to comprehend the depths of his despair. "Whatever I can do, let me know. Anything."

"I need a place to crash for a while."

"No problem. You can stay here as long as you want."

"I appreciate that, I really do. I'm completely wiped. I need some serious sleep."

I stared at him, the questions bouncing around in my head. I wanted some answers, and—selfishly—I wanted them right now. I vacillated between being pissed and trying to be understanding about what Finn had survived. And he had *survived*. "Come on, I'll get you set up." I grinned as I thought about how happy Uncle Phil and Aunt Vera were going to be, right along with my own parents and Izzy and everybody else. Cousin Finn was back from the dead.

I got Finn settled in his room and practically watched his eyelids droop shut. I told him to find me in the morning, and I'd take him to breakfast, then get him cleaned up. Haircut. Shave. Maybe a trip to the clinic to get checked out. I didn't tell him that I expected a full rundown of where he'd been. Of course, it wasn't really my business—Finn was an adult and certainly wasn't accountable to me. But his disappearance and subsequent radio silence had utterly devastated me and the people I cared about. We were owed something, weren't we?

Back in my room, I thought about calling my sister Izzy to tell her. She hadn't been as close to Finn as I'd been, but I knew she'd be ecstatic to hear he'd returned. However, once I told her—no matter how much she promised to keep it a secret—there was little chance the news would remain a secret. She'd tell her husband Russell, and maybe one of my nieces would overhear and ask an innocent question in front of another family member. Unlikely, maybe, that the word would get back to Uncle Phil, but if it did, Finn would be apoplectic. And Uncle Phil would be supremely pissed at Finn.

It seemed to be a fact that the more sensational the news, the harder it was to keep secret. And while Finn's reappearance wouldn't be making any CNN headline, in my family, it was just about the biggest news I could imagine short of someone dying.

I supposed Finn was right; his parents hadn't heard from him in years; what was another few days? I turned on the TV, surfed around a bit, then hit mute, content to watch images of some nature documentary while I pondered the bombshell news.

I remembered a distinct change in my relationship with Finn right about the time I went off to college. He was a year behind, so he still had his senior year to complete, and I was caught up in my new adventure life. New friends, new situations. We drifted apart.

The next year, he graduated high school but chose not to go to college, disappointing—and angering—Uncle Phil. Instead, Finn tried out a few jobs, working in retail and as a server at some DC restaurants. I'd known he'd left the nest, aiming to couch surf and crash with friends until things panned out.

We'd text every so often, but we each had our lives. I'd assumed he was getting along okay.

A few years later, he left the area.

Every so often at the beginning, anyway, there'd be some cryptic message. A voice mail or an email. *Okay, just sorting through some things.* Or *on the road, no worries.* And the ever-popular: *Can you put money in my account?* My mother would relay this information to me with great care, I'm sure, with the goal of reassuring me that Finn was okay. I'm not certain it worked. I think I felt the longer it dragged on, the worse the outcome would be.

Predictably, the interval between contacts got longer, and they turned exclusively into requests for money until they petered out entirely after about two years.

All my relatives were heartbroken. At the time, I remembered thinking Finn's disappearance was more tragic than if he'd been killed in some horrible accident.

The not-knowing was horrific.

Shortly after the messages stopped, Uncle Phil hired a private detective who tried diligently to find Finn for almost two years, without luck. Again, all this family gossip came by way of my mother, so I never really knew how much of the story she was keeping from me. Probably the uglier parts—shielding your children from terrible news was part of the job description, after all.

I was still in shock. Although we'd never heard definitively that he'd died, we all assumed it.

And now he was back, six years later. Alive.

On the TV, a hippo lurked in some African river, waiting for its unwitting prey to come swimming by.

So many memories. One time, when I was about seventeen, Finn and I persuaded some random guy to purchase us two six-packs of beer—I think an extra twenty bucks was involved. We took our contraband to a dilapidated tree house on this vacant lot near his house and polished them off. As we left, the rotten wood on the ladder gave way under Finn's foot, and he took a nasty tumble, cracking his head on a rock.

It bled like crazy. We didn't know what to do, so we ended up sneaking into Finn's basement, where we found a bag of rags, which we used to staunch the gash. Then, we put about thirty band-aids over the cut.

I recalled us spending half an hour concocting some outrageous story to explain to his parents what happened. When we finally went upstairs, Uncle Phil and Aunt Vera were sitting in the living room, half-soused themselves. They barely looked up as we passed through, and they sure didn't ask Finn what had happened. We were a little bummed out we didn't get a chance to tell them our alibi story, but we filed it away for future use.

Funny that they became so interested in his welfare after he'd flown the coop. Of course, I wasn't being fair. There was a gargantuan difference between having a cut on your forehead and running away and severing ties with your family.

Despite my day-to-day disagreements with Uncle Phil, I still empathized with his loss. Even though I had trouble being in the same room with him for more than ten minutes, I loved him.

Finn's reappearance was great news, *fantastic* news, but I realized it was going to take some time to accept that Finn was really here and willing to become part of the family again.

I pushed aside thoughts of Finn and texted Lia to see how her big story was shaking out.

She called me ten seconds later. "Hi, Mess." I pictured the moon-shaped scar on her chin dancing as she spoke to me.

"Hey. How's your story going?"

"Oh my god. You'll never believe it."

"Tell me," I said.

"How about I tell you in person?" she countered.

She read my mind.

Chapter Four

I'd just about cleared all the crap out of my room—tossing it into the office next door—when Lia arrived. After a brief but delicious hug, she eased into the only chair in the room. "Oh man, what a day. Did you hear the news?"

"No." I wasn't a newshound. If it crawled along the bottom of the screen of whatever sport I was watching, then I'd see it. Otherwise…

"Webster Claypool was murdered. Last night, in his home. In Oakton. Not too far from here, in fact."

I plopped down myself on the bed. "Oh, shit. That is big news." Claypool was one of the largest real estate developers in the region and an outsized character, always making headlines. He had a reputation as a ruthless businessman and as a player on the social scene. He had his hands in everything. At one point, many years ago, he even tried to buy the motel from my parents. He'd wanted to raze it to build upscale condos.

"Yeah, it is. And my editor assigned me as the lead reporter."

"I'm not surprised." Lia's star was rising after her recent big story. "Do they know who did it?"

"Nope. And the cops are in a frenzy. Claypool is a high visibility case, all right."

"He wasn't the most liked guy around. I imagine the suspect list would be miles long," I said.

She nodded and pushed some hair off her face. "Yeah, that's the impression I got from the detective. So far, they haven't issued many official details, but unofficially, they don't have any witnesses. A few neighbors heard some activity, but nobody saw anything more than shadowy figures making their getaway."

"Oakton's usually very quiet."

"Yep. Not a place where people typically get murdered." Lia wheeled her chair over to the bed. "If I wasn't so tired…"

"I've got a Coke in the fridge if you think a shot of caffeine would help."

"Oh, Mess, I'd love to spend the night, but I really am exhausted, and I've got another big day tomorrow." She gestured around the room, as if she was on a game show about to give away a bedroom set. "And you live in a motel room. Still having a little trouble getting used to that."

Living in a dumpy motel room with two twin beds was a definite turn-off. For the most part, we spent our together time at Lia's, but for the next couple of weeks, a roommate's mother from Ireland was staying with them. Having someone's mother around was also a definite turn-off. "I get it. Maybe tomorrow, you'll feel more energetic."

"Hopefully." She smiled, and I forgot where I was for a moment. "Enough about me. What about you? Anything interesting happen today?"

I ran a motel, so there were plenty of interesting things happening on a daily basis, but most were of the *badly interesting* variety. But not today! "As a matter of fact, something notable did happen. My cousin Finn showed up." I was about to explain the whole Finn story when Lia exploded.

"Oh my God! The one you thought had ODed in a gutter someplace? He's back? That's so awesome!" She launched herself from the chair and dove on top of me. "And he's doing okay?"

"I thought you were exhausted."

"I still am. But I'm exhaustively happy for you. I bet your aunt and uncle are thrilled."

"They don't know yet."

Lia raised an eyebrow. "Really?"

"Finn's involved, so I'm sure there's some convoluted explanation. He said he'd fill me in tomorrow. He's sacked out a few rooms away."

"That's great news," Lia mumbled, then her eyes slowly closed, and she nodded off to sleep in my arms.

* * *

The next morning, my buddy D'Marvellus Jackson and I sat in Hole Lotta Love, the bagel place adjacent to the motel property. It was owned by Sandy Beech, a Navy vet, and she ran it with her daughter Crystal as if it were a ship in the fleet. Vell and I ate there so often we'd memorized all the choices, but we checked out the menus anyway, just in case Sandy had slipped something new into the rotation. Lia had cleared out early—back on her story—and I'd invited Vell over to listen to Finn's tale, which was bound to be entertaining.

More importantly, Vell had a very highly developed BS meter. I'd gotten some weird vibes from Finn yesterday, and I wasn't sure if that was simply Finn's baseline weirdness or if something else was afoot.

"He just appeared, poof, out of the blue. No warning. No call-ahead. No nothing?" Vell asked.

"Yep. And he's been in town for a month. My family is nothing like your family. Where your family is warm and inviting, mine is distant and cold. And very, very judgmental. Izzy and I are trying to break that mold, but we've got the gene pool of generations of starchy forebearers working against us."

The door to the bagel place opened, and Finn stepped partway in. He wore a wide-brimmed bucket hat and sunglasses. Did he think we were going fishing? I waved him to our booth.

He motioned for me to come over to where he stood. I waved him over again, but he shook his head and held his ground. Motioned again, more urgently.

"I'll be right back," I said to Vell as I got up and walked over to Finn. "What's going on? Come join us for breakfast."

He glanced over his shoulder. "How about if we grab something to go and eat it someplace else?"

"Why? Where?"

"Please, Mess. I'd love to go on a little picnic. Get some fresh air. Enjoy nature."

Picnic? "Uh, okay. Sure. We'll get takeout." I turned to go tell Vell, but

Finn grabbed my shirt. I spun around. "Yeah?"

"Get me some kind of breakfast sammie, okay? I'll meet you over there." He pointed across the parking lot. Without waiting for a response, he slipped out of the restaurant.

Vell came over. "What's going on?"

"Wish I knew. Hope you like picnics."

A few weeks ago, my ancient Civic died, so I bought an old Corolla on some no-brand online used car site. Best things I can say about the Corolla: it didn't smell too bad, and the AC worked much of the time. I was hard on my cars, and they got a lot of rough use—I loaned them out to my invited guests from time to time.

At the moment, the car was not being used, so we piled in. Vell rode shotgun, and Finn crawled into the back. He buckled up, then slid as far down in the seat as he could while still being able to see out the window.

"You okay back there?" I started the car and put it in reverse.

"Yup. Nice wheels, by the way."

I exchanged glances with Vell. Everything was relative, of course, but if these were nice wheels, what was Finn used to? A forty-year-old AMC Gremlin?

"Any requests for where to have our picnic?"

"I'm easy," Vell said.

"Anywhere with lots of trees is good with me," Finn said. "Isolated, preferably."

I drove to a nearby park with lots of trees, and we found a picnic bench not far from the parking lot. There was one other car in the lot, but we didn't see another person.

We took our seats and unwrapped our sandwiches. Dug in.

"I didn't realize you were a picnic guy," I said between bites.

"People change, you know," Finn said.

I'd had enough preamble and small talk. "So, time to fill me in, Finn. What have you been doing the last six years?"

Next to me, I could practically feel Vell turn the sensitivity up on his BS meter.

Finn sighed. Then he sighed again. Once more, for good measure, in case we hadn't noticed the first two. "The last six years have been tough ones. I'm not going to lie. But I've finally straightened out, and I'm ready to reconnect with all those people I've left in the dark for so long."

"That's great to hear." Of course, I noticed he didn't answer my question. If I'd thought Finn was going to recap his missing time linearly and logically, one year at a time, I was mistaken. This was going to take some effort and finesse on my part. "Must have been difficult, getting straightened out. How were you able to do that? You must have found some generous people who helped, huh?"

"I don't wish what happened to me on my worst enemies." Finn took a huge bite of his sandwich and worked diligently to chew it down.

I tapped Vell under the table with my foot.

Vell took the hint. "So, Finn. Mess said you'd just gotten back into town, what, a month ago? That right?"

"Give or take. More or less." He took another bite of his food.

"Since you've been back in town, have you been staying with friends?" Vell asked.

"You could say that."

I took over, tag-team style. "Old friends or new friends?"

Finn shrugged. "You know how it is."

Actually, I had no idea. "Where are you coming from most recently?" I was trying to get some picture of Finn's life, and maybe if we worked backward, we could—eventually—get the entire picture.

Finn shrugged again. "Not important where I've been. It's only important where I'm going." He gazed into the distance at the trees. "Nature is so peaceful, isn't it? Puts things into perspective."

"You seem to be dodging our questions," Vell said.

Finn removed his sunglasses and set them on the picnic table. Then he narrowed his eyes at Vell. "I've lived through some bad times, and I don't wish to rehash them. Of course, my life story really isn't any of your business now, is it?"

Vell held up his hands. Smiled in his disarming way. "Relax, dude. Just thought you wanted to get some stuff off your chest. If you want to hold it all in until your insides rot away, that's up to you."

I interjected before things got out of hand. "Finn, I understand—or at least I think I understand—that the time you've been away has been full of bad experiences. And I don't mean to pry. But I care about you, and I want to help, moving forward. If I know what some of your issues were—or are—I'd be in a lot better place to do that." I tried to peer inside Finn through his eyes, but he wasn't giving anything away. I'd noticed the same expression on many of the street people I brought in to stay at the motel. "You know I'm on your side, right?"

"I do."

"And you also know your parents are going to pepper you with these same questions, and they're not going to give up until they think you're telling them the truth. I guess I'm trying to give you an opportunity to tell your story to a more sympathetic ear."

Finn's eyes met mine. "I appreciate your concern, Mess. I really do. But the details are just too depressing. If you imagine I've been through the worst things, suffered all kinds of indignities, endured the most miserable circumstances, you probably wouldn't be far off." He put his shades back on. "I'm trying very hard to put the past behind me and get my act together. You'll have to trust me on that. Now, if you don't mind, I'd like to go back. I'm not feeling too good."

Chapter Five

We returned to the motel, and Finn holed up in his room. Vell and I stood outside, talking.

"He's a piece of work, all right," Vell said. "You think he isn't feeling well because of withdrawal? Or maybe he's using again?"

"He said he's clean, but who really knows? He's been through a lot. I think I'd be out of sorts, too, if I was in his shoes."

"Here's the thing, man. You'd never be in his shoes. You've got a lot of faults, lord knows, but basically, you're a good, reasonably responsible dude."

"What faults?"

Vell frowned. "On the other hand, your cousin…"

"Okay, so Finn didn't make a very good first impression. But I think we need to cut him some slack. The Finn I remember was a loyal guy and easygoing. It hurts to see how living hand-to-mouth has taken it out of him."

"Uh-huh." Vell made no attempt to hide his skepticism. "And what's with the hat, anyway? You may not see it, or you may see it and not want to acknowledge it, but your cousin is hiding something. Afraid of something, too."

Nothing ever got past Vell. I hoped I'd find out the true score sooner rather than later. "Let's change the subject."

Vell raised his head and opened his arms wide. "Nice weather we're having."

"Funny. Did you hear about Webster Claypool?"

"I sure did. Hell of a thing," Vell said. "Met him once at a charity event. Seemed nice enough, but now that he's dead, people are turning on him—at least if you read between the lines. Usually, it's the other way around. When a guy dies, everyone praises him, even if he was an SOB."

"Well, the people are right. He was not a nice man. But that's not the good part. Lia got assigned the story."

Vell clapped once. "Oh man, that's cool. Movin' on up to the big time. Good for her."

"Yeah, except it means she'll be scarce for a while."

"You're strong. You'll survive." Vell chucked me on the shoulder. "Means more time for us, though, right?"

"Lucky me."

"You got that right. Listen, I gotta bounce. Maybe dinner tonight?"

"Don't you have a social life?"

"Now I do. Later."

Vell took off, and I walked over to the registration office to see how things were going.

Cesar greeted me with his usual, "Hello, Mess."

"Hey, Cesar. Anything going on that needs my attention?"

"The gutters need to be cleaned. The pothole on the far end of the parking lot is getting bigger. You promised to review my proposal to replace the registration software, and the guest in Room 3 was singing at the top of her lungs at five a.m." Cesar gave me a tight smile, one of his specialties. "How much longer will she be staying with us?"

Mrs. Williams had to be closer to ninety than eighty, and she couldn't have weighed seventy pounds, even with three pounds of hairspray shellacking her hair. She'd been kicked out of her daughter's home where she'd been staying and didn't have any place else to go, except for social services. She was the aunt of a friend of a friend, so how could I have turned her away? I knew what the system did to folks who weren't always their own best advocates. "I'll talk to her."

"And the rest of the action items?" Cesar asked.

"Yes, of course. I'll get right on it. In the meantime, if you want to get started, that's okay with me. I'm sure you'll be judicious with our limited maintenance and facilities improvement budget."

"In other words, only do those things that are absolutely necessary?"

"Cesar, what would I do without you?"

"I'd be afraid to find out," he said, sotto voce.

"I'll see you later."

"One more thing, Mess. That guest who checked in last night. Under the name Thomas Cruz, with a Z?"

Finn hadn't wanted to use his real name, and I didn't press him. But Tom Cruise? "Yeah?"

"Not that it's any of my business, but he looks very familiar to me." One of Cesar's eyebrows arched.

"Oh?" I feigned ignorance.

"Long lost relative, in fact. Yours, not mine." Cesar had worked for my father since the beginning. He knew Finn, of course. And he also knew Uncle Phil quite well.

"Right. Well, you know how families are. He hasn't told Uncle Phil or Aunt Vera yet."

"After all these years? I assume he will be informing them, how shall I put this, that *he's still alive?*" Cesar raised his voice, clearly upset at Finn. I didn't see Cesar's feathers ruffled very often, and I had to admit, it made me uneasy. It also made it clear that I needed to persuade Finn to do the right thing, and soon.

I'd take another run at him later.

* * *

As a child, Finn was always sweet and sensitive, much more than I was. He got into mischief a fair bit, but he was never malicious. Every so often, our two families went away on vacation together. One time, we went to some fancy resort—nothing but the best for Uncle Phil—and me, Izzy, and Finn had been shuffled off to the kid's club for the day, along with every other kid staying at the resort, it seemed.

There were arts & crafts and sports and meals and everything a kid could want, all in a tropical setting. Soon after we arrived, Finn noticed a kid off in the corner by himself, obviously anxious about being away from his parents, and he befriended him, but not without some effort. Finn displayed extraordinary sensitivity and patience, finally persuading the boy to participate in the fun, and they teamed up in the ping-pong tournament. They ended up winning the whole thing, and Finn kept the tiny plastic trophy he got for years.

From then on, I tried to be more like Finn and be sensitive to others while exercising more patience. I struggled at times, but I tried.

Now, though, it had been three hours since we'd come back from the picnic, and I couldn't wait any longer. I needed to talk to Finn. I strode down the walkway that fronted the rooms and was about to knock on his door, when it swung open. Only Finn's face was visible in the dark, and it held a look of fear. "Who was that?" His panicky voice matched his expression.

"Who was who?" I turned around in time to see a white SUV leave the lot, making a right turn on Route 50.

"That guy. He was in the registration office."

"I don't know. Customer who wanted a place to sleep and realized this place was a dump?"

Finn receded into the shadows. "Come in, quick. And shut the door."

I stepped in and flipped the light switch. Finn made a strangled sound and covered up his face with an arm. Maybe he'd turned nocturnal in the past six years.

"Must you?" he screeched.

"Yes, I must. It's the middle of the afternoon."

Finn took a few steps backward, then collapsed onto his unmade bed. The room was surprisingly neat—I would have expected a total dumpster fire—but I guess when you didn't have many belongings, there wasn't much to mess up. A battered backpack rested on the floor, in the corner. "You sure you don't know who that guy was?"

"Hang on." I took my phone out and called the front desk.

Cesar answered. "Yes, sir."

Sir? Cesar got ultra-formal when he was torqued at me. I wondered what

I'd done, except ignore his list of to-do items. I made a mental note to speak to Mrs. Williams after I was done talking to Finn. "Who was the guy in the white SUV?"

"Sales guy. Hotel supply company. I told him what our annual budget was, and he left without even trying to sell me anything. Just said, and I quote, 'Oh my.'"

"Okay. Good."

"Good?"

"Never mind. Thanks. Gotta run." I clicked off.

"It was a salesperson," I said to Finn, as I pulled the chair out from under the desk and sat. The chair sagged to the right, and I made another mental note to replace it with one that wasn't busted. "What's going on, Finn? And the truth might be nice. You're practically shaking in your socks."

Finn ran his hand over his face and shook his head a couple of times, as if whatever was hounding him could be shrugged off if he tried hard enough. "Okay, man. You've always had my back, right? Blood brothers, right?"

"Well, blood cousins. What's going on?"

"I think some bad people are after me."

My stomach dropped a floor. "Who? What for?"

"Don't know who. Not sure about the *what for* either."

Most likely, this was just some paranoia. I'd seen it often among the homeless, where a suspicious, almost paranoid, mindset was a survival skill. "Start at the beginning and walk me through it, okay?"

"Sure, sure." Finn sucked in a deep breath. "I was walking along night before last, minding my own business, when a couple guys started yelling at me. Wanted me to stop. I figured they wanted to mug me, so I took off. Managed to run to my car and get away. I'm sure they think I'm somebody else, but I'm still pretty freaked out."

"Your car? Where's your car?" There wasn't any unaccounted-for car in our lot.

"I left it parked at the mall. I think they might have been following me, so I drove there and managed to lose them in the parking area. Dumped my car and ran away on foot."

"You dumped your car at Fair Oaks Mall? You have to admit, it sounds weird that two muggers would want to follow you in a car, doesn't it?"

"Well, I *thought* they were muggers."

"Did they say why they wanted you to stop? Did you know these guys?"

Finn licked his lips. "No."

"I'm confused." And I was. "Two guys were yelling at you to stop. You thought they were muggers, and now you think they're after you? No offense, man, but what could you possibly have that they would want?"

"That's the mystery, bro."

"Is this why you were wearing that ridiculous fisherman's hat and wanted to picnic in the park?"

"Yup." Finn's voice had reduced to a whisper.

"Sounds to me like you're spinning some kind of wild conspiracy theory. Maybe they thought you'd run over their flower bed or something. Maybe they'd had too much to drink, and you were the first person who wandered by."

"Maybe." Finn shook his head. "But I don't think so."

"What's the end game here? Spend the rest of your life in a dark motel room using a fake name?"

Finn shrugged.

"Would you feel better if we called the police? I have a contact there." I'd gone to high school with Eric Ostervale, who was now a detective on the force.

"No police," Finn practically yelled. "No cops."

"The police are our friends."

"If you'd been in my shoes the past six years, you wouldn't think that at all. The cops never believe guys like me; they hassle guys like me, and I'm sure this time wouldn't be any different."

"Okay, what do you suggest?"

"I was hoping you had a plan. This is your town, after all."

I exhaled. "Why don't we start by getting your car?"

Finn pondered the idea. "I guess we could do that."

* * *

I wasn't sure what frame of mind Finn was in, so I thought about calling Vell to help by driving Finn's car back from the mall. But after a brief discussion with Finn, I accepted his assurance that he could drive the three or four miles without incident. Besides, I wasn't sure Vell wanted to be around Finn; my buddy didn't want me to be taken advantage of, and I knew this because if our roles were reversed, that's how I'd feel.

We hopped into the Corolla and drove to the mall. Once we got there, Finn directed me to the area where he'd parked, and after a few wrong turns, we located the lot near Macy's.

"Stop right here," Finn said.

I pulled over to the side. "What?"

"We need to be careful. Someone may be watching for me."

"Seriously? You think somebody is staking out your car?" I glanced at the rows of parked cars. It was crowded for a weekday afternoon.

"Get out and let's check."

I opened my mouth to argue, then figured it would be a whole lot easier just to go along, so I took the first parking spot I came to. "You do know this seems crazy-town, right?"

"Follow me, and don't act suspicious."

I locked the door and followed Finn as he walked toward the mall entrance. Out of the side of his mouth, he said, "Two rows over. The yellow Honda Fit. With the artwork on the side."

I turned my head and spotted the car Finn was referring to. Bright yellow, with a ginormous picture of a pepperoni pizza on the side. The restaurant's name, Paulo's Pies, was emblazoned above the picture in Day-Glo pink. "What about it?"

"That's my car."

I tried not to laugh. "Well, it sure does blend in."

"So now you know why it's easy to spot."

"Why are you driving a pizzamobile?"

"I got a job there."

"I didn't know you had a job. Good for you."

"I'll explain later, okay? Keep walking and see if you can tell if it's being watched."

We made it all the way to the mall doors without noticing anything suspicious. Finn kept going, right into Macy's. I followed.

He stopped in Men's Shoes. "Okay, so far, so good. We'll make one more pass down the rows on the other side. If it's clear, then we're golden."

"Do you really think that this—"

"C'mon." Finn put down the loafer he'd been inspecting and walked out the door. I followed.

We cut to our left, then began to traverse the row of parked cars. We'd gone about twenty steps when Finn's hand shot out and tapped my elbow. "Don't look, but there's a black sedan, a Beamer or Audi maybe."

"And?"

"And there's two guys in it. Staring at my car."

Chapter Six

I wasn't sure how I was supposed to corroborate his sighting if I couldn't look, so I snuck a quick glance. Hard to tell at this distance, in this light, but it looked like there were two guys in a dark Audi staring at Finn's bright yellow pizza car. Of course, I imagined a lot of people stared at the bright yellow pizza car. But in this case, I thought Finn might be on to something.

"Okay, I've got a plan. You walk behind my car, stop, then bend down to tie your shoes. If they seem super-attentive when you stop behind my car, then we'll know," Finn said.

As plans went, it wasn't the worst one I'd heard. "Fine."

Finn drifted off to the side a bit, trying to get an unobstructed view. Then he leaned against a concrete pillar and pulled out his phone, pretending to be engrossed in something. I cut between some cars until I came to the right row, then slowly walked until I came to Finn's car. I stopped and bent over to tie my shoes, then straightened. I casually glanced at the Audi. Empty.

My heart thumped. I whirled around and searched for Finn. He was no longer leaning against the pillar. I caught the backs of two men hustling into Macy's.

I hustled after them.

Into the store. Past Men's Shoes. I figured Finn would head for the main part of the mall, where he could go in a hundred different directions to try to lose his pursuit.

I jogged through the store, ignoring the sharp looks from the other shoppers. I noticed several employees heading for the aisles, and I figured having men tearing through their store was bound to cause some alarm. I hoped Finn had a good head start.

I made it through the store and out into the mall proper. Took a second to look around. The usual assortment of shoppers: A group of mall walkers. A mother pushing a stroller. Two older men pausing to look at the Victoria's Secret display window. But I didn't see Finn or his pursuers. I loped down the concourse, hoping to spot some signs that they'd been through. At the next side shoot, I saw movement at the far end. Finn, running up the down escalator. One of the guys was right behind him, while the other was on the up escalator, but he was stuck behind a large family.

I raced in that direction, then dashed up a staircase, taking the steps two at a time, keeping my eyes glued to the action.

Somehow, Finn managed to get to the top just seconds before the other guy did. Finn veered left and turned on his afterburners, and I adjusted course so I could intercept him.

The goon chasing Finn was gaining ground, but I'd also closed the gap between us. Finn was concentrating on his escape, so he didn't notice me, and the other guy behind him was concentrating on Finn, so he didn't notice me either. He was tall with a shaved bald head, and he didn't look happy.

I let Finn speed by me, then I lowered my shoulder and drove it into the tall guy. I didn't have to put much into it; his speed worked against him as we collided. He went sprawling.

His partner wasn't quite as big—with shorter legs—but he'd built up a head of steam and had almost caught up to us. He must have thought his buddy had accidentally crashed into me, because he didn't slow down one bit—and he didn't perceive me as a threat. He was going to catch Finn, no matter what.

Except...I pivoted and repeated my maneuver. Lowered my shoulder, anchored my back leg, and let his momentum drive him into me. He doubled over with a yelp as the air escaped his lungs, but he didn't go down.

Until I kicked his legs out from under him.

Then I sprinted after Finn, who had just rounded the corner. I yelled to him, and he slowed, and we scrambled down the first stairway we found.

Then we doubled back to Macy's, raced out the door and to my car, and laid skid marks as we tore out of the parking lot.

* * *

We didn't take any time to catch our proverbial breath. From the mall, we drove directly to the nearest hair salon that took walk-ins. Finn got shampooed, shorn, and shaved, and when the stylist finished, he looked so much better. And different. Hopefully, he'd now be unrecognizable to the guys chasing him. I paid for it all and left a very generous tip.

Time to head back to the motel.

Despite what my parents would hint at from time to time, and despite what my sister would say once in a while, and despite what Uncle Phil told me on a regular basis, I wasn't a complete idiot.

Finn was holding out on me. There was no way two hoodlums were staking out his car, simply because they didn't mug him properly the night before. Finn was flat-out lying, and I really shouldn't have been surprised. Although he was a loyal cousin/friend, he'd always been adept at spinning yarns. Back when we were kids, however, he saved his storytelling for those in authority—his parents, his teachers, the cops on occasion. I didn't remember him lying to me a single time. But maybe he had, and I hadn't been sharp enough to pick up on it.

Now, after living the past six years who knew where, I figured his deception skills had only gotten better.

When we got back, I fully expected to grill him about last night and about the last six years. Things were rapidly going downhill, and the sooner we got a handle on things, the smoother everything was bound to go.

We got out of my car, and I walked him to his room, figuratively rolling up my sleeves, ready to get dirty.

He didn't invite me in.

"We really need to have a conversation, Finn. And it needs to be now."

"I know I owe you an explanation, but I'm too stressed. Tonight, Mess. I promise. Right now, I need to lie down for a bit. I'm sure you understand."

I didn't, but I only nodded. *Patience. Understanding. Remember what he'd been through.* "Fine. Later. But I'm going to hold you to your promise."

"I expect nothing less. And thanks for the spa treatment." He practically closed his door in my face.

Sometimes it was your family members who pissed you off the most.

* * *

I managed to persuade Lia to join me for dinner, and it only required a minimum of begging on my part. She met me at the motel, and before we actually went out to eat, we turned off our phones and got re-acquainted with each other.

Which was very, very nice.

Afterward, we went to the Krab Shack, the site of our first date, about three months ago. The place was a dive, but the food was good.

"Can I ask you a question?" she said after we were seated.

"Sure."

"Don't you get tired of eating out all the time?"

"I live in a motel. Where else would I eat but *out?*"

"Funny, but that's not a good answer," she said.

"The food part gets old, but when I get to dine with such great company, I actually look forward to it."

She hit me with a perfect smile. "*That's* a good answer."

I returned her smile. "Thanks."

We chowed down. Dinner was delicious. And, of course, the company was great. I folded my napkin and set it on the table. "Back to my place? Watch something on Netflix?"

"I wish I could, Mess. But this story calls."

"Fill me in. Have the cops figured out who killed Webster Claypool?"

"Nope. But not for lack of trying. They canvassed the neighborhood, door-to-door, hoping to find someone who saw or heard something."

"Any luck?"

"Nothing concrete. A couple of people reported hearing some

commotion—people yelling in the street and then cars zooming off—but they think it was probably teenagers. Nothing to do with the murder."

"Where in Oakton is this?" Oakton was an affluent area, but some parts of it were *very* exclusive.

"There's a residential enclave of about twenty uber high-end homes, only a few streets. Big houses on relatively small lots—kinda squished together, really. Right off Vale Road. That's where Claypool lived." Lia paused, glanced around the restaurant. Everyone else seemed to be involved in their own conversation. She lowered her voice anyway. "You know who one of his neighbors is?"

I was about to give her some sarcastic answer, but she must have sensed it because she quickly said, "Headstomper Thorpe."

"That was going to be my first guess." I smiled. "Who's Headstomper Thorpe? Leader of the local Boy Scout troop?"

"Ha-ha. I didn't know either, but evidently, he's a big deal in MMA."

I watched a lot of ESPN, but whenever mixed martial arts came on, I switched off. Too barbaric for my tastes. If I wanted to see people act viciously toward each other, I'd watch C-SPAN. "Do the authorities think he killed Claypool?"

"No. He was out of town on some publicity tour. But can you imagine that neighborhood block party? Whoa. Anyway, I know they're doing a lot of legwork, and they haven't released the forensic data—and probably won't. I've been relying on my contacts there, but they really don't share much from an open investigation. Tomorrow, I may try to interview some of the neighbors. If nothing else, they can provide some background and context."

The thought of Lia cold-calling strangers made me uneasy. "Sounds like it could be kind of uncomfortable, trying to get neighbors to open up after someone's been killed. You sure you'll be okay?"

"You're sweet, Mess." She chuckled. "Maybe I should have you tag along as my photographer."

"Just say the word."

"You'll be the first one I call."

"Okay. By the way, how much longer is your roommate's mother going to be staying with you?"

"That roommate's name is Yaz. And, bad news: her mother came here on a one-way ticket. You know there's not much I can do about it, right?"

I took her hands in mine, stared deeply into her eyes, and said in the sincerest tone I could, "I do."

She jerked her hands back. "Stop doing that. It freaks me out."

Truth be told, it freaked me out, too. The entire idea of marriage did. But I enjoyed getting Lia going.

"Time to get out of here." Lia slapped me on the shoulder. "You're such a goofball."

"But I'm *your* lovable goofball."

"Who said anything about lovable?"

I drove Lia back to the motel to get her car, said goodbye, then returned a bunch of emails and texts. With motel business done for the day, I googled Headstomper Thorpe.

There were thousands of hits.

If only half of what I read was accurate, Headstomper was a bad dude. He was a top-ranked fighter in the Ultimate Fighting Championship—UFC—but there were so many events sponsored by so many different factions, I was quickly confused.

All I needed to know was that in one fight, he knocked his poor opponent into a coma lasting six weeks.

Like I said, bad dude.

And, evidently, a rich dude. Not only did he make money fighting, but he made a lot of money endorsing products. I watched a few interview clips. Good-looking guy, well-spoken, possessed a definite air of menace, but somehow, he also seemed to exhibit a soft underbelly.

There were hundreds of photos of him with different women, who all had one thing in common—they were all very, very attractive.

I was about to close my laptop when I noticed one woman on his arm more often than others, and when I checked the dates, I discovered it was his wife. Her name was Alluree Escalante, and she was, according to a photo tag, one of the world's leading supermodels.

Weird to think this celebrity couple lived nearby in normally staid Oakton.

An hour later, there was a knock at my door. If there was an issue with a guest, Cesar or Fareed would text me, then if I didn't answer quickly, they'd call me.

Only in dire emergencies would they knock on my door.

I jumped off my bed to see what was going on, fully prepared for some minor emergency. I flung the door open, and Finn was standing there, a can of soda in his hand.

"Hey, Mess." He glanced over his shoulder. "Can I come in?"

It was pretty late, but I was learning I needed to interact with Finn on his schedule or not at all. "Sure. Come on in."

He looked around for a place to sit. Clutter, everywhere. "Why don't we go next door, into my office?" I led the way through the adjoining door. It wasn't much neater than my room. I removed a book of carpet samples from a chair and gestured for Finn to sit.

I rolled the chair out from behind my desk and sat myself. "So, what do you want to talk about? The Nationals?"

"Well, I thought—"

"It was a joke. We're going to talk about what's going on with you. Because if that's not what you wanted to discuss, I'm going to ask you to leave so I can get some sleep."

"Okay, man. I get it. I haven't been one hundred percent truthful, and I owe it to you. It's something I'm working to improve, but I guess I still have a ways to go."

"Hit me."

"Those guys last night weren't trying to mug me. I think they were going to kill me."

Chapter Seven

K*ill him?* I was starting to get used to Finn yanking my chain, but this was another level. "Why would they want to kill you?"

"Because they think I saw them kill someone else."

"Who?"

"That real estate guy, Webster Clayton, or whatever."

"Webster Claypool?"

"Yeah. Him."

So many questions zipped through my head. I closed my eyes and tried to get centered. "Okay, Finn. Why don't you start at the beginning?"

"Sure, sure. Good idea. When I came to town, I needed a job, so I figured I could get a job delivering pizzas, right? Probably don't need many references for that. Had to go to a couple of places, but I took a job with Paolo's Pies. It's not far from here."

I was familiar with the place. Pizzas were decent, if a bit overpriced. Heard good things about the owner, Paolo, too. "Yeah, I've been there."

"So they gave me a car to drive, for deliveries."

"They just gave it to you?"

"Well, no. I use it to make deliveries while I'm working, then if the schedule pans out right, I can keep it overnight and use it the next day. I figured it was a way I could have some wheels to run errands without actually having to buy a car. Money's a little tight right now."

"That actually makes sense."

"Anyway, I was delivering an order—two large, one cheese, one pepperoni, and a wowie brownie—when these guys started running and yelling at me.

I hopped in my car and took off. The next morning, I heard the news about the dude's murder."

I noodled it through. "Let me see if I have this right. These guys yell at you, then when you don't stop, they chase you. You take off in the pizzamobile and ditch it at the mall, because you're afraid these murderers saw you and think maybe you witnessed what they did. Under the assumption that if they kill you, they'll eliminate a possible witness."

Finn pointed at me and nodded. "Yes. Exactly, that. I was afraid these murderers thought I'd seen what they did and were afraid I'd rat them out. So they wanted to kill me."

"Then why ditch your car that night?"

Finn cocked his head. "I don't follow."

"You said you heard the news the next morning, right?"

"Yeah."

"Then you didn't know a murder occurred that night. Hence, you had no idea these men were murderers."

Finn's eyes narrowed, and I could tell he was seeing if my logic made sense. "These guys were yelling at me and chasing me. I had a feeling they were bad men."

"But you had no reason to think they might be *murderers* since you hadn't even learned about the murder yet."

Finn's voice shrank. "I was scared, Mess."

Fear made people do all kinds of desperate things, but I wasn't buying Finn's account. "I'm sure you were scared. Any normal person would have been in the situation you've described. But your story doesn't make sense, not to me." I stood. "Get out, Finn. When you want to tell me the actual, real, honest-to-goodness truth, then come back. But know this: you only get so many chances, and then you're on your own. I don't appreciate being lied to."

I waited a moment for Finn to spill his guts, but when nothing came spewing out from between his lying lips, I went to the door and opened it. He got up and shuffled out, and I made sure to slam the door behind him.

Then I returned to my room. Could Finn have been in Claypool's neighborhood delivering a pizza at the time of his murder?

Possible, I guessed. If it wasn't true, or at least true-ish, why would Finn say it was? What could he possibly have to gain by getting mixed up in a high-profile murder? I thought it was clear that something frightened him enough to ditch the car at the mall. And it was obvious those two guys in the Audi were waiting specifically for Finn.

The facts, as Finn laid them out, sort of fit. Except for the reasoning.

I replayed the scene Finn had described, and I tried to piece everything together logically, but it was like putting together a jigsaw puzzle using a very fuzzy picture as a guide. After a few minutes, a solution dawned on me. Everything Finn said would make sense, *if* he changed one tiny detail. Finn said he believed the two guys thought Finn had witnessed the murder. What if Finn actually *had* witnessed the murder? Then he'd be plenty scared enough to ditch his car and come hide away at the Inn and wear the ridiculous fishing hat.

And it made sense the two killers would go to great lengths to find Finn, including staking out his car. It also followed that if Finn had indeed witnessed the murder, and the murderers had spotted him, then Finn's life could be in danger.

Of course, if Finn had witnessed Claypool's murder, the killers weren't the only ones who would want to talk to him. The police would be extremely interested—an eyewitness would be the break they needed.

And a certain newspaper reporter would also love to interview him. I picked up my phone and was about to text Lia, when a terrible thought struck me.

A truly *terrible* thought.

What if Finn wasn't just an eyewitness? What if he was somehow involved in the murder himself?

I couldn't talk to Lia quite yet.

I went to bed instead, and it took me about two hours to fall asleep, and I dreamed of killer pizza delivery guys in flying cars on their way to a picnic.

* * *

When my parents gave me the keys to the motel slightly over a year ago, I was a bright-eyed idealist. Still liked to think I was, although some of the luster had worn off. I figured I'd pick up the hospitality industry quickly. After all, I was a fast learner.

Plus, the motel business was in my blood. But the time I spent in my childhood and teen years hanging around the motel, doing maintenance, odd jobs, and the occasional stint behind the registration desk hadn't fully prepared me for all the minutiae involved in running a first-rate operation. Or a third-rate one either, it turned out.

In those first days, I was overwhelmed. Cesar kept the day-to-day operation rolling, and he helped me the best he could with the budgeting and financial planning. And, I had to admit, Uncle Phil helped teach me the ropes, too, even through his gigantic Lens of Judgment. Of course, the stuff he didn't approve of—me opening up the doors to the less fortunate, primarily—didn't begin until a few months after I'd taken over. After he'd taught me what he could.

People asked me why I decided to go that route, to allow those seeking refuge from bad situations—or even just a warm bed on a frigid night—and I always gave a generic answer: *I want to help those in need.* Which was undeniably one hundred percent true.

But there was a more personal driving force, too. Every time I was able to give a room to someone who really could use one, I felt I was helping Finn—or, more accurately, someone in dire straits like Finn. I mean, if I couldn't help my cousin directly, then this was the next best thing. *Pay it forward. Good Karma. Good deed of the day.* Or, however you wanted to think about it.

The catch was that I needed to do what I could—within reason, of course—to make enough money to keep the doors open.

To that end, I dove into the monthly expenses, trying to find another few hundred dollars I could squeeze out. But my mind kept going back to Finn.

It was almost nine a.m., and he was probably awake. More than anything, I wanted to march down to Finn's room and read him the riot act. But my compassionate side took over. If he *had* witnessed a murder and if he *did* think the killers were after him, then I could understand him lying about it. Maybe to protect me, or maybe because he was afraid I'd insist he go to the police. Either way, if I was going to try to help Finn do the right thing, I'd have to approach him the way I'd approach a baby bird who'd fallen out of the nest. Carefully, slowly, and non-threateningly.

As for telling Lia about everything, I really wanted to. But until I knew the level of Finn's involvement, I'd have to put that off. I'd feel terrible if I led the lamb to the slaughter, at least until I got the full story from the lamb. I was just tired of having to pick my way through sheep shit.

The phone rang: Lia. Had we developed some kind of bizarre ESP-type connection? I think of telling her something, and she calls me? I answered. "Good morning, good looking."

"May I speak to Mess Hopkins, ace photographer?"

I imagined Lia's scar beckoning as she smiled. "Speaking."

"While I'm waiting for more details from the investigators, my editor wants me to prepare a background piece on the street where Claypool lives—*lived*. Not only is there that Headstomper guy, but there's a college basketball coach and a retired actor living there. Who knew there was a neighborhood with so many celebrities, right in our back yard?"

"I guess you need to make some bank to afford the houses there."

"For sure. Anyway, I've got several appointments set up for today. I'm sure it won't be anything hard-hitting—in fact, it may not even be very interesting—but I figured it would be a way to spend some time together. We've been real busy the last couple of weeks. And, if you play your cards right, I'll let you take me out to lunch. There's that new tapas place I've been wanting to try." She paused. "If your boss will let you play hooky, that is."

I was pretty sure she meant me, but I pictured the frown on Cesar's face when I told him I couldn't make our weekly meeting. Of course, if I simply texted him, I wouldn't have to actually see his mask of disapproval. "You're on. Except I don't have a camera."

"Don't worry, your phone will be fine. I doubt if we'll use any of your pictures, anyway. Remember, I've seen some of your photos."

Forty minutes later, we pulled up in front of Claypool's next-door neighbor, Headstomper Thorpe.

Lia turned to me before we got out of the car. "Listen, Mess. Photographers should be seen and not heard. And not really seen, either. Stay in the background, ask if you may take a photo before snapping one, smile, and say thank you when we're finished. Okay?"

"Sure thing. Won't say a word." I wasn't sure exactly what I was looking for, but I was hoping to get some sense of the neighborhood, enough to identify the parts of Finn's story that might be bullshit and which parts might actually have a kernel of truth to them. This may be a road to nowhere, but at least it beat stewing in my room at the Inn—and it definitely beat talking to Cesar about soap dispensers.

Plus, I'd get to take Lia out to lunch, so there was that to look forward to.

The gate across the driveway was open. As we made our way up to Headstomper's front door, I observed the neighborhood. Very large houses, set back from the street a ways. But the lots were no more than an acre. Most of the yards were fenced, and while there were some decent-sized trees, it wasn't like other parts of Oakton, which seemed to have been carved out of forests.

This seemed more like a newer development built on already-cleared land, with the intent of creating an exclusive enclave of executive mansions, primarily for people who wanted a big, showy house but didn't want the headaches that went with trying to maintain a large property.

The kind of place that appealed to new money, if I had to stereotype it.

At the front door, Lia rang the video doorbell, and I hung back a bit, the ever-respectful photographer. I had a jolt of panic when I imagined Headstomper recognizing me as a motel operator and blowing my cover, but it only took a millisecond for me to realize that a guy who lived in this house would never, ever have been to the Fairfax Manor Inn. I was safe.

Lia was about to ring again when the front door opened, and we were greeted by a tall brunette with amazing green eyes. Dressed in a tight white t-shirt and even tighter jeans—with platform sandals—it had to be Mrs. Headstomper, the supermodel.

"Ah, you must be the reporter. Lia, isn't it?" She looked past her, to me.

Hit me with a smile that almost blinded me. "And you are...?"

"He's my photographer, Hopkins."

I had a retort ready to go, but I swallowed it. *Hopkins* wasn't going to screw up his girlfriend's interview.

"I am Alluree. Please, come in. We can chat in the solarium."

Alluree led us past the living room, the dining room, a home office, a family room, a home theater, another family room, a library, another office, a trophy room that must have held fifty MMA and boxing trophies, and finally into a bright room overlooking a nice pool in their back yard. We didn't pass a kitchen, but I'd bet there were at least two in the house. I wasn't sure what kind of home I expected from a man named Headstomper, but this was very tastefully decorated, and there were no mangled bodies anywhere. That I could see, anyway.

Alluree gestured to a wicker furniture grouping. "Have a seat. I'll let my husband know you're here." She sashayed off, and Lia and I sat in matching armchairs. Although they were wicker, they had very thick seats and arm pads, so they were quite comfortable.

"Nice place, huh?" she said.

I made a face. "Eh, seems like it would require a lot of upkeep."

"That's what staff is for. I don't think you'd make a very good rich person."

After seeing Uncle Phil—and my parents, to some extent—attain a net worth I never would, I knew Lia was right. And, in a poor man's way, I was proud of that. "Well, I wouldn't mind trying." I didn't know how to spend millions on myself, but I could think of a lot of places to donate any excess funds.

Floor-to-ceiling windows and a quartet of skylights let the sun in. Flowering plants—and vases of cut flowers—occupied all the nooks and crannies of the room. Outside, the yard wasn't huge—and much of it was taken up by the pool and stone deck—but it was landscaped expertly. A seven-foot fence enclosed the entire property, and it seemed very private— even though I knew there were executive mansions on either side and one behind.

I wondered if the Headstompers spent much time in this room, enjoying the ambiance.

A few minutes later, Alluree returned with Headstomper. I'd seen pictures of him on the Internet when I'd done my Google research. And, not surprisingly, his face looked exactly like those photos. Square jawline. Close-cropped hair. A diamond stud sparkling in each earlobe.

But online, he'd often been photographed in the ring, without a shirt and with a sheen of perspiration adding gloss to a heavily inked torso. In person, you could still make out his impressively muscled physique underneath his button-down shirt, but he looked more like a gym rat than a mauling machine who went by the modest name of Headstomper.

And he wore tortoise-shell glasses, which made him look a little like a gym rat accountant.

Lia and I rose, and he extended his hand. "Timothy Thorpe. Call me Tim. Or Thorpe. Just not by my nickname. That's simply for show. Please, have a seat."

I knew names were simply names, but Tim? *Tim?* Tims worked in a library. Tims sold neckties at the department store in the mall. Tim made up more than half the word *timid*. Tims were Tiny. Thorpe wasn't tiny in any way whatsoever.

Timothy wasn't any better. Half the parishes across the country had a Father Timothy, a gentle soul who guided people to spiritual enlightenment. I'd seen more than a dozen video clips of Thorpe demolishing the faces of his opponents with brutal efficiency, and he wasn't a Tim or a Timothy. He was a Headstomper all the way. After seeing the violence, I'd never think of him in any other way. But I could compromise by calling him Thorpe.

Thorpe and Alluree sat next to each other on the loveseat and held hands. An everyday thing, or were they posing for the press?

"Alluree tells me you're with the Fairfax Observer." Thorpe's voice was mellifluous, completely opposite to the one I'd heard in a YouTube video when he was threatening to rip the lungs out of his opponent in the most painful of ways.

Lia leaned forward. "Yes, that's right."

"You should know I don't usually do interviews for local papers. Or, really, for print media at all. But Alluree handles all of my branding, and she thought it would be good for my image—and my local interests—if I opened myself up more. So here I am, opening myself up. Ask away."

"Thank you so much for granting us this time. I'll try not to waste it." Lia smiled and I noticed Alluree tightening her grip on Thorpe's hand. "I know you've spoken to the police about Webster Claypool's death, and I really don't want to dwell on it, but I feel like I have to at least give you a chance to go on record with your thoughts about it."

"Yes, of course." Thorpe flashed a tight smile. "A terrible tragedy. He was a good neighbor and a vital member of this community. I trust the police will find those responsible, and our justice system will impose the appropriate consequences." He disengaged his hand from his wife's and made a fist. "If I had been here that night, and I had seen the killer, I would have delivered my own brand of justice."

Alluree jumped in. "That comment was off the record. Neither of us was home that night. Tim was at a promotional appearance in Atlanta, and I was on a girl's getaway in New York. Obviously, we have no knowledge of the incident, and we really have nothing more to say about it. Now, please, let's continue with the interview."

Lia proceeded to ask a bunch of questions about how they met, how their marriage worked with two incredibly demanding careers, about their upbringing, and about their growing role in the local community. They'd recently formed a charitable foundation to help children's literacy and afterschool programs in the entire DC area, and they spent much of the next fifteen minutes talking about that.

I kept my mouth shut the entire time, as requested.

After Lia finished the interview, Thorpe and Alluree posed for a number of pictures, in the solarium and several other rooms. I did my best to appear as if I was a real photographer and knew what I was doing, pretending to take into account the light and angles and all the photographic stuff.

I gave them stage directions, repositioned them, tapped some buttons on my phone, and frowned. They cooperated, responding like they'd done it before. And being celebrities, I'm sure they had. I mean, Alluree was a professional model, but I think I had her convinced I was a pro photographer.

We took a few final pictures in the trophy room, and I realized that I'd initially underestimated the number of trophies, awards, plaques, belts, ribbons, and plates that Thorpe—in his guise as Headstomper—had won. There had to be hundreds. When Lia asked about them, Thorpe shrugged. "For some guys, fighting is their life, their identity. For me, it's a means to an end. Yeah, I'm good at it. Yeah, I enjoy dominating my opponent. But when it's time to hang things up, I don't think I'll look back. Getting beat on isn't always so pleasant. I've got many other interests, as I hope you've learned during the interview. Thanks for doing the piece on me. If you have any more questions, Alluree will be able to help you. Have a good day." Tim Thorpe, the Headstomper, walked out of the room, and when he left, he seemed to suck some of the air out with him.

"I'll show you out." Alluree led us back the way we came, and the house was no less impressive leaving as it was coming in.

At the door, she bid us goodbye, but before she closed the door, I finally spoke up. "I have a question."

"Yes?"

"Where do you get your pizza from?"

Alluree looked as if I'd asked her a question in Urdu. "I guess it's almost lunchtime, isn't it? Well, we don't really eat much pizza, but I understand Georgio's is the best place near here. That's what all the neighbors get— the Georgio's pizza delivery guy is here frequently." She lowered her voice. "You'd think educated people—everybody in this community, at least—would eat healthier. I mean, your body is your temple, right?"

She glanced down at my slightly out-of-shape temple, and I thought I detected the smallest of frowns.

"Thanks." I was hoping she'd say Paulo's Pies, which might lend a bit of credence to Finn's story, but I knew her answer didn't mean much, either way.

I took a bunch of pictures of the neighborhood, from a variety of angles and zooms. I thought maybe I could show them to Finn, and he could point out exactly where he'd parked and where the guys chasing him had come from.

When we got back to the car, Lia turned to me. "What was that about the pizza, Mess? I thought you were taking me out for tapas."

"I am. Just curious about something."

"What?" She gazed deeply into my eyes, and I knew exactly what I needed to do.

"We'll go to lunch, but we need to stop at the Inn first," I said. "I need to introduce you to my cousin Finn."

Chapter Eight

We found Finn in his room, watching a cooking reality show where the celebrity chef yells at the contestants until they cry in their soup. He got up off the bed to greet us.

I made the introductions. "Lia, this is my cousin Finn. Finn, Lia. She's a reporter for the local newspaper."

"Nice to meet you."

Finn stood there, unsure what was happening. I know he'd wanted to remain anonymous, and a reporter was probably the fourth-to-last person he'd want to meet, after a cop and both of Claypool's killers.

"Don't worry, she doesn't bite," I said. "We'd like to talk to you."

"When?"

"Right this very minute."

"I don't know, Mess. I'm not feeling too good."

I eyed him. He always seemed to feel ill when I wanted something from him. "Sit back down. It won't take long."

Finn sighed as he reclined on his bed. Lia sat in the room's only chair, and I remained standing.

"Okay, Finn. You need to know that not only is Lia a reporter, but we're seeing each other. So what you tell her as a source is doubly protected. By the reporter-source confidentiality, and by the fact she's not going to burn you because we're dating."

"Mess, I'm not sure—"

I interrupted. "She's not going to tell anyone what you tell her, unless you say it's okay." I nodded at Lia. "Isn't that right?"

"Well, I can't make any ironclad promises. What's all this about, anyway?"

"Webster Claypool's death." I tried to deliver the line flatly, without any trace of the dramatic, but I'm not sure I succeeded.

Lia's eyes grew. "What?" Her beautiful brown orbs returned to their normal size as she turned to Finn. "No offense, but what could you possibly know about Claypool's murder?"

"That's not a very reporter-like stance, is it?" I pointed out. "Aren't you supposed to listen to what your sources say with an open mind?"

She was speechless for a moment but recovered nicely. "You're right. I just didn't realize Finn was a source. Now that I understand he might be, I'm all ears." She cleared her throat and spoke in a newsperson's steady voice. "Okay, Finn. What do you know about Webster Claypool's murder?"

Finn had been watching me and Lia verbally spar, but now that it was his turn to speak, he fumbled. "Well, you see, I happened to be…I mean, I was in the…"

"Oh, spit it out, man," I said.

"I was there," Finn said. "Delivering a pizza in the neighborhood that night. Two guys started yelling and chasing me. They must have been the killers." Once Finn started, the words came flooding out of his mouth, as if they'd been imprisoned there, and it was jailbreak time.

"You were chased by Claypool's murderers?" she asked.

"I believe so."

Lia blew out a big breath. "Okay, you'll have to start at the beginning and take me through it, step by step. Can you do that?"

"Sure." Finn recounted what he'd done that night and what he'd seen, same as he'd told me. Getting yelled at and getting chased. Dumping the car at the mall. Us going back the next day to retrieve it and seeing the two guys staking it out. The chase through the mall, although he omitted the part about me leveling the two guys. Both versions—the one he told me and the one he told Lia—were identical.

"I can vouch for the last part. There were definitely two guys staking out Finn's pizzamobile. And then they chased him."

"Now I know why you asked Alluree about the pizza." Lia sat perfectly still, and I knew she was thinking it through, trying to see what angles Finn might be playing. I'd done the same thing, and I wondered if Lia would eventually arrive at the same conclusions. Namely, that Finn either witnessed the actual murder or he was involved in it.

Finally, she spoke. "If you didn't see the murder itself, how do you know the two guys chasing you were the murderers?"

I almost blurted out, *Yes, exactly*, but I kept it in check. It was nice to know that Lia and I had both spotted Finn's erroneous logic. Maybe *she'd* have more success getting to the truth.

Finn licked his lips. "If you had seen them, you'd know they had just killed *someone*."

His statement was, of course, ludicrous. I was about to call him on it, but Lia was too quick.

"Okay," Lia said. "When you saw these guys, had you already delivered your pizza?"

"Uh, yes. That's right."

"To which house?"

"Hmm. Let's see, I'm not sure exactly."

"Okay, I guess we can check the records at the pizza place."

"I'm guessing I don't have that job anymore, and I'm also guessing my boss isn't very happy with me. Not sure he'd be in the cooperating mood."

"How would you describe those guys?" Lia asked.

"One guy was tall-ish. And bald. The other guy was…normal. Both guys were white."

"Is that based on seeing them that night or the next day at the mall?" Lia asked.

Finn looked puzzled. "Um, both? Although it was dark, and I was running for my life the night before, so I guess I saw them more clearly at the mall. Mess saw them, too."

"But you don't know for sure they were the same guys, do you?"

"Not for sure, sure." Finn tilted his head, as if he was watching the events of that night on instant replay. "But pretty sure."

"And you don't know for *certain* they had anything to do with Claypool's murder, right?" Lia sounded like a defense attorney on every TV lawyer show I'd ever watched.

"I 'spose not. But it sure seems likely."

Lia didn't press the issue. "When you went to the cops, what did they say?"

Finn swallowed, glanced my way. Lia picked up on it, and she looked at me, too. I shrugged. "She's asking you, Finn."

"I didn't tell the cops. Me and them don't get along."

I sensed Finn starting to get irritated. And that would only make him *less* cooperative. "We get it. Just a few more questions, okay?"

She shot me a look, then continued. "Did they have guns or knives or anything?"

"That night?"

"Yes, that night." Impatience colored her words.

"Like I said, it was dark. Mostly I only saw two shadowy figures."

"Hang on." I pulled my phone out and scrolled through the pictures I'd taken of Claypool's neighborhood. "Got some streetlamps. Those old-fashioned ones, like in London. Maybe they shed some light. Think back, Finn."

Finn made some faces as he tried to remember. "I think they might have had something in their hands. Maybe phones? Maybe something else?" He shrugged. "I've told you all I can remember, I swear."

Lia's phone buzzed. She checked it, then looked up. "Gotta run. Chairman Young and the Chief of Police are holding a press conference in half an hour. Boss wants me to cover it, ask some questions about Claypool's murder investigation. It's not like I get any good answers, but he wants some visibility for me—and the paper. All in a day's work. Raincheck on the tapas?"

"Sure."

Lia gave me a quick peck on the cheek, then rushed off.

"I like her," Finn said. "I really like her."

Chapter Nine

With my lunch date gone, I had two choices. Eat lunch with Finn or do some investigating. Easy decision. I called Vell.

"Whassup, Mess?"

"Hungry?" I asked.

"Always."

"Let's get some pizza."

"If you're buying, I'm eating," Vell said. "I'll be right over."

Vell parked at the motel, and I drove us the few miles to the "downtown" City of Fairfax. Not a downtown like most major cities, with high-rise office buildings and traffic jams and, well, lots of bustle. The City of Fairfax's downtown was little more than the City Hall and Municipal Building, the library, and a smattering of townhouse professional offices.

It wasn't far from George Mason University, so there were a fair share of cheapo restaurants and college bars and more than a fair share of *here today, gone tomorrow* coffee houses.

We found a parking spot in a public lot and walked two blocks to Paulo's Pies.

"Been a while since we've been here." Vell opened the door, and we were immediately hit with the distinct smell of wood stove pizza. "Too long, in fact."

The hostess led us to a booth along the side wall. There were about ten tables in the place, and most of them were occupied. There were half a dozen chairs up front by the register to accommodate people waiting for their carryout orders. Any decent pizza place near a college campus was bound to do well, both eat-in and delivery.

The hostess handed us the menus. "Enjoy."

She started to leave, but I stopped her. "May we speak to Paolo, please?"

Her brow furrowed. "Is there a problem?"

"No. We just had some questions."

She stood there for a second, no doubt trying to come up with some way to make us happy without having to bother the boss. Finally, she gave us a little shrug and an even littler smile. "Sure. I'll send him over."

When she was out of earshot, Vell whispered, "*Is* there a problem?"

"Only trying to get some answers. This is the pizza place Finn works for."

"I knew there had to be a reason we were here. I feel used."

"So you don't want to enjoy a tasty lunch, on me?"

"Oh, I don't feel *that* used. Carry on." He picked up a menu and buried himself in it.

A couple of minutes later, a guy dressed in shirt and tie, sleeves rolled up, came over. "I'm Paulo. I understand you wanted to see me. Is there a problem?"

I guessed it was nice to see that the staff wanted to address any problems, but what did it say—about the restaurant or about society—that the first thing everyone assumed was a problem? "Nope. I'd just like to ask you a few questions, if that's okay?"

The manager exhaled audibly, and the muscles in his face relaxed. "Sure. What can I help you with?"

"You deliver, right?"

"Of course."

"To Oakton?"

"To the part closest to us. But we don't get a ton of business from there. Most of our delivery is to the university. You know how it is, hungry college kids who don't want to cook."

"Do you have a guy named Finn working for you?"

Paolo's face tightened. Anger? Or concern? "I keep my employee information confidential. Why do you want to know, anyway?"

"I'm his cousin. He's, uh, not feeling too well and couldn't make his shift.

Wanted me to come in and apologize in person."

Paolo stared at me for the longest time. "You're Mess Hopkins, aren't you?"

"That's right."

"Finn mentioned you. And your reputation precedes you." Paulo smiled, two rows of white, although crooked, teeth.

That sounded a bit ominous. "My reputation?"

"As a kind and generous soul in the community," Paolo said. "May I sit?"

I exhaled. "Sure."

Vell slid over, and Paolo lowered himself into the booth. "Finn didn't show up the other night. Abandoned one of our cars. I had to send someone out to pick it up. I tried calling him, but he never answered. He's sick, huh?"

"Under the weather." Which was true. "How did you know where the car was, anyway?"

"I put GPS trackers in them, so I'll know if there are any delivery issues or security issues or whatever. Comes with this cool phone app. Can't be too careful, right?"

"Right." I exchanged glances with Vell. "Do you still have the tracking data from two days ago?"

"I guess so."

"Would you mind showing me? I'm trying to corroborate some things."

"Does this have anything to do with the guy who called me yesterday evening and wanted to know the names of my delivery drivers?" Paolo's features had hardened.

My heart skipped a beat. Those two goons were persistent. I wondered if they were staking out the pizza place. "What did you tell him?"

"Don't worry, I didn't divulge anything. I pride myself in my ability to judge a person's character, and I could tell the caller was trouble. Something fishy is going on. Care to enlighten me?"

"That's what I'm trying to find out myself. Right now, the working theory is that Finn saw something he shouldn't have."

Paolo stared at me again. Must be his thinking mode. Finally, he said, "Underneath it all, Finn is a decent guy who could use a few breaks. Whatever he's mixed up in, I'd like to help, if I can. As long as it's nothing illegal. That's where I draw the line."

"As far as I can tell, he was just in the wrong place at the wrong time."

"Good to hear," Paolo said.

I smiled. "Maybe the data will help shed some light on things."

Paolo pulled out his phone, opened the app, and after poking around a bit, came up with the info. "He parked Anchovy—that's the name of the car he drove—in Oakton at 7:08 pm. It stayed there until 11:52 pm, when it took off. Then…"

On the screen, I saw a map, and a squiggly blue line, that—evidently—was the route Finn took after leaving Claypool's neighborhood. Paolo swiped a couple of times, then pointed at the map. "Looks like he parked it here, at the mall, about twenty minutes later. That's the last movement." He looked up. "I don't monitor the cars' whereabouts unless there's some kind of issue. That's why I didn't notice it was at the mall until the next day, when Finn was late for his shift."

Paulo tapped the phone some more, getting lost in the data. Then he looked up. "Two things. First, we didn't have a delivery in Oakton that night. And since he was there for four hours, I'd say he was there on some personal matter."

"You let them use the car for personal things?" Vell asked.

Paulo's face shaded. "Well…sometimes the people we hire—college kids and the like—don't always have their own vehicles. So I'm flexible on letting them use the cars for whatever. As long as they show up for their shifts and work hard, I'm okay with that. See, I'm the son of an immigrant, and when my father came here, he relied on the generosity of strangers who helped him out. Just trying to pay it forward, you know?"

"Very generous of you."

"I try to do what's right."

"You mentioned there were two things."

"Yes. According to the tracker, Finn was parked in that same Oakton neighborhood the night before, too. All night long." Paolo smiled. "Maybe he's got a girlfriend there. He deserves some happiness."

Vell started coughing as if he had something caught in his throat, and I figured I knew what it was—a big wad of disbelief.

If Finn was there two nights in a row, not delivering pizza, then something was up. I had no idea how this all dovetailed with Claypool's murder, but I was going to find out, one way or another.

"Like I said, Finn seems like a good guy, and I know he had to overcome so much just to get back on his feet. After hearing his story, I wanted to help out in any way I could. I have a son myself. That's very important to me—I try to help out as many people as I can. I guess maybe you and I are kindred spirits."

It was nice to know what I'd heard about Paolo seemed to be true.

"Thank you so much, Paolo. You've been very helpful. Hopefully, Finn will be, uh, feeling better soon."

"Sure. When all this gets straightened out, he needs to come back to work. We miss him." He got up, noticed the table was empty. "You boys hungry? Please, be my guest. Pizza on me. Large pepperoni okay?"

"That would be awesome," Vell said. "Thanks."

Chapter Ten

We downed the pizza quickly, and Vell was patient enough to wait until we were back in the car before letting loose about Finn. "Two nights in a row, in that neighborhood? Sounds mighty suspicious. One night to case the joint, the next night a burglary gone bad? Then he makes up some story about being there and being chased in case someone saw the pizzamobile fleeing the scene of the crime? All fits."

"Do you think if someone was going to commit a crime, they'd drive around in a brightly colored car with giant pizza pies on it?"

"Nobody said criminals were smart."

"Finn is not a criminal." I inhaled a deep breath and let it out slowly. "At least he's not a murderer."

"Maybe not. But maybe so. I'm getting some real bad vibes here, man. I hope I'm wrong, but things seem to be heading in the wrong direction for your cousin." Vell exhaled sharply. "And do I need to bring up the possibility he was involved in Claypool's murder?"

I started the car and headed back to the motel. It was times like these I wished I owned a polygraph and I could find an excuse to hook Finn up. "I'm going to confront Finn with what we learned from Paolo. I think we need some definitive answers. Jumping to these wild conclusions isn't helping anyone."

"Amen, brother." Vell shot me a steely look. "Right now?"

"Finn's a slippery one. I need to ease into it, find the right time and place."

He scoffed. "You can be such a chicken sometimes."

Vell wasn't wrong.

* * *

I hadn't had a chance to ask Lia what she was planning to do about Finn's story, so I called her. "Hey, busy?"

She laughed. "You could say that. Working on a recap of the press conference. But I've got a minute. What's up?"

"Well, we haven't talked about our conversation with Finn today. I know he wants his name kept out of any story you might print. I didn't think it was a problem; you journalists always protect your sources, right?"

Lia laughed again, but it seemed she was laughing more at me than with me. "Seriously, Mess? I don't know your cousin, so I hesitate to call him a liar, but…come on. That story he told was just that—a story. And frankly, not even a very compelling one."

"What about those two guys at the mall? I saw them chase Finn, and they were serious about catching him." I, too, left out the part about me derailing those guys with my shoulder. No need to worry her.

"Oh, I don't doubt there were two guys looking for the driver of the pizza delivery car. But I doubt they were murderers. More likely, they got into some kind of road rage incident with Finn and were looking for revenge. Or maybe Finn owes them money. Or maybe Finn's selling drugs and he infringed on their turf. There are a million more probable reasons two guys would be after Finn than because they're murderers. Now, if his story made better sense, well, that's another thing altogether. So, don't worry. I don't plan to use *anything* Finn told me. At least not until someone comes forth with some actual facts. I have my reputation to think about."

"You could be right."

"Without more information, we'll never know. Hey, I gotta run. Sorry. Maybe we can connect soon, huh?"

"Sure. Good luck with the story. Talk to you later."

We clicked off. What Lia said made a lot of sense. Was I too close to Finn to be as unbiased as I should be? At least she didn't think Finn was involved somehow—that thought still was lodged in my mind.

My sister Izzy invited me over for dinner tonight, and I was planning to bring a surprise guest. I'd been anticipating the look on her face ever since Finn showed up.

I figured that reconnecting with Izzy while devouring some home cooking—such that it was, Izzy wasn't the best chef—would make Finn feel more comfortable. Show him his family loved him, unconditionally. Plus, spending time with my cutie-patootie twin nieces was bound to put anyone in a good mood. When he'd left town, they were toddlers.

It was time Finn was welcomed back into the family fold. Past time, if you asked me.

He could thank me later.

✳ ✳ ✳

I parked in Izzy's driveway.

"I thought you said we were going to dinner at some great place," Finn said.

"After this stop."

"Fine. I'll stay in the car." Finn pulled out his phone and started tapping. He had no clue we were at Izzy's place. When he'd left town, she'd been living in Alexandria.

"Come on. Not sure exactly how long I'll be."

"Do I have to?" Finn said it while actually pouting.

"You sound like a child. Now, get out of the car. *Please.*"

Finn harrumphed as if he were an eighty-year-old, then he capitulated. We walked up the flagstone path to the front door, and I remembered the last time I'd brought an uninvited guest to Izzy's for dinner. It didn't go too well. This evening, though, I expected a much warmer welcome from Izzy's husband, Russell.

I rang the bell and listened to the sonorous chimes within. Izzy lived in a very nice house in McLean, not too far from Uncle Phil. Despite the proximity, I wasn't sure how often they saw each other. Uncle Phil liked to spread his judgment around almost as much as he did his money. Made him feel like a big shot.

The door swung open, and I had to look down to see who had answered it.

"Uncle Mess!" Emma and Olivia screeched. "You're here!"

"Uncle Mess? Uncle Mess? Who is this Uncle Mess? I am Sir Galahad." I bowed and executed an elaborate arm flourish. "And this, Princess Emma and Princess Olivia, is the great knight Sir Phineas."

The twins each curtsied. "Welcome, Sir Phineas. Whoever you are."

"We have slayed the terrible dragon and have now come to dine with you and Queen Izzy."

The girls giggled. Then they turned and fled back into the house, "Mom, Uncle Mess is here. And he brought some knight named Sir Finnegan."

"Come on, Sir Finnegan," I said. "Let's go see the queen."

When we entered the kitchen, Izzy was bent over the oven, checking on something. The girls had disappeared, and Russell was nowhere in sight. I cleared my throat.

"Is the temperature of this chicken supposed to be two hundred degrees?" she said without turning around.

"I think it's done." I didn't do much cooking—hard to cook in a motel room—but that sounded plenty done to me. Wasn't two hundred and twelve boiling?

"I think so, too." Izzy pulled the casserole dish from the oven and set it on the stovetop. I wished I could say it smelled good. On the other hand, I'd smelled a lot worse coming here for dinner. Finally, she turned around, wiping her hands on her apron.

She smiled at my guest and held out her hand. "Hello, I'm—" She stopped midsentence. "Holy shit, is that Finn? Finn Hopkins? You're alive!" She practically threw herself at him, engulfing him in a giant hug. A few tears dripped down her cheeks. I got the make-a-mess genes in the family, and she got the bear-hugging ones.

After what seemed like five minutes, they broke apart. "Oh my God, I'm so glad to see you." She turned to me. "How come you didn't tell me, jerkwad?"

Then she spun back to Finn. "How long have you been back? Where were you all this time? I bet Uncle Phil and Aunt Vera are so, so happy, huh? Where are you staying? What's the—"

I held up a hand. "Slow your roll, Sis. You've got all evening to interrogate Finn. For now, why don't we celebrate with a toast?" I glanced around. "Where's Rusty?"

Izzy gave me the evil eye. "Don't start, Mess. Not tonight. Not with such great news to celebrate!" Russell hated it when I called him Rusty. To be honest, I didn't usually say it to his face. He was bigger and meaner than I was. "He's on his way home. Called a while ago from the road."

"I'll try to behave."

Russell was a high-priced lobbyist who worked in D.C. He was a hard worker, a good father and husband, and a bit of a condescending prick. But he made Izzy happy, and he sired two adorable kids whom I loved dearly, so I couldn't really hate him. I was sure he remembered Finn, although I doubted he'd be giving his long-lost cousin-in-law any bear hugs or shedding any tears of joy.

Izzy found a bottle of sparkling wine and poured us drinks. In the background, I heard the *boopity beepity* noises of a child's video game. My nieces were already gaming wizards at seven years old.

"To family and to homecomings." Izzy held her glass high.

We echoed her sentiments and sipped our wine.

Izzy stood there with the biggest grin, shaking her head as if she didn't believe it. I debated telling her what kind of trouble Finn might be in, but I wasn't sure she could really help, and the idea of bumming her out bummed me out. I supposed she'd find out soon enough, so why ruin her reunion tonight?

Emma and Olivia came roaring into the kitchen as if they'd been transported by a hurricane-force wind. "We're hungry. When's dinner ready?"

"We'll eat in a minute. I want to introduce you to someone." She kneeled and corralled her two girls. "This is Finn. He's my cousin. Which means he's your cousin, too."

"Hi, Finn."

"He's Uncle Phil's son."

They stared at him, then Emma turned to Izzy. "Can we eat *now?*"

Izzy sighed. "Sure. Wash your hands and take your seats. Daddy will be home shortly, but I guess we can get started."

The girls scampered off to the bathroom.

"You, too. Wash your hands."

"Yes, Mom," I said.

Finn followed me to the bathroom, and we had to jump aside to dodge the girls beelining for the dinner table.

"You're awful quiet," I said.

"A bit overwhelmed, I guess."

"There's a lot of energy in this house, that's for sure. But Finn, people are genuinely glad to see you. And to see you're okay. The Hopkinses may argue from time to time, but when things get serious, we stand up for each other." How often had I heard my father use those exact words?

"Are you suggesting I tell my parents I've returned?"

"Yes, that's exactly what I'm suggesting."

When we got to the table, Izzy already had a place set for Finn. "Why don't you sit here, right between the two girls?"

That was my usual seat of honor, but I guessed I could relinquish it for Finn. At least this one time.

Izzy brought the food to the table and served the girls. "Okay, dig in."

We all got our food—chicken, asparagus, and potatoes that had been baked about three days too long. I was pushing it around on my plate, deciding which overcooked item to attack first, when I heard the garage door rolling up. A moment later, Russell strode in.

"Hello, family." Russell sounded happy, which I didn't recall happening very often. He entered the dining room, and his huge smile faltered. "Hey, everybody. Um, who's this?"

"Who do you think it is?" Izzy asked.

Russell apprised Finn, but recognition never came. "I, uh…" He shrugged. "I'm sorry."

Izzy got up, put her arm around her husband. "It's Finn."

"Finn?"

"Phil's son. Cousin Finn."

Russell's jaw dropped. "I thought…I mean, we thought you were…" He looked at me as if I had some kind of answer. I gave him a small shrug of my own. He nodded at Finn and smiled broadly, Mr. Man-of-the-Manor. "Welcome home, Finn."

The dinner conversation revolved around Finn, and as expected, Izzy led the way, peppering Finn with question after question. Most of his answers were vague—sketchy details, a lot of "I don't remembers," and some very adroit change-of-topics. Having already experienced Finn's stonewalling, I was paying close attention, trying to glean any relevant pieces of information from the stream of ambiguousness.

But you couldn't get blood from an overcooked turnip, or something like that.

At the end of the table, Russell played on his phone, like he often did at dinner, a man so important he couldn't even shut down his availability for fifteen minutes to eat with his family.

And, as usual, dinner itself was barely this side of edible.

Emma and Olivia ate fast and, completely uninterested in Finn's story, asked to be excused quickly. Izzy granted their request, and soon thereafter, the sounds of the video game started again.

Izzy stopped her inquisition long enough to bring dessert to the table. She'd made a bundt cake, and judging from the neon-colored icing in some sort of abstract pattern; my nieces had helped. Before she had a chance to call them back in, the doorbell chimes sounded.

"Expecting company?" Izzy asked Russell, who sat there with a weird smirk on his mug. "I'll see who it is. Can you call the girls in, please?"

Russell bellowed for his daughters, and Izzy went to answer the door. Dinner at Izzy's was always a bit disjointed, and it reminded me of dinners growing up, which were also full of energy, served with a dollop of screaming and heaping side dishes of judgment.

A moment later, Uncle Phil stalked into the dining room. He stood there, mouth agape, staring at Finn. He didn't say a word, and although the girls had now returned to the table, the silence was absolute.

Finn stared back, and his face had gone so pale, I could practically see through his skin to the bones in his face.

Even motormouth Izzy was quiet.

I expected Uncle Phil to rush over and hug Finn, sobbing with unbridled joy, the son he thought was dead. But he continued to stand there, mesmerized. I supposed it was impossible to anticipate how someone would react to seeing their dead son come back to life.

Still, even in a family where repressing feelings was the norm—for males, at least—I expected some sort of reaction from Finn, from Phil. The incredibly awkward silence stretched on.

Finn sat there between my nieces, frozen in terror. I couldn't say I blamed him.

Finally, *finally*, Izzy spoke in a whisper. "Finn's back, Uncle Phil. Isn't that great?"

Uncle Phil's upper lip twitched, just a hair. "I can see that. I had to get a text from Russell here—the only considerate one, it would seem—to tell me that my son, the son who I haven't seen in six years, the son who I feared was *dead*—is alive and enjoying dinner at a house in McLean. A house that isn't mine." He took a step toward Finn. "Do you have any idea what you put your mother and me through? Didn't we raise you with love and attention? And this is how you treat us? I didn't tell your mother yet; I wanted to make sure it was true. Had to see it with my own two eyes."

I could feel Uncle Phil's fury from five feet away, like being near an erupting volcano. Hot and unrelenting. I supposed I could understand his anger about the torment Finn had put them through, but wasn't there also some absolute joy? Maybe after the anger faded, he'd feel some happiness. I glanced at Russell, who seemed to be relishing this. Figured he'd be the one to rat on Finn. Not sure why he did what he did sometimes. Was it because he thought he knew best how Finn should behave, or was it because he liked stirring up family trouble?

"I...I..." Finn began.

I wasn't sure what Finn expected from his parents when he returned, but I figured he thought he'd be greeted with warmth *before* he got reamed out.

Phil reached into his pocket, removed his phone, and held it out to Finn. "You need to call your mother, right now."

Although Finn was thirty years old, Phil was giving him orders as if he were ten.

I waited for Izzy to say something to lighten the situation, but she seemed as stricken as the rest of us.

Finn stood, but instead of reaching for Phil's phone he brushed right past him, heading out of the dining room. "I need to go to the bathroom," he called out over his shoulder.

Phil remained rooted to the floor, staring at us as if this was part of a dream. The wrinkles in his face seemed deeper, and the bags under his eyes more pronounced. It wasn't a feeling I had often, but right now, I felt sorry for my uncle.

"Finn seems good," Izzy said. "I know this must be quite a shock."

Uncle Phil opened his mouth to say something but closed it without uttering a thing. Emma and Olivia were squirming in their seats, and I doubted they'd ever witnessed anything so emotionally charged that wasn't accompanied by lots of shouting and crying.

Izzy popped out of her chair and dragged it over to Phil. "Here, have a seat."

She gently eased him down. I'd seen people in shock before, after an auto accident or witnessing some horrible event. But I couldn't recall ever seeing Phil seem so unlike his usual self. On some level, he was right; Finn had treated him and Aunt Vera unforgivably. But wasn't that part of being a parent? Forgiving your children when they behave unforgivably?

"Girls, let's get you some dessert, okay?" Izzy said, returning to the table and holding up the plate with the bundt cake. "Isn't it beautiful? It was a group project."

"Looks fabulous," I said.

"Absolutely. Great job, girls," Russell said.

Izzy cut slices and served them, and the girls dug in, like locusts. In a matter of seconds, the cake was gone, and each had a purple-pink-green icing moustache. "Can we please be excused?"

"Yes, yes, go," Russell said.

The girls vanished in an instant, and the adults' attention returned to Phil. Slumped in the chair, a mixture of shock and exhaustion on his drawn face. I had to believe that once things got settled down, he'd be ecstatic. But Phil had a perpetually dour outlook on life. Maybe he'd somehow twist Finn's return into some kind of giant negative.

Where was Finn, anyway? I got up and tossed my napkin on the table. "I'm going to check on him." I hustled to the powder room and knocked gently. "Finn, you okay in there?" I could only imagine what was going through his head. He'd wanted to tell Phil on his own terms, and jackhole Russell had messed that up. And worse, much worse, was Phil's angry reaction. I prayed I was never so heartless to my kids, assuming I'd have kids someday.

I knocked again. "Finn. Come on out. I'm sure your father's anger will fade."

No sound came from the bathroom.

"Finn? You in there? Finn?" Images of him lying on the floor, wrists slit, leaped into my mind. I turned the knob and opened the door. Empty.

I opened the door to the garage, peeked out. No sign of him. Had he walked out and kept on walking? I found the girls in front of the TV. "Hey, kiddos. Let's play a little game. I think Finn might be playing hide-and-seek. First one to find him wins something special."

That got their attention.

"What?" Emma asked.

"Something super special."

"You're just saying that. We know you, Uncle Mess. You want us to go find Sir Finnegan, don't you?" Olivia.

"Yes."

Emma made a face, and she reminded me of Izzy when she was a girl. "That'll be kinda hard."

"Why?"

"Because he left." Olivia pointed to the window. "I saw him going down the driveway a few minutes ago."

"Yeah," Emma said. "And he was running pretty fast, too."

Chapter Eleven

I left Izzy to deal with Uncle Phil—maybe it was a cowardly move on my part, but it was Russell's fault for summoning him in the first place. I drove around awhile, looking for a dejected guy walking along the side of the road, but I gave up after about twenty minutes. Hopefully, Finn called himself an Uber and was back in his room, watching heavily scripted reality TV.

I called Cesar, but he hadn't seen Finn return.

When I got back to the motel, I saw Mrs. Williams sitting in a chair outside her room, smoking, and I realized I'd never had my chat with her.

I wandered down. "Evening, Mrs. Williams. How are you doing?"

She blew some smoke at me. Not a cigarette, but a cigarillo. One with a weird cherry smell. "Fine, just fine."

"Have you spoken to your daughter lately?"

"She's dead to me. Kicking me to the curb like that. Who needs her?"

Mrs. Williams needed her. "I know you don't mean that. I'm sure you'd like to go back. Be with your daughter. Family's family, right?"

"Screw my family. They don't care about me at all."

"That's not true." I paused, then snapped my fingers as if I'd had a brainstorm. "How about this? How about if I call your daughter and arrange a conversation between you two? If it helps, I'll even stick around and make sure everything goes smoothly." If I could broker a make-up and get Mrs. Williams out of the Inn and home again, everybody would be happier, and Cesar would be off my back.

Mrs. Williams eyed me through a haze of smoke. "You'd do that? For me?"

"I would." I smiled. "But only if you tell me your first name."

"It's Norma Rae."

Of course, it was. "Well, Norma Rae, why don't you give me your daughter's name and phone number, and I'll get it set up?" I knew Cesar already had this information, but I read someplace that getting someone to actively participate helped to ensure their cooperation and increase their desire to achieve success.

She took another drag, then exhaled very, very slowly. "You know, you're a pretty nice guy. Lettin' me stay here and all. Offerin' to help patch things up with Rosie—that's my daughter. Got two sons, too. They live all the way in California, though." She shuddered, as if the idea of living in California was repulsive. To some, I guessed it was.

"I'll call her first thing in the morning, maybe try to get us all together for lunch, my treat? How does that sound?"

"Sounds fine." She reached out, grabbed my arm. Gave it a squeeze. "A handsome fella like you, I bet you're spoken for, huh?"

I gently wiggled my arm free. "Yes, I am. I'll see you tomorrow, Mrs. Will—I mean Norma Rae. Sleep well."

I retreated as fast as I could without being too obvious. I stopped in front of Finn's door and banged on it for a while—no answer. I stood there for a few minutes, leaning against the wall, simply observing. The traffic whizzing by on Route 50. A plane flying overhead, on its way into Dulles. Two women out for a late evening exercise walk, each one with two pink dumbbells in their hands, pumping them as they motored along.

Still no sign of Finn.

I reached into my pocket, pulled out my wallet, and slid out the master passkey. Inserted it into the slot in Finn's door and entered. "Finn, you in here?"

I flipped on the lights, an image of Finn lying in bed, eyes staring at the ceiling, causing my heart to race. But the room was unoccupied. Just some of his clothing strewn about. I checked the bathroom, and it was empty, too. I exited quickly, then skulked back to my room. I never used my passkey unless there was a very strong suspicion that something serious required my attention. I guessed I was more worried about Finn than I wanted to admit.

I called Lia, but she was worn out from spending all day trying to interview Claypool's business associates.

Another night alone. Before turning in, though, I texted Finn for the tenth time to see if he'd returned. No response. I opened my door and looked down the walkway fronting the rooms. No activity, so I quietly shut my door and engaged the locks.

I went to bed, but my mind raced. Was Finn gone forever? Back to those places he didn't want to talk about? Back to the life he was trying to escape? He was afraid killers were after him, and now he was probably afraid his own father wanted no part of him. Must be hell to come home to the one place on earth where you figured you'd be taken in and loved unconditionally and then get rejected.

I drifted off to sleep as dueling images of Uncle Phil berating his own child and Finn living on the streets escorted me into dreamland.

* * *

First thing the next morning, I repeated my actions of last night. Texted Finn—no response—and banged on his door—no answer. This time, I refrained from going in uninvited. I went to check in at the registration desk, praying that no issues had arisen during the night.

When I got there, Abraham Lincoln Ruiz—Cesar and Diego's ten-year-old kid—was sitting in one of the lobby chairs, feet dangling a few inches above the floor. His backpack rested on the chair next to him.

"What's going on, big guy?"

"I'm very excited. We're going on a field trip today."

"Oh? Where?"

"The Air & Space Museum."

"Ah, going downtown? Nice."

"No, Mess. We're going to the Udvar-Hazy Center. It's near here. It has a whole bunch of actual planes and things. There's even an old space shuttle.

It's number four on my list of favorite museums."

"You have a list of favorite museums?"

"Yes, of course. There are twenty-two on it right now."

I didn't think I'd even been to twenty-two museums, and I was three times as old as Abie. "Very impressive. What's your favorite museum?"

Without missing a beat, Abie said, "The Met in New York. Followed by the downtown Air & Space Museum, followed by the Museum of Natural History. Then comes the Udvar-Hazy, then—"

"Okay, I get the picture. You like museums."

He looked at me weird. "Don't you?"

"Uh, sure. Museums are great."

"What's your favorite?"

"Well, I like the Museum of Unidentified Flying Objects."

"Where's that?"

"In Nevada. In the desert."

"Never heard of it. I think you're making that up."

I brought my hand to my chest and tried to look offended. "You never heard of it because it's super-secret. Only a handful of people know about it, mostly government officials and brilliant scientists."

"And *you*?" Abie said. I couldn't be sure, but I detected a subtle eye-roll.

"As a matter of fact, yes. I may seem like just a guy who helps run this Inn, but I've got a lot of other interests, too. Outer space being one of them. The museum displays actual spaceships and extraterrestrial space suits and even some technical manuals written in whatever language aliens use. Martian, I think." I glanced around and put a finger to my lips. "You can't tell anyone what I just told you. They'll revoke my museum privileges if you do."

"You know, Mess, I might have believed you when I was a young kid. But I'm ten now, and I know when people are not telling the truth."

"You think I'm pulling your leg?"

"I think you're pulling both legs and both arms." He popped up from his chair. "I'll text you a picture from the museum, okay?"

"Sure." I turned around, and Cesar stood there, hands on his hips, frown on his face. "Oh, hey, Cesar. Good morning."

"Good morning, Mess." One eyebrow arched.

"How long were you standing there?" I asked.

"Long enough. I didn't realize you had such a fascination with outer space. And extraterrestrials."

"I guess you learn something every day."

Cesar glared at me. "Sometimes I wonder who the child is around here."

I wondered the same thing, but I just shrugged. "FYI, I spoke to Mrs. Williams, and I'll be arranging a mother-daughter meet-up to smooth things over. With any luck, she'll be on her way back home today."

"I hope you're not relying solely on luck, Mess. It's been my experience that strategy is a losing proposition in the long run."

"Perhaps my negotiating skills will help."

"I shall pray for luck."

"Funny. Anything happen overnight I need to know about?"

"As a matter of fact, there is something I wish to discuss with you." Again with the eyebrow.

"What?"

"Phil. He keeps calling. Wants to know if his son has returned. Wants me to promise to notify him the minute I see him. I know that both you and Finn do not wish Finn's whereabouts to be divulged." Cesar held his hands out. "You see my predicament. I've known Phil a long time, and I am forever indebted to your father—and, by some extension, to Phil. However, you are running the show now. I feel as if I am caught in the middle of a tug-of-war, a position I do not appreciate."

"Okay, I get it." And I did. Cesar was loyal to both me and Phil, and I didn't blame him one bit. "I'll try to figure this out. At the moment, though, I don't have the foggiest idea where Finn is. For all I know, he's back in the wind again, never to return."

"I hope that is not the case," Cesar said. "Family support is so important, especially when you're in trouble. And I sense Finn is in some serious trouble."

"I'll keep you posted." I'd been preoccupied, but I now noticed that Cesar was dressed casually today. "Aren't you working?"

"No. I will be accompanying Abraham on his field trip. Fareed will be here any second."

"Great." I thought about asking Cesar where the Udvar-Hazy ranked on his list of favorite museums, but I was afraid he'd have an answer. "Have a good time. Remember to stay with your group; we don't want any chaperones to get lost, do we?"

Cesar didn't even crack a smile. "Goodbye, Mess."

Chapter Twelve

When I was a teen, before Sandy started Hole Lotta Love, I ate at Denny's. A lot. It was only a few blocks from the motel, and I'd hit it during my work breaks. I'd never been a food connoisseur, which was practically a prerequisite when you were eating at Denny's. They provided greasy, grubby, gassy hi-caloric excess at a rock-bottom price.

Perfect for the growing teenager.

Over the years, though, my tastes had changed, and my periodic cravings for a Grand Slam had waned. Nonetheless, the convenience of the nearby Denny's and the fact that there was never a wait for a table came in handy. Besides, an occasional greasy meal wouldn't kill me.

It seemed like the perfect place for Norma Rae's reunion with her daughter, Rosie. When I arrived with Norma Rae, Rosie was already settled into a booth, glass of iced tea in front of her. When she saw us enter, she offered a half-hearted wave, then took a giant slurp of her drink. Rosie had to be in her seventies, and if you squinted, she and Norma Rae could have been sisters.

"Hi, Ma," Rosie said as we slid into the booth opposite her.

"Hi, hon," Norma Rae said.

Before we even got into a conversation, the server came over.

"Ladies, this is my treat. Order whatever you want," I said.

The ladies ordered the ham steak lunch special, and I ordered a burger. At Denny's, you didn't want to order something too far off the beaten track. The server scooped up our menus and stalked off.

"How you been, dear?" Norma Rae's voice had that scratchiness unique to heavy smokers.

"It's only been a few days. I'm the same. What were you expecting?" Rosie eyed her mother.

I jumped in before things went off the rails. "Ladies, I asked you both here today to make up. Family ties are too important to take for granted. You need to work on strengthening the bonds. I know Norma Rae has been missing you, and—"

Norma Rae made some sort of raspberry noise.

"—and I imagine that you, Rosie, have been missing your mother. What would have to happen to get you two reunited?"

"She needs to treat me better," they both said in unison. Then they smiled at each other.

"Okay, Ma, come on home. I'll make a deal with you. You treat me better, and I'll treat you better."

"Deal." Norma Rae glanced around. "Where's my drink? I'm parched."

* * *

At quarter to five that afternoon, there was a knock at the door, and when I answered it, Finn came rushing in. He took one look at the mess in my room, then passed through the adjoining doorway into my office and flopped on the loveseat. I followed him in, working hard to appear nonchalant by trying to mask my relief. "Well, look what the cat dragged in."

And it looked like something *had* dragged him in. His clothes were filthy and torn in spots. Black smudges covered half of his exposed skin. A few scrapes decorated one side of his face. A definitely unpleasant smell emanated from him as he sprawled there.

"Are you okay?"

"Do I look okay?"

"You do not. Can I get you some water or something?"

"That would be great."

I went to the mini fridge in my room and grabbed two bottles of cold water. Returned to the office and handed him one, then watched him empty two-thirds of it before coming up for air.

"Can you tell me where you—"

He held up his hand, then chugged the rest of his water. "I'm done, Mess. Done. Living on the streets, hustling, hustling, hustling. Done with it all. I don't care what happens, but I can't do it anymore. I'm ready to face whatever may come my way, whatever I deserve and probably some of what I don't, but I can't spend another night sleeping in an alley with one eye open. Can't do it. Won't do it. I am ready to face the consequences." He tossed his empty water bottle across the room in the general direction of the trash can.

"What can I do for you, Finn? If you're in trouble, maybe I can help. You know you can stay here as long as you want." I thought back to the summers when Finn and I were practically inseparable. I would have done anything for him then, and I'd do just about anything for him now. Our bond went deep, and I still felt the connection, even though he hadn't reached out anytime in the past six years to tell me he was still alive. Life was funny sometimes, and relationships with family members were inexplicable.

He gave me a wan smile. "I saw those two guys kill Webster Claypool. In cold blood."

I was surprised, but not as surprised as I otherwise might have been. I'd already considered that Finn could be a possible witness. "And they spotted you?"

"I think maybe. But they sure saw me running from the area, and I certainly ran faster when they started chasing me."

"You weren't delivering pizzas there, were you?"

Finn licked his lips.

"Vell and I talked to your boss at the pizza place, Paolo."

Finn sat up straighter. "You did what?"

"We kinda thought your story didn't make sense, so we, uh…" I held my hands out, palms up. "We were trying to help."

"By doubting me? By going behind my back to my boss? Or should I say, my ex-boss. I didn't call out sick or anything. Just abandoned the delivery car."

"He seems to really like you. Wants you back at work when you're ready."

Finn's anger dissipated. "Seriously?"

"Yep."

He shifted on the loveseat. "Well, if I live through this, maybe I'll go back. I know delivering pizzas sounds like a bullshit job, but after what I've been through…The people there are nice. And supportive."

"You should go to the police. Tell them what you saw."

"If I do that, I'm a dead man." Finn started shaking his head, slowly at first, then more rapidly. "I don't trust the cops. I can't tell you how many times they did me wrong over the years. And it's cops everywhere. They treat those down on their luck like trash."

"I'll go with you. I'll stay with you, every step of the way. I have a buddy on the force. Maybe he can help."

"Thanks, man. But I can't go to the cops." Finn reclined, closed his eyes, and moaned several times.

I rose and retrieved the orange Nerf ball from under my desk. Took a few shots at the hoop I'd hung over the closet door. Vell and I would play H-O-R-S-E every so often, banking the ball off the walls and ceiling, calling our shots. I'd sometimes fool around trying to create new shots as I noodled through problems. How far did I want to press Finn for the details? Given his declaration that he was done running and living on the streets, was he now ready to tell me the truth? One way to find out. I tossed the Nerf ball at the hoop one last time and took a seat again.

"Finn?"

He grunted.

"Can you please sit up? I'm going to help you out of this jam. But I need you to cooperate by telling me exactly what you saw that night, okay?" As far as I knew, Claypool was found dead, inside his house. How had Finn witnessed that?

Finn slowly rearranged himself into a sitting position. "Okay. I'll tell you. But I'm not telling the cops."

"Fine. Maybe I can think of some way of getting this information to them, without involving you."

"Right. And maybe it was all a dream."

"Please tell me what you saw, and let me handle the rest." I figured, if nothing else, Lia would be very, very interested in what Finn had to say, even if she didn't know where the information came from.

"I wasn't delivering pizza. I was next door and I looked through Claypool's window into some basement room or something, and I saw a guy tied up in a chair. Must have been Claypool himself. It seemed as if these two guys were there, but I couldn't see them clearly, they kept walking in and out of my sight. I stayed frozen in place, mesmerized, as if I was watching some kind of TV show. In fact, at first, I thought maybe it was some kind of thing they were filming. Not real, you know?" Finn blinked rapidly.

"Go on."

He licked his lips and continued. "After a minute or so, the two guys had disappeared from view. I thought maybe they'd left. Then Claypool's head jerked forward, and his chin rested on his chest. I heard a muffled shot, too. I watched for another few seconds, but he didn't move. For a while, nothing. Until one of the guys looked out the window, and I think he spotted me." Finn closed his eyes, and his breathing accelerated, as if he was reliving the entire scene.

"Then what happened?"

Finn's eyes popped open. "Then I ran like hell! They saw me. I could have been next! When I got outside, these guys were coming outside too, and they started chasing me."

"Let me get this straight. You were at the house next door. Which one?"

"The one on the right, as you look from the street."

"Headstomper Thorpe's house?" I wasn't sure, but my jaw might have dropped.

Finn nodded.

"What were you doing there?"

Finn stared at me. Swallowed.

"Before you try to spin some kind of crazy story, I should tell you that Paolo told me you were there that night *and* the previous night."

"Paolo? How does he—"

"He's got GPS trackers in the delivery vehicles. He said it's to help provide information about when pizzas might get delivered." I exhaled, and Finn would have to be completely oblivious not to sense my extreme disappointment. "You were casing the place the first night, then you broke in the next night. Thorpe didn't say anything about being robbed, so I'm guessing you bolted before you could steal something."

"It wasn't exactly like that," Finn said.

"But it was something like that," I countered.

"Yeah, I suppose it was." Finn chewed on his lip. "That's another reason—the biggest reason—I can't go to the cops. I shouldn't have been there."

"You're in some shit, Finn."

He cocked his head. "Hold up. You talked to Thorpe? When? Why?"

I explained how I accompanied Lia on her interview. "Why did you pick his house to burgle, anyway?"

"What difference does it make? Two murderers are trying to find me. And when they do, they'll kill me. I think that's what we should be concentrating on, don't you?"

I was transported back to when I was about ten, and Finn and I had ducked out of my house, against my mother's wishes. We were waiting to leave to go to some family party—some decrepit relative's birthday or something—so we were dressed in nice clothes, but I persuaded Finn to run down to the creek with me to look for tadpoles. He was afraid we'd get in trouble, but I persisted until he gave in. We ran across a couple of fields, down a dirty embankment to where a tiny creek meandered through the woods. Slick, irregular-shaped rocks and brown, murky water do not mix. I slipped and fell in, ruining my new shoes and tearing my pants. When we got back to the house, my mother took one look at me and blew a gasket, yelling until I went deaf. Finn stepped up and said he practically dragged me down to the creek and that I hadn't wanted to go, afraid I might wreck my clothes.

Finn also came up with a whopper about a bigger kid named Brett Something, someone we thought went to the middle school, who pushed me into the creek, then ran away laughing. I wasn't positive, but I think my mother believed him because she stopped yelling and just told me to go upstairs and change.

What stuck with me: Finn was a loyal friend and cousin, and he would throw himself under the bus for me. Also: he was a very skilled liar. I remembered his face clearly when he spun that story about the middle school kid named Brett Something.

It was the same expression I saw on his face now.

"Mess? You still there?"

I snapped out of the past. "Yeah. Sorry. Did you actually see them kill Claypool?"

"Not really. But does it even matter? They *think* I did, and they're out to silence me. Permanently." A look of fear descended on his face, and I bet he was picturing himself in that chair, about to get one in the back of the head.

I only had one idea about ensuring Finn's safety. If the cops caught the bad guys and put them in jail, then Finn could sleep easy. And the best way to do that was to tell them what Finn saw. The trick was not getting him involved directly.

"Okay, Finn. I think you're safe here, for now. I'll remind Griff to keep an eye out." Griff was our 6XL-sized security representative. I liked to think of him as the Inn's bouncer. "In the meantime, I'm going to tell Lia what you saw. Maybe she can somehow float this information to the cops without using your name."

"You can't do that. If my name gets out there, I'm as good as dead. Sounds way too risky."

"You're a walking billboard for risk. I didn't tell you to rob a guy named Headstomper's house, did I? Your best bet is to go hide in your room and let me handle this, okay?"

Finn stared at me, and I waited for some kind of wise-ass retort, but he just nodded twice and shuffled off.

Chapter Thirteen

It was a pleasant evening, so Lia and I decided to go for a walk in a nearby townhouse community. Two or three blocks wide, not far off the main drag of Route 50, built when squeezing homes into any available tract of land was the cool thing to do. It was quiet in both noise and activity. We strolled along the sidewalk, side-by-side, and we each carried a water bottle. Hydration was important.

"So, what's the latest with your investigation?"

Lia filled me in. The police had finished canvassing the neighbors and hadn't learned anything else. They were still in the process of obtaining and reviewing all the doorbell and security cam video footage, and they were processing all the forensic data gathered at the scene. As she waded into the weeds with the police procedure stuff, her face took on an excited glow. I felt happy for her—this was her passion, and she was getting the opportunity to pursue it. Which, unfortunately, not everyone could.

When she took a breath, I seized my chance. "I learned something very interesting today. About your case."

She had her water bottle to her lips, but she stopped and brought it down slowly. "Oh? What was that?"

"I know you investigative reporters are all about protecting your sources, right?"

"This again?"

"It's important."

"In most cases, yes." She was laser-focused on me now, and I could practically feel the temperature of my face increasing. "What's this all about?

More Finn nonsense?"

"He saw what happened. He watched Claypool get shot."

Lia shook her head at me like I was a dolt. And maybe I was, when it came to trying to slide stuff by her. "Now he claims he actually saw what happened? How come he didn't say so before?"

"Finn is…well, he's been through a lot these past six years, and he's understandably skittish."

She put her hand on my forearm. "I know he's your cousin, and I'm not trying to be mean, but Finn seems like what we in the business call an *unreliable witness.*"

"You don't know him like I do."

"Living on the streets changes a person, Mess. You haven't seen him in a long time."

I nodded. "Maybe. But please hear me out, okay?"

"Fine."

"I know I'm in no position to ask this, but can you promise you won't out Finn as the witness? At least not until I figure some things out first. Okay?"

"What makes you think I'll even believe him? You have no idea how many people claim to have seen crimes. They like to be in the middle of the action, so they make up all kinds of nonsense. One of my jobs is to determine who's telling the truth. Can you imagine if I printed something, and it turned out to be false? That would seriously damage my career." She was clearly miffed. But I also believed she wouldn't let her annoyance ruin what might turn out to be a big break—or at least an interesting one—in her story.

"I understand. But it wouldn't hurt to hear what he said he saw, right? Then you can make your mind up how you'd like to proceed."

"Sure. Tell me."

I sucked in a deep breath, knowing I was going to face some skepticism. "Finn claims to have seen two men kill Webster Claypool. He was tied up in a chair in his house and then got shot in the back of the head. Finn ran and then was pursued by these two killers. He's pretty sure these were the two guys who chased him at the mall."

"From what I know of the crime scene, that would fit. Where was Finn when he saw this? Was he in the house with them?" Her voice pitched higher, just thinking that might be the case.

"Finn wasn't in Claypool's house, but he had a clear line of vision to see what was inside."

"So, lurking in the bushes? Maybe a lookout for the killers who's now had a change of heart?"

"No."

"No, not lurking? Or no, not a lookout for the killers?"

I shook my head. "No to both."

"The only other place would be in a neighboring yard. Or house."

"All I know is Finn said he saw these two had Claypool tied up in a chair; then he was dead. He didn't give me any details about where he was when he saw it go down." I felt uncomfortable shading the truth with Lia as I strived to not implicate Finn in a burglary.

"He's probably making this all up to get attention."

"I don't think so. I know it's a lot to ask, but can you preserve Finn's anonymity as you look into this? Pass the info along to your detective contact without divulging where you got it?" I thought about calling my buddy on the force, Detective Ostervale, but this wasn't his case. And I'm not sure he'd be as sympathetic to the whole "protect your source" credo. On a case this important, I might find him at my doorstep with a search warrant. We were buddies, not BFFs.

Lia and I had hit a dead end, so we turned around and headed back down the row of townhouses. A man with a dog emerged from the house next to us, and the dog began barking. We waved, and the dog barked louder, until the owner barked his own command, and the dog went quiet. "My contact is going to want details. An unsubstantiated description from a phantom witness won't fly."

I'd figured Lia would say something along those lines.

"Why won't Finn come forth and tell what he saw? This is a cold-blooded murder we're talking about. These are very dangerous people walking the streets." She showed me some teeth, but it was far from a smile. "Oh, wait. I know why Finn won't come forth. Because he's full of crap. Making a false report to the police is a crime. And what was he doing there, peering into someone's windows?"

"Look, I know how this all sounds. Some sketchy guy who's been away for six years suddenly reappears and witnesses a murder. But I know Finn, and while I wouldn't swear to it, I think his account bears investigation."

Lia pursed her lips, and it was times like these when I wished I knew what she was thinking. "Mess, letting killers walk around isn't the right thing to do. Coming forth and telling the authorities what you've seen is. I can't believe you think talking to me is better than going to the police. I'm just a reporter, and I can't print something I don't know is true. Finn is your cousin, and from what you've told me, you might be the only one he'll listen to. You've got to convince him to come forward. If he's telling the truth, of course. Which I highly doubt." Lia began walking faster, and I increased my pace to keep up. "I need to get going. Got a big day tomorrow."

* * *

When we got back to the Inn, Lia took off, and I checked on Finn. He was tucked away in his room, just chilling, laying low. For a second, I thought about seeing if he wanted to talk about what had happened at Izzy's, to see if venting would help him feel better, but I decided not to for fear of stirring things up. There'd be plenty of time to swap stories of our dysfunctional relatives. Besides, I imagined the last few days had wiped him out, physically and emotionally, and it would do him some good to rest without any expectations—from cousins or parents. I told him I'd stop by in the morning to see how things were going.

Back in my room, I fired up my laptop. Ordinarily, I wouldn't care a whole lot about someone's murder. Not that I didn't find murder reprehensible, but hearing the details didn't fascinate me the same way it did others. There was nothing I could do about some random guy's murder, and honestly, watching the news was one bad thing after another. It depressed me.

But Claypool's murder was different. Finn claimed to be a witness, and he was hiding here at the Inn, and Lia was the Observer's lead reporter on the story. This murder investigation had everything to do with me.

So it behooved me to learn more about it.

I'd already read Lia's articles about the murder, of course, but there were a whole lot more on the Internet. Most were posted by reputable news outlets. I read the first twenty listed. None had any new information to share. Claypool had been murdered in his house. He was probably targeted. The murder weapon had not been divulged. There were no suspects yet. Most importantly for Finn, there was no mention of any witness. The investigation continued.

Not all the articles posted were from recognized sources. The Internet had given birth to a bourgeoning cottage industry of conspiracy theories, fake news, and flat-out lies. At least the headlines were amusing.

Webster Claypool Killed in Satanic Ritual

CIA Involved in Claypool Death

Claypool Dismembered by Sasquatch, Disguised as Murder to Prevent Public Panic

I skimmed some of the sensational articles and wondered how much more productive society would be if these lunatics spent their time doing something worthwhile. On the other hand, maybe keeping these nutcases in their basements on their computers was better than having them run amok in public.

A number of the articles—opinion pieces, mostly by local bloggers with axes to grind, I imagined—speculated about motive. Who could have wanted Claypool dead? Several people mentioned another prominent real estate developer. Two were convinced it was some kind of mob hit. Another mentioned a gambling ring. One mentioned Jimbo Young, a local politician getting ready to make a run for Congress.

I spent some time diving down Internet rabbit holes. Articles, blogs, videos. On YouTube, I was watching Jimbo Young, the current Chair of the county Board of Supervisors, give a campaign speech, which wasn't that unusual. The unusual part began when I saw Webster Claypool step up next to Young, grab his hand, and lift both their hands up in the air, the same way a boxing referee holds up the champ's hand after a bout.

Things got downright alarming when I noticed two men on the stage, in the background. One tall, with a head shaved bald.

Coincidence?

Possibly. But my gut was bucking strong. I bookmarked the page to show Finn in the morning. The video had been recorded a few years ago—maybe during the last election cycle, and it sure looked like Claypool and Young were on the same team. Which made it even more unlikely the two guys in the background—and from the mall—were the ones Finn said he saw kill Claypool.

I googled Jimbo Young. He'd been elected about twenty years ago and had shepherded the county as it increased development *responsibly*—the big catchword. Increasing business while still maintaining the level of public services an affluent area demanded. I'd always thought he'd done a good job, although I had to admit I often felt the city's social services could be improved.

I nosed around online for a while longer, concentrating on Claypool, trying to get a sense of what kind of guy he really was and what he was into. And if I identified an enemy with a motive strong enough to kill him, then all the better.

Nothing popped. I closed my laptop.

Stared at my phone. Thought about texting Lia to apologize, but I figured that would go better if I did it in person, so I sent her a text asking if she could break away sometime tomorrow.

Then I stared at my phone, waiting for her reply, heart beating fast.

Sure. How about coffee in the morning?

I responded: *Great! G'night.* Then I exhaled and went to bed.

* * *

Unfortunately, when I woke up, there was a text from Lia canceling our coffee. Some government official was giving a public update on the case, and she needed to be there asking questions and taking notes. She didn't ask for a rain check or suggest lunch or dinner, or afternoon tea. I tried not to take it personally, instead telling myself it was nice my girlfriend was so dedicated to her very worthwhile job.

I considered telling her about the men in the YouTube video, but I took to heart what she'd told me—she wouldn't print anything that hadn't been confirmed, verified, corroborated, and double-sourced. She was delivering news, not conspiracy theories based on smoke.

I went down to Finn's room and showed him the video. He agreed with me that the two guys in the video were likely the same two guys from the mall. Looking at it again, I was pretty sure myself, but not positive. The video was a few years old, and they were dressed differently, and there really wasn't anything remarkable about them. I left him watching some stupid movie from the 90s.

Back in my room, I called Vell. "Hey, you busy?"

"I'm always busy, man."

"I'm going to nose around a bit, wanted some company. If you can break away, that is."

"Be there in ten."

I could always count on Vell. While I waited, I walked over to the registration office. Cesar was behind the counter, tapping away at the computer. He raised his head, saw it was me, then went back to what he was doing. I bothered him anyway. "Hey, what's up today?"

"Are you just being polite, or do you really want to know?"

Fifty-fifty. "I want to know if you want to tell me."

"Things are fine." Tap-tap.

"How was the museum? Abie sent me a picture of the Enola Gay. Seemed educational."

Cesar didn't look up. "Everyone had a wonderful time."

"What are you working on?"

"Trying to balance the accounts."

"I thought that was my job," I said.

"I did, too. Yet…"

I guessed I was a couple of months behind. "I was going to get to it yesterday, but I had the thing with Mrs. Williams. Who is now back at her daughter's place, thank you very much."

Cesar raised his head. Smiled. "Well done, Mess. A gold star for you. I'm sure that is the last we'll see of her."

Did he know something I didn't? Wouldn't be the first time. "Yes, well, I've got some errands to run, so I'll see you later. Unless there's something you need from me before I go."

He flashed me one of his fake-o smiles, which I think he reserved solely for me. "Everything is under control, boss. Have a splendid time."

Chapter Fourteen

Vell and I parked in the vast Fairfax Government Center lot and walked into the impressive-looking building, erected right around when I was born. Thought by some to be a massive boondoggle, it nonetheless housed many of the county's bureaucratic offices—and a county as large as Fairfax County had a lot of bureaucracy. Personally, I didn't have too much interaction with Fairfax County officials. The City of Fairfax, where the Inn resided, was an independent city within the county. But the City did rely on many county services—schools, libraries, sheriff. I was often confused about all the jurisdictional quirks, County versus City, and I'd lived here all my life.

We consulted no fewer than three wall directories and maps to find the Board of Supervisors' offices. "Some use of taxpayer money, huh?" Vell said. "I bet you could think of better ways to spend the dough. I know I could."

There were people waiting at the elevator, so we took the stairs. Halfway around the semi-circular building and we'd found Young's office.

"Have you ever met him?" Vell asked.

"Actually, I did once. He was gladhanding at a July Fourth parade years ago, before he was the Chair. Back when he was campaigning as a man of the people. Seemed like an okay guy then, and actually seems like an okay guy now."

"Can't judge a book by its title."

"Something like that." I opened the door into the outer office, and we strolled in. Three people sitting at three desks each lifted their heads. The one in the middle spoke. "Welcome to Supervisor Young's office. How may I help you?" She was young, attractive, cheery, and spoke with clear enunciation.

Vell and I hadn't really rehearsed anything. I guessed we hoped we'd just see the two killers standing guard by Young's door. "Well, I, uh, is there a listing of all the people who work for the Chair?"

Her smile didn't falter a bit. Well trained. "There's a directory of key staff on the website. Is there someone or something specific you're looking for?"

A tall bald guy and his regular-sized buddy? Or, more to the point, the two men who killed Webster Claypool? I figured we might as well go with the truth. I pulled out my phone and showed her a still frame from the video. "Do you know either of these two men?"

The woman took my phone. Looked intently at the picture. "I don't believe they are employed by Mr. Young. At least not as far as I know." She turned to the man at the desk next to hers and handed him my phone. "Steve, do you recognize these men?"

"I think they work—worked—for Claypool. Saw them at one of their joint appearances. Pretty sure that's what I remember." He turned his attention to me. "Why? They do something bad?"

"Why would you say that?" I asked.

He shrugged and handed me my phone. "They look like tough guys, I guess." He rose and spoke to the woman in the middle, who seemed to be the gatekeeper-in-charge. "I'm going on break. Back in ten."

The boss lady's smile still shone, as if it were the main fixture lighting up the room. "Anything else I can help you with?"

I looked at Vell, and he shook his head. I turned back to Ms. Sunshine. "No, we're good. Thanks for your help."

"That's why I'm here. To help Supervisor Young's constituents."

I didn't fess up that we didn't live in his jurisdiction. Afraid the smile would turn into a frown.

We left, but before we got twenty feet, Steve, from Young's office, waved us over to where he stood, in a shadowy alcove by the stairs. "Hey."

"Hey," I said.

"Hey," Vell said.

Steve glanced up and down the concourse. "You didn't hear this from me, but I saw those two guys talking to Supervisor Young a few weeks ago. Right here in the cafeteria."

"Is that unusual? I mean, Young and Claypool do events together, right? Maybe they were simply coordinating things?"

"Maybe." Steve paused, and it looked like a canary was about to come bursting out of his mouth.

"What?"

"Maybe they were talking about something else." Again, Steve glanced around as if he was expecting a SWAT team to come charging in.

Vell shifted, and I could tell he was tired of this little dance. To be honest, I was too. "Look, if you've got something more to say, I would seriously love to hear it. But we don't know enough about these two guys or what the Chair is working on to play this guessing game."

Steve's tone changed from teasing to straightforward. "Supervisor Young and Webster Claypool did do a bunch of joint events, back during the last election cycle. But in the past year, Young has been under a lot of pressure to rein in some of the big developers and move to a different paradigm. Smart development, responsible development, compassionate development. Whatever you want to call it, gung-ho developers like Claypool are feeling the heat. There was talk that Claypool wasn't going to support Young in the next election. Even if he was an ass, Claypool's support was significant, and Supervisor Young will have to hustle to make up what he lost. And if Claypool supported Supervisor Young's opponent, well, that would be doubly detrimental."

Doubly detrimental? This guy had a way with words. "And you think, what, these two guys were trying to extort Young? Be nicer to developers, or I'll support your opponent?"

"All I'm saying is Young and Claypool weren't as chummy lately as they used to be. And those two guys in the picture? I heard they were Claypool's muscle."

"Muscle?" Vell asked.

"Guys like Claypool don't get where they are by playing patty-cake all the time. Sometimes you gotta flex, know what I mean? I need to get back. Gentlemen." Steve walked off, probably disappointed we didn't want to play Twenty Questions.

"Maybe we should pay a visit to Claypool's office. Find out who these guys are," I said.

"Sounds like a plan." Vell held out his fist, and I bumped it.

I figured a big company like Claypool's wouldn't shut down because of his death, but what did I know? I could picture Uncle Phil swooping in to run the Inn the next day, if something happened to me.

I pulled out my phone, searched for Claypool Development. Called the number, figuring we'd need an appointment to talk to someone. There was a big difference between a public servant like Young and a private land baron.

I got transferred a handful of times, until I finally wound up talking to someone in Community Relations. She read me the party line about everyone being devastated by Claypool's death, and that only essential operations would be running in the foreseeable future. Then she asked me if my matter was essential.

"Well, it could be."

"Thank you for your understanding. Goodbye." She clicked off.

"No dice," I said to Vell, who'd been watching my face as I talked on the phone and already knew I'd struck out.

"Now what?"

"Know anybody who works for Claypool?" I asked. Vell never ceased to amaze me with his extensive network of friends and acquaintances. He was always calling himself Vellipedia, and not without good reason.

"I can ask around."

"Okay, thanks. In the meantime, I think I'll try the big gun."

* * *

I dropped Vell off at Mama's—he had his network to connect with, and that started with his grandmother, who everyone called Mama—and I drove back to the Inn, thinking. I knew what Steve meant about Claypool not playing nice as he made his way to the top, in very broad terms, but it would take more time than I had to dive into local politics to learn enough about what was going on to form any conclusions. However, knowing that the two guys Finn might have seen were bad guys—or at least tough guys—lent more credence to his claim of witnessing Claypool's murder.

Getting killed by two guys whose paychecks you signed? Not unheard of—et tu, Brute?—but a harsh lesson in loyalty, or lack thereof.

Whatever was going on, I was clearly trying to play catch-up.

When I got back, Cesar texted me before I got out of the car. I guessed he'd been watching for me. I ambled over to the registration office, girding myself. One of the things about running a motel was that you never knew what was going to happen next.

I opened the door, and the bell dinged overhead. I'd wanted to get rid of that, but Cesar overruled me. Something about "embracing the quaint charms of being old school."

"Hello, Mess. How were your errands?"

"Fine." I glanced around. Nothing seemed to be on fire. "You summoned?"

"Mrs. Williams."

"Oh? Did she call to thank us?"

Cesar smiled indulgently. "If she wanted to thank us, there is no need for her to call."

I raised one eyebrow. "Did she send us a card?"

"If Mrs. Williams would like to thank us, she can do it in person. She has returned."

"What?" I looked out the window, across the parking lot at the rooms. She wasn't outside, smoking. "What happened?"

"She said something about her ungrateful, good-for-nothing progeny. I'll spare you the exact vocabulary she employed." He shot me an I-told-you-so look, which I got every time one of my invited guests did something he didn't approve of. "I put her back in Room Three."

"Thanks." I wondered what Norma Rae had done to Rosie to get kicked out again. Didn't really matter, though. Norma Rae was my problem for the moment. "I'll try to figure something out."

"You always do, don't you?"

I opened my mouth to respond, but I wasn't in the mood for sparring with Cesar, although it *was* often entertaining. At least for me. "I'll be going out again shortly."

"Goodbye, Mess. Do not worry. I have everything here under control. And if Mrs. Williams needs anything, I'll be sure to give her your number."

* * *

I had told Vell it was time to pull out the big gun, so I called the big gun. She picked up right away.

"Hey, *dahling,*" she said with an indistinguishable accent.

"Hi, *dahling* yourself. How's the investigation?"

"Going great. The detectives released some of the forensic details. They often don't, but this case has mushroomed into something huge. There's a ton of pressure—from the public, from the government—to get this thing solved quickly. I guess the police divulged more information to keep us off their backs. Whatever. Better for me. Anyway, what's up with you?"

I told her about the video, and I told her about our trip to Government Center. When I told her what Steve said about the two guys working for Claypool, and about me calling Claypool Development to follow up, she interrupted me.

"Interesting. I called over there and got a similar message. But my editor wants me to dig in and get more background on Claypool. Come up with an enemies list. Let me try again to get an appointment. Now that things have died down—excuse the pun—they may be more receptive. I've got a literal press pass. Sometimes, that opens up doors, especially if I threaten to say they 'refused to comment' in a story. People don't like to look uncooperative. Makes them seem guilty."

"Great," I said. "Can I tag along?" I worried that maybe she was still torqued at me for not persuading Finn to go to the cops.

"Well, I do need a good photographer," she said. "But I'll settle for you."

Chapter Fifteen

L ia and I sat in Danielle Sakai's top-floor corner office, one door removed from Webster Claypool's. The rug was Persian, the desk large and mahogany, and the art on the walls was worth a heckuva lot more than my Corolla. I sat on the leather couch and tried not to move— if I scratched something, I would cause thousands of dollars of damage. When we first arrived, Lia explained that I was the photographer and that she would be the one asking the questions. Another be-seen-and-not-heard situation. If I was a sensitive guy, my self-esteem might have taken a hit.

Out the window, Tysons Corner sprawled. High-rise office buildings, condos, high-end retail, Metro rails, and highway interchanges interwove to connect this city-in-the-suburbs with the entire DMV region.

Danielle was the COO of Claypool Development. She was about thirty-five, and judging by the first ten minutes of our conversation, she'd attained her lofty position by merit. Slick as a real estate sales brochure. She displayed just the right amount of grief over Claypool's death, anger at him being murdered, concern for the welfare of the company moving forward, and irritation at us for taking up her valuable time. She regurgitated some background information about the company and about Claypool, but it wasn't anything we couldn't have learned after spending five minutes on the internet.

Her talking without saying anything struck me as very professional, in a stonewalling, obfuscating, corporate kind of way. Maybe I was a tad too cynical when it came to cutthroat business types.

"I'm not sure what else I can tell you, Ms. Katsaros, that I haven't already told the police. It's a damn tragedy, and we—I'm speaking for the officers of the company and all its employees—have no idea who might have committed this heinous act. I do appreciate your position here—doing your job and all that—but I'm afraid I really don't know anything that might prove valuable to your story."

Lia shifted in her seat. "This is an important piece. Your boss was a well-known businessman with significant ties to the local community. I want to make sure that I portray him in the most accurate way possible, so if it seems as if I'm asking some of the same questions as the police, it's because I might be. But I can assure you that what I do with the information will be a whole lot different. Over the years, many things have been written about him, some of which were undoubtedly hit jobs. However, I can paint a picture of the real Webster Claypool. But I need your help." Lia smiled, and while that smile might have melted my heart, it also seemed to soften Danielle's, because, for the first time, she smiled back.

"Sure. I know everyone here would like to set the record straight about what kind of guy Webster was."

"Why don't you tell me?" Lia said.

Danielle launched into a long monologue—a eulogy, really—about all of Webster Claypool's sterling qualities. According to her, the man was generous, warm, loyal, ambitious, brilliant, and a dozen other wonderful adjectives. I didn't hear cutthroat, backstabbing, conniving, ruthless, or any of the multitude of other adjectives I'd read in the articles about him. I guessed it was all about perspective.

Lia asked more questions, gently trying to steer the interview in the direction she wanted, but I recognized her strategy. Get the subject talking, and something interesting was bound to emerge. Especially when discussing such a complex individual as Claypool. My attention wandered out the window to take in the view. How many of these high-rise buildings comprising Tysons Corner had Claypool built?

How many hundreds of millions of dollars had he made from them?

I turned my focus on Danielle as she spoke off the cuff, quite eloquently, and wondered how much she stood to benefit from Claypool's death.

A lot, I imagined. But murdering your boss to get it seemed far-fetched, especially if you were already roaring down the fast track.

Danielle paused for air, and Lia was able to slip in a few more questions. "What was Claypool's interest in politics? Was he planning to run for office? And what was his relationship with Jimbo Young?"

Danielle needed only a millisecond of thought before she spoke. Maybe *she* should be running for office. "Webster had no interest in public office. He liked money, and he hated bureaucracy, two excellent reasons to stay away from politics. He involved himself in local affairs only as much as he needed to for the business. Jimbo Young is pro-business—or at least he *was;* the tides are ever-changing—so Webster supported his campaigns as much as the law allowed. Why do you ask?"

We'd printed a still photo from the YouTube appearance, and Lia pulled it out and handed it to Danielle. "Here's a picture taken at one of Young's campaign stops a couple of years ago."

She glanced at it and set it down. "Well, like I said, Webster supported him."

"Do you know those two men on the stage behind him? The tall bald one and the guy next to him?"

Danielle took another look, and for the first time since we'd landed in her office, I noticed she wasn't one-hundred percent confident when she spoke. "No, I don't believe I do. Do you know who they are?"

"Just curious if you did. A colleague of mine wanted to know."

Danielle stared at Lia, and Lia stared back, as if each one knew the other was lying.

"I think that's all the questions I have," Lia said. "Unless you have an idea who might have killed your boss?"

Danielle stood. "If I had, I already would have told the detectives."

"Right. Do you mind if we get some pictures? Of you? The office?"

We rose.

"Not at all. Be sure to get my good side." Danielle didn't smile when she said it, nor did she smile in any of the pictures I took.

She was all business.

* * *

Lia went into the office to start working on her story, and I returned to the Inn. I needed to check in with Finn and Norma Rae and Vell, but first I needed to touch base with Cesar.

As soon as I entered the registration office, he looked up from his computer. "Hello, Mess. Nice of you to drop by. I hope running this place isn't infringing on all the personal things you are always taking care of."

"No. I mean, it's a hassle running this place, but things seem to be going okay, wouldn't you say?"

Not even a smile. "If you've come for a status report, everything is status quo." Cesar adjusted the knot in his necktie.

"That bad, huh?"

"Mrs. Williams is complaining about the loud vehicular noise."

I looked around, half expecting to see a cement mixer in the parking lot. "What noise?"

"Evidently, the traffic going by on Route 50 is too noisy for her. She's having trouble getting her beauty sleep."

"It's the middle of the day."

"Who am I to argue with her? I told her I'd ask the passing motorists to drive more quietly." He arched an eyebrow, a look I'd seen all too often.

"Anything else?"

"There's always something else. But I saved the best for last." He gazed at me expectantly.

"What?"

"No guesses?"

"Not in the mood."

The sides of Cesar's mouth curled up infinitesimally. "Since when is Mess Hopkins not in the mood for a fun game?"

I smelled a trap, but I bit anyway. "Okay, I'll guess. You spotted Griff practicing his ballet."

"Close. Phil came by looking for Finn."

"Oh crap." I looked out at the parking lot, this time expecting to see blood on the pavement.

"Oh crap, indeed," Cesar said.

"What happened?"

He sighed. "I told you I didn't want to be in the middle of this, and you said you'd take care of it. I do not consider having Phil show up and scream at me, taking care of it."

"I'm sorry, Cesar. I really am. Did Uncle Phil and Finn get into it?"

"They did not. Primarily because Finn is not here."

Finn's shenanigans were getting old. "Where is he?"

"I do not know. I am not my boss's cousin's keeper."

"Did you see him leave? Take an Uber? Hoof it?"

Cesar locked eyes with me. "I did not see him at all. I wish only the best for him, and I truly hope he reconciles with Phil and Vera. Despite how they act sometimes, they only want what's best for Finn."

"I know. You're right. And thanks. I really do mean it, Cesar. You should not be in the middle of this, at all. This is between Uncle Phil and Finn, and somehow, I've been drafted as a referee. If Phil comes by again, tell him to see me."

"That's what I told him *this* time." One of Cesar's eyebrows arched again, and I wished he'd stop doing that. Made me feel guiltier than I already felt.

"I'd better talk to Uncle Phil then. Strike preemptively."

"Good luck, Mess."

I turned to go, then spun around. "You got a minute?"

"For you, Mess. I have five."

"What do you think about how Phil treated Finn?"

Cesar narrowed his eyes. "I assume you are talking about before Finn left."

"Yes."

"I am reluctant to judge, because I do not know all the facts."

Nor did I. All I knew was what Finn told me, that Phil wasn't very accepting of his being gay. So much so that Finn felt compelled to go far away. "That's fair. If I'm being too personal, just let me know, but were your parents accepting of you?"

Cesar nodded. "I have wonderful parents. Very accepting. Of course, they believe they knew I was gay before I did, or at least that's their claim. I am lucky, though. Many parents are not as supportive. Nor are other relatives, for that matter. Poor Diego hasn't spoken to one of his aunts in fifteen years." He smiled. "It's her loss. She has never met Abie."

"That *is* her loss."

Cesar's smile faded. "However, sometimes it takes time. People learn. People grow. People change. From what I can tell, Uncle Phil has made an effort. Hopefully, he and Finn can work things out. He's overbearing and pretentious and controlling, but he does have some good qualities, too. I truly believe he loves Finn. I'm sure I don't have to tell you this, but people are complicated, Mess."

Boy, were they ever.

Chapter Sixteen

When I was a kid and my parents bought the Fairfax Manor Inn, I didn't care about the motel. Not one iota. Just a boring place for strangers to stay for a day or two. But I was *ecstatic* that, as part of the deal, the motel came with an adjacent miniature golf course promising an exciting adventure: *See the World in 18 Holes!*

I played those eighteen holes quite a lot until I knew every slope, twist, and dead bumper. I spent a good deal of time helping my parents run the place, too. They put me in charge of keeping the place clean, and as I got older, I graduated to sitting in the hut, taking customers' money, and handing out putters and balls. Not a bad gig for a twelve-year-old.

A couple of summers, Finn helped me run the place, and we turned it into our little fiefdom, a pair of hotshot operators and mini-golf hustlers. Those were two of the happiest summer vacations I'd ever spent, and I think if you asked Finn, he would agree.

But everything had a life cycle, including mini-golf courses. My parents closed the place years ago, and the fiberglass structures have been, very slowly, deteriorating. We'd built a tall chain-link fence to surround the entire thing—with green mesh to shield the eyesore from the roadway and a padlock on the gate to keep out drunk teens looking for fun.

I came over here sometimes to think, relying on the memories of happier times to ease my mind. I could almost hear the cries of joy after a hole-in-one and smell the popcorn we sold in those flimsy paper cones. Memory was a funny thing.

Now, I sat on the bench in front of the hut, pondering the events since

Finn had beamed back into my life. I needed to talk to Phil, tell him to chill down and meet Finn on his own terms. Being a completely rational person, a father to a child who'd been missing for six years and presumed dead, of course, Phil would retreat to his BarcaLounger and invite Finn to visit.

And I had a bridge to sell.

Perhaps I could impress upon Phil that Finn had been through hell and back and that, having been there himself, no doubt, he could be a little more understanding. Although I figured each of them probably thought their ordeal was worse.

This would require some finesse, something Phil most definitely did not appreciate. I thought about calling Izzy and begging her to tag-team Phil with me. Both of us working together were bound to have a greater chance of success. But was that being fair to her? I was closer to Finn—always had been—and Finn was here, for the time being.

And, oh yeah, he'd unburdened himself to me about being a witness to a murder.

I thought it might be easier to approach Aunt Vera. I just assumed Phil had called her in Minneapolis or Portland or wherever she happened to be visiting to tell her that her son was alive and back home. I knew that if I were in her shoes, I'd be on the next flight. But I hadn't heard that she'd returned. Of course, she and Phil might be plotting some kind of hostage rescue operation at this very moment, for all I knew.

Screw it. Someone wiser—and more motivational—than me said to meet challenges head-on. I pulled out my phone and called Phil. It rang and rang, and I was about to hang up when he answered. "Hullo."

He didn't sound so good. "Uncle Phil? You okay?"

"Me and Johnnie Walker are having an in-death conversation. Although I have to say, there isn't much talking going on, on, on."

I assumed—hoped—he meant in-depth. No denying Phil liked his booze. That wasn't unusual. That he was toasted in the middle of the afternoon was concerning. "Listen, maybe you and Johnnie should call it quits for the day."

"Well, Benjamin, maybe you and your stupid friend Cesar should call it quits for the day, day, day."

"Is Aunt Vera there?"

"Where?"

"There. With you?"

"No, sir. She's visiting one of her many sisters. She's got a lot of 'em, you know."

I did know. "Did you tell her about Finn?"

"Biggest thing to happen in my wife in the past six years? Of course, I called my life."

Oh boy. "Is she coming home soon?"

"I tole her Finny doesn't want to see us. You know what, when I came by today, your silly friend said he wasn't there. Then I insisted we go to his room, and you know what? He wasn't there. Gone again, little Finny. Goodbye again, little Finny. I'm hanging up now, Mess."

And he did.

I couldn't remember ever hearing Uncle Phil in such pitiful shape. When I was a kid, he was always larger than life, and even as I realized he was a bombastic blowhard, I was still intimidated. I thought about driving out to his place to make sure he was okay, but Izzy lived so much closer. I hadn't wanted to bother her, but this seemed important. *Family.*

I called her. "Izzy, can you do me a favor?" I explained the situation, and after a few choice words in response, she agreed to go check on him. "It's probably not a good idea to take the girls," I added, but she'd already hung up. Just as well, she didn't need Captain Obvious giving her parenting advice.

I sat there gazing at the Statue of Liberty, wishing I could check out for a while. Maybe go to New York and see the real deal. But I knew I needed to go joust with Norma Rae Williams. Luckily—at least I hoped it was luckily— I was saved that fate by a text from Vell telling me he had something big and was coming over.

So much for checking out for a while.

* * *

I returned to my room to wait for Vell. He didn't bother knocking. One minute I was alone, lounging on my bed, and the next he was sitting in my desk chair staring at me.

"Hello, Vell."

"You will *never* guess what I found out. Never, never, never."

"Webster Claypool is a CIA operative and was killed by a foreign government."

"No."

"Close?"

"Not really."

"I could keep guessing," I said. "But why don't you just tell me? Save us both some time." I was tired of everyone's guessing games.

"You used to be more fun."

I shrugged.

"Okay, I put the word out, and a buddy I have who installs windows got back to me." Vell beamed like he'd just won two hundred dollars playing scratch-offs.

"I'm listening."

"You sure you don't want to guess?"

"Vell…"

"Okay. This guy was working on a house across the street from Claypool's a few months ago. And he was there early one morning, inspecting something or other, and he saw someone on a walk of shame leaving Claypool's house. A barefoot, halfway-dressed woman."

According to a local magazine, Claypool was a perennial finalist on the Washington Area's Most Eligible Bachelor list. And he had a reputation as a player. When you were a handsome, unattached mega-millionaire, women seemed to pay attention. "That doesn't sound so earth-shattering."

"This woman was attractive. *Very* attractive. Supermodel attractive. And she went into the house next door."

Now, that *was* earth-shattering. "You're saying that Alluree was sleeping with Webster Claypool?"

"Seems so."

"Her next-door neighbor?"

"Convenience *is* important," Vell said.

"Is your source solid?"

"As granite. And after he told me, I asked Mama to put her feelers out. She knew some people who corroborated what he said. Alluree and Claypool were doing it. Nothing like next-door nooky."

"I don't think I'd want to sleep with the wife of someone named Headstomper. Doesn't seem like a good thing for one's long-term prospects."

Vell laughed at me. "Dude, I keep telling you, rich people think differently. They believe they are invincible and that if something bad does happen, they can just throw money at the problem."

"Not sure how money will stop an MMA fighter from ripping off your head, but what do I know? I could barely afford a ticket to one of his fights." Dozens of thoughts bounced around in my poor-person brain.

Vell voiced one of those thoughts. "Finding out a guy was having sex with your wife is a time-honored motive for murder. Convenience works both ways."

"Except Headstomper was out of town that night."

"That's even better, having a good alibi, right? Be seen at an event a thousand miles away? He could have hired some guys." Vell punched the air with a fist. "I bet he knows a few who could get the job done."

It didn't add up, at least not on its face. "The two guys from that video? They seemed to be working *for* Claypool."

"Maybe those guys don't actually work directly for Claypool. Maybe they are rent-a-muscle types," Vell said.

I thought aloud. "Well, if they'd worked together, they could get close to him without arousing suspicion. They'd be perfect killers."

"On the other hand, I'd think a guy like Headstomper would want to handle something like this himself. With his bare hands," Vell said. "An honor code kind of thing."

I'd talked with Headstomper—as his much tamer real-world persona Tim— and while I understood he was on his best behavior for the interview, I didn't get any 'roid rage vibes—or rage vibes of any kind. He actually seemed in control. But having a wife cheat on you with a neighbor might cause even the mildest guys to Hulk out. "It definitely is a wrinkle in this whole thing. I should tell Lia. Does your friend want to talk to a reporter?"

"I didn't ask him, but I would say absolutely." Vell paused. "*Not.* As in no way, no how. He likes his job, and publicity like that might get him canned. You'd best go with an unnamed source."

I wondered if there was a limit on the number of unnamed sources you could have in any one article.

Chapter Seventeen

The next morning, Lia and I sat in Tim and Alluree's solarium again. I'd told Lia what Vell had told me, and she'd been able to arrange an interview with Alluree alone this time on the pretense her editor wanted to turn it into a celebrity-couple-dealing-with-fame piece.

Alluree could only spare about half an hour, and this morning was the only time available before she flew to New York for a photoshoot later in the day. Somehow, Lia had gotten her to agree to see us before she took off. She was an expert at friendly persistence.

The Headstomper and the Supermodel were quite the jet-setting pair.

As before, I was officially there to take pictures. But Lia and I had two ulterior motives. We wanted to determine if Alluree had indeed been sleeping with Claypool, and we wanted to confirm Finn's story that he could see through one of Claypool's windows from Thorpe's house. Our strategy was to divide and conquer. She'd go after the affair, and I'd work on Finn's claim.

Today, Alluree wore a snug white sundress that accentuated her super-model curves. I wondered what it would be like to have a job where one's appearance was so important. I sometimes wished I could present a bit nicer, but I was a slob, through and through. I wouldn't even know where to begin. I was lucky if I could find clean clothes to wear every day.

Lia set her phone down and pressed record. "First, thank you for agreeing to this follow-up. After seeing a draft of my piece, my editor thought we could expand the story to focus on what it's like for two mega-celebrities to live together, right here in not-so-glamorous suburbia. He thought it would be interesting—and enlightening—if I interviewed each one of you separately. See if your answers matched." Lia chuckled when she said it, as it was clearly a joke.

"Of course," Alluree said, but I wasn't sure she saw the humor.

"Great. I know you're on a tight time frame, so let's get started."

Alluree flashed a dazzling smile, the same one you'd see on lip gloss ads. "Perfect."

"I just had a couple more questions about the murder, before we get into the lifestyle stuff," Lia said.

Alluree's smile dimmed. "Sure."

"How well did you know Webster?"

If I hadn't been laser-focused on Alluree's face to gauge her reaction, I might have missed the tiniest chink in her poise. But it was there. Sadness? I wasn't sure if it was over losing someone you cared for, or over the loss of *anyone*, but it proved to me she wasn't a plastic Barbie doll. "We've lived here for four years, and he moved in about six months after we did. We knew each other about as well as neighbors do. Seemed like a nice guy." Her voice caught slightly, but again, unless you were looking for it, you might not have noticed. "A terrible shame what happened."

"Did you and Tim ever socialize with him? At charity events, perhaps?"

"Once in a while, yes. We like to support as many worthwhile causes as we can, and Webster did, too."

"Didn't I see a photo of you and Webster at an event a few months ago? Children Cancer Survivors or something like that?"

Alluree's smile tightened. "Probably. The paparazzi love those things. That's one of the reasons we decided to move here. To suburbia, as you call it. To avoid the paparazzi and the stalkers. To try to live a normal life, as best we can."

"Did Tim get along with Webster, too?"

Alluree crossed her long legs. "Yes, of course."

"Sometimes neighbors have squabbles. Anything like that going on in the neighborhood?"

Alluree uncrossed her long legs and sat forward. "I'm not sure what you're getting at."

"Just trying to get a sense of the neighborhood, for context. I think my readers would like to know that celebrities face all the same things with regard to their communities that regular people do. Would you say that's true?"

"This is a fine neighborhood. Quiet. Everyone is friendly, but nobody's really in anybody else's business. Which is exactly how Tim and I like it." Alluree glanced at her watch.

"Since we're crunched for time, would you mind if Hopkins started taking some pictures. Maybe he can start on the back deck? By the pool and spa?"

Alluree's brow furrowed as she considered Lia's request. Of course, we'd planned for her to ask. I wanted to discover exactly what Finn could see from Thorpe's house. "Sure, I guess so." She pointed behind her. "You can go right through there. Watch your step. Sometimes it gets slick."

I got up and left Lia to continue her interview. Neither of us expected Alluree to come right out and admit having an affair with Claypool, but we were hoping her body language or facial expressions might give us a clue.

The door at the back of the solarium led directly out to a two-level deck. Below me, on the ground level, the patio surrounded an elaborate pool. It wasn't gigantic, but one side had an impressive rock formation that gave way to a waterfall. Water jets shot into the air on the other side. A swim-up fire pit seemed suspended over the water.

A dozen chaise lounges provided ample seating, and across the pool, there was an outdoor kitchen with an oversized grill. A covered bar area nestled between the kitchen and the house, and above the bar hung a large TV, presumably to watch all the MMA bouts while sipping drinks and enjoying the great outdoors.

The pool and adjoining bar area were designed for entertaining, but the smaller and more intimate upper deck seemed like Thorpe and Alluree's private spot. An all-weather loveseat abutted the house, and off to one side— closest to Claypool's house—was a circular hot tub. A retractable awning could extend over the hot tub to provide shelter from the elements.

I pulled out my phone and started taking pictures. First of the pool below, then I shifted around until I was right next to the hot tub. I gazed up at the sky, then back at my phone, pretending to check the light levels in case Alluree was watching through the window.

I spied Claypool's house next door, about twenty yards away. There was a hedge of trees blocking much of the view, but it was thinner in spots, as if some of the plants had succumbed to a disease.

And if I leaned over a bit, I could see through a corner of a window. Right into the first level of Claypool's house. Pretty clearly, in fact. A family room. I could see some furniture, the corner of a TV or entertainment center. At the top of the window was a shade. If I was going to kill someone, I'd make sure I had the shades drawn, but it was dark, and maybe they figured no one would be next door leaning over at precisely the right angle to spot them. Of course, no one ever said hitmen were geniuses.

I craned my neck to examine the side of Thorpe's house. No windows. So if Finn saw something, it would most likely have been from approximately where I stood on the deck.

There was nothing here to disprove Finn's story. He could have seen Claypool getting killed if he'd been on the deck at the right time, in the right spot. But if he was there to steal stuff, what in the world was he doing out by the hot tub? One answer led to another question.

I took a series of shots featuring Claypool's house from this vantage point, so I could show Lia and Vell and whoever else might want to check out Finn's story.

Information gathered, I resumed my photographer ruse and moved around the deck, taking more pictures—of the nicely landscaped back yard— before going inside. Lia and Alluree were finishing up, and judging by the thick tension in the air, things hadn't gone any smoother. Had Alluree picked up on the fact Lia wasn't really doing a puff piece on their idyllic home life?

"All done with the pictures?" Lia asked me.

"Yep."

Lia turned to Alluree and extended a hand. "I guess that's a wrap. Thank you so much for your time. I know it was last minute."

"Yes, it was. I'll show you out now. Please, follow me." Alluree took off without looking back.

We waited until I'd driven out of the neighborhood before speaking, as if Alluree could hear us five hundred yards away.

"She was definitely having an affair with Claypool." Lia turned to face me as I drove. "She didn't come right out and say it, but I know."

"And Finn could definitely have seen the murder," I replied, sticking out my fist, which she bumped lightly.

"Maybe Thorpe found out what was going on," Lia began.

"And a guy named Headstomper might take things into his own hands," I finished, sticking out my fist again.

Lia bumped it. "Now *we* just need to figure out what's going on."

Yeah, that.

* * *

We decided to continue with our divide-and-conquer strategy. Lia returned to her office to try to dig up more information about Alluree's personal life, looking to confirm she'd been having an affair with Claypool. Basing our suspicions on an early morning sighting by some random home improvement contractor was kind of shaky, and our spidey-sense about Alluree maybe wasn't the most reliable indicator. Lia had some contacts in the upper-class society world of DC from an article she wrote last year, so she was planning to hit the phones to see what she could scare up.

I was going to delve more into the life of Thorpe, but the idea of doing it alone seemed foolish. Even with Vell by my side, I knew we were probably outgunned if things turned physical. And with a guy named Headstomper, getting physical seemed like a foregone conclusion.

I called Vell, and he agreed to ride shotgun—as long as we had a pre-excursion planning meeting that involved lunch.

Chapter Eighteen

I didn't want to argue with Vell about where to go to lunch, so I stopped by Hole Lotta Love and snagged a couple of loaded meat sandwiches, to-go. Once in a while—I guessed when the inventory got unbalanced— Sandy offered loaded meat sandwiches as daily specials. A mix of whatever struck her fancy, no two sandwiches were alike. I wasn't sure that was the best marketing strategy—didn't people return to restaurants to order their favorite meals?—but it worked for me and Vell. Our favorite meals often involved extremely large portions of assorted meats.

I met him at Mama's, where he was finishing up some chores for her while she was at some church lady meeting. He said he was way more productive when she wasn't there peering over his shoulder, offering suggestions.

He opened the door wearing a shirt decorated with paint drippings.

I held up the bag with the sandwiches. "Sustenance has arrived."

"Perfect. Come on in. I just finished painting the guest room."

We attacked our lunches in the breakfast nook. "So my buddy was right? Supermodel was sleeping with super developer?" Vell spoke through a mouthful of assorted meat.

"She was giving off some guilty vibes. But she could have just been annoyed at us for bothering her again." I took a bite of my sandwich. Roast beef, pastrami, and turkey, with a generous slather of Russian dressing.

"You do have a tendency to annoy people."

"Thanks. Lia got the same sense, though."

"She's too sweet to annoy anybody." Vell put down his sandwich, removed the top slice of bread, and rearranged the slices of meat. Then he reassembled.

"Point is, we need to figure out if Thorpe found out about the affair and took care of the problem."

"Okay. How do we do that? Ask him?" Vell said.

I took a gulp of water. All that meat needed some lubrication to work its way down the gullet. "First, we check out his alibi. He said he was at some charity function. Then we ask around, see if he has a temper outside the ring. I imagine there would be tons of stuff on the internet if he was involved in numerous altercations."

"And if all that doesn't give us an answer?"

I shrugged. "I guess we could follow him. See if he hangs around with any unsavory characters."

"Sounds like a complete act of desperation to me." Vell took another bite of his gargantuan sammie.

"Got a better idea?"

He shook his head and wiped a smear of dressing off his face.

The creak of the front door got our attention. Vell's eyes went wide. "Quick," he said. "Hide your food."

"Hello?" Mama called out. "Mess? You here? That your car out front?"

Before we could get our sandwiches wrapped up and tucked away someplace, Mama swooped into the kitchen. She scowled at us like she'd been a scowling major in college. "Well, what do we have here?"

"I thought you were at church." Vell swallowed the last bit of food in his mouth.

"Jeanmarie wasn't feeling well. Ended the meeting early." She stepped forward, pointed at the sandwiches on the table. "I can't believe you brought this into my house. I would have made you boys lunch. You don't need this…this…*stuff*."

"You weren't here," Vell said.

"You could have called."

"I didn't want to bother you." Vell's voice got softer.

"I'm sorry, Mama," I offered.

"Oh, Mess, honey, this isn't your fault. You might not know better, but

Vell sure does. Ain't that right, child?"

"Yes, ma'am."

Mama scooped up what was left of our lunches and dumped them into the trash can under the sink. "Now, how about I fix you two something tasty? I bet you'd like that."

Vell and I exchanged glances. I'd already devoured about a pound of meat, so where was I going to put another lunch? One of Mama's big meals, to boot? Just thinking about it made my stomach hurt.

But we really didn't have a choice. One of Mama's great joys in life was feeding those she loved.

Vell smiled. "Sure, Mama. That would be great."

She beamed, and I knew I'd figure out a way to clean my plate. "Wonderful. Give me about twenty minutes, okay? Now, run along, and I'll call you when it's ready."

Vell and I retreated into Mama's den to do some research. You could find anything on the Internet. It didn't take long for us to find a few celeb photos from the charity event Thorpe attended the night of the murder. No surprise. If he was indeed Claypool's killer, I would expect him to make sure his alibi was airtight. Thorpe didn't strike me as an idiot.

It also didn't take very long to uncover a number—a large number—of photos taken of Thorpe, mostly in his Headstomper persona—acting physical. I'd seen some the other night when I'd done a search, but now that we were specifically looking for acts of violence, they seemed more apparent. And more abundant. And more vicious.

"This dude is a serious headcase, man." Vell ran a hand through his hair. "Wouldn't want to meet him in a dark alley, alone or otherwise."

Despite his insane, killer façade, Thorpe didn't strike me as unhinged. Or violent for violent sake. "Maybe."

"What? You see all these incidents, right?"

I did. "I just wonder how much of them are staged to make him seem like a bad-boy MMA fighter. Build up his street cred."

Vell flexed his biceps, and I could see a slight bulge under his shirt. "You see that guy's guns? Staged or not, he's packing."

I went to Thorpe's website, pretty sure I wouldn't find any paparazzi-style pictures of him harassing others or getting harassed. I was wrong. It seemed these altercations bolstered his image of a bad boy and also bolstered my suspicion that many—if not most—were staged. After all, I didn't see any evidence of lawsuits or arrests for assault.

I stumbled onto his Events page. Alluree and Thorpe weren't kidding about attending a lot of local events to help the community. There were dozens of appearances listed on their upcoming schedule, and he happened to have one this afternoon at Children's Hospital. I wanted to talk with him in the most non-confrontational way possible to see what he knew about Alluree's dalliance with Claypool. No time like the present. "Want to go for a ride?" I asked Vell.

"Will I be putting my body in harm's way?" he asked.

"Possibly."

"Then I'm in." Vell licked his lips. "After lunch, of course. Don't want to make Mama mad."

* * *

After we crammed lunch number two down our throats—and it *was* delicious—we drove to Children's Hospital and lucked into a parking spot with a view of the main entrance. I figured Thorpe would want as much coverage of him doing something charitable as possible, so he'd enter and exit through the front doors to accommodate the paparazzi. I also figured we'd have a better chance of getting the information we wanted if we didn't corral him in front of reporters or photographers.

After my last visit to the Thorpe home, I didn't think I'd be invited in again.

Our plan was to meet at his car and persuade him to join us at a nearby coffee shop where we could have a conversation. Private, yet in view of the public. We didn't feel the need to discover firsthand why they called him Headstomper.

We waited in the hospital lot patiently, no pun intended.

"Ever been in a fistfight?" Vell asked.

I'd been in more than my share of scuffles, usually breaking up a fight between motel guests. "Yeah, I guess. More wrestling and pushing and shoving than throwing punches. You?"

"Some. Hurts like hell, though. Not like in the movies. Punching someone in the face hurts your fingers and your hands. Violence is rarely the answer, my friend."

I glanced over at him. "What's wrong with you?"

"Nothing. Just being introspective. Inevitably, violence escalates the problem. Makes a peaceful resolution more difficult to attain." Vell put his hands together, prayer-like.

"Very Ghandhi-like of you. Where do you stand on pugilistic sports?"

"Like MMA?"

"Yeah."

Vell shrugged. "Far be it for me to judge how one makes their living."

"But?"

"Not a fan. I used to watch some boxing as a teen, but I've given up on it. Same with UFC stuff. Too brutal. Bloodthirsty."

"But you watch pro football?"

Vell grinned. "They've got pads on, bro. And helmets. And the goal is to win the game, not kill your opponent. Big difference."

"If you say so."

Vell pointed. "There he is."

The front doors of the hospital had opened, and Thorpe emerged, accompanied by a few people. A publicist, maybe, and another guy snapping pictures. A nearby security guard observed the goings-on with little interest.

Thorpe posed with a sharply-dressed woman—hospital administrator, if I had to guess—then shook hands with everyone there, and the small group said their goodbyes and disbanded.

"Now?" Vell asked, hand on the door handle.

I watched Thorpe weave his way through the first two rows of parked cars. If we jumped out, we could probably intercept him before he left. But did we really want to have this conversation in the middle of a parking lot?

He'd be a lot more inclined to blow us off, and all he had to do was drive away, and we'd be standing around like a couple of losers. Plus, I didn't like the presence of a security guard. Too easy for Thorpe to call him over and say he was being harassed.

"Why don't we follow him instead? Find a better place to talk with him."

I could feel Vell's eyes on me. "What if he goes straight home?"

"Then I guess we'll have to come up with some other angle. I'm getting some bad vibes here."

"Okay, man. I know better than to argue with your vibes."

Thorpe made it to his car, some sleek all-electric job, and slowly backed out of his spot. Then he headed for the lot's exit. I started up my dumpy Corolla and followed.

It wasn't hard keeping up with Thorpe. His flashy car stood out from the rest, and he had no reason to believe anyone was following him. We stayed a few cars behind him for about ten minutes, heading vaguely west, back toward the Northern VA suburbs, until he made an unexpected right turn. North. Into Maryland. When we got to the Beltway, he went east instead of west.

"I guess he's not going straight home," Vell said. "As usual, you were right."

We followed Thorpe farther and farther away from the city. The neighborhoods got increasingly worse, and seedy strip shopping centers became the norm, not the exception.

"Any idea where he's going?" Vell asked.

"Not a clue."

"Maybe he's got some side action." Vell snorted. "Which would mean he's crazier than I thought. His wife is a supermodel, you know."

"It's not all about looks, my friend." I tapped my heart with my fist. "It's about love."

Traffic was lighter here, so we hung back more. There was no indication he'd spotted us, but maybe that's why he'd left the well-beaten path—to lure us out here so he could stomp our heads without witnesses.

Thorpe drove past a junkyard, a check-cashing place slash pawn shop, and a storefront pet hospital. The setting did not inspire confidence if I had a sick cat.

Finally, he pulled into the parking lot of a seedy motel, The Clamshell Motor Lodge, and drove to the far end of the strip of rooms.

What the hell?

Chapter Nineteen

Instead of following him into the Clamshell's lot, I turned left into a 7-Eleven and took a spot with a view of the motel. Thorpe parked his fancy car, taking up two spaces, and it stuck out, well, like a fancy sports car in a lot sprinkled with fifteen-year-old rusted-out pickups.

"Classy," Vell said.

Across the street, Thorpe emerged from his car. He now wore a dark gray hoodie, with the hood up over his face, obviously trying to hide his identity, although there was nobody around at all, let alone anyone paying attention.

I was familiar with many of the independent motels in the DC area. I knew a lot of the owner-operators, and I was a sometime-participant in a listserv where indies would trade best practices and bemoan the general lack of business.

However, I'd never heard of the Clamshell. Eighteen units, one long strip. Built in the 1970s or so, back when motels were springing up like toadstools. Usually situated closer to the interstates. Usually motels that old had undergone some sort of renovation. Usually ones like this hadn't been in business for years.

Which meant a couple of things. Either it was a pay-by-the-hour flophouse, or it was some kind of front for illegal activities. Off the main roads like this, it could have been either. Or both.

"If he's meeting his sidepiece, she must have very low standards," Vell said. "On the other hand, there's not much chance of anyone recognizing him here."

"Some kind of drug deal?"

"Who knows? Celebs would go to great lengths to keep something like that quiet. And MMA fighters strike me as crazier than most, and that's saying something." Vell shook his head in disgust.

I'd spent some time with Thorpe, and he didn't seem crazy. He also didn't seem like the guy to risk messing up his body—his ticket to stardom—with substances.

Vell swiveled to face me. "Okay, what's our move here?"

"We need more info."

"How do you propose getting that?"

"Going to rely on my brotherhood. Wait here, okay? If Thorpe shows his face, text me." I hopped out and crossed the street, headed for the registration office, which occupied the last unit on the left. A stereotypical red neon light blinked VACANCY. I opened the door, and a guy sitting on a stool behind the desk glanced my way. When he saw I was a potential customer, he sprang to attention and stitched on a smile. "How can I help you?"

I smiled back. "How's it going?"

"Fine, thank you." He was about forty—in age and in hours since his last shower. Greasy black hair framed an ashen face with sunken eyes. Didn't look like he got out much.

"My name's Hopkins, and I'm an indie operator, too. Run the Fairfax Manor Inn in the City of Fairfax."

"Okay."

I'd been hoping to use our common quest—providing affordable lodging to the masses—to forge a bond, but he simply stared at me. I ran my hand along the countertop. "Been running this place long?"

"A dozen years or so." He jutted his chin at me a fraction. "Would you like a room?"

"Oh, no. I don't need a room."

"Then why are you here? This is a motel, you know."

"I make it a point to meet other motel operators, especially local ones, whenever I can."

"Are you here to steal my trade secrets?" he asked without a trace of irony.

I wondered what type of trade secrets a place like this would have. "No, of course not. I just thought it would be nice to make your acquaintance. By the way, are you on the DMV listserv of motel and inn operators?"

"No."

"You ought to look into that. We're a friendly bunch."

"I don't really need any friends," he said. "No offense."

I glanced around the registration desk. "Do you have a card?"

"No card." He reached under the counter and pulled out a yellowed brochure with a photo of a much newer-looking Clamshell Motor Lodge on the front. "You can have one of these."

"Thanks. Is your name on it?"

"No."

Things weren't going very well, but the more he stonewalled, the more determined I became. "What's your typical occupancy rate for this month?"

"It varies."

"How much do you charge for a room?"

"It varies."

"What sort of discounts do you provide? How do you increase visibility? What marketing techniques have you found to be most effective? What's your policy on late checkout?" I tried to tamp down the irritation in my voice and failed miserably.

"It varies, of course." He cocked his head. "If you're trying to sell me something, I'm not interested."

I exhaled. "Not trying to sell you something, simply trying to connect. It's been my experience that when I meet people in our business, I always learn something new."

"And what are you learning now?"

What a jerk you are. "I learned that despite a poor location and a property desperately in need of a facelift, you're still in business. Are you a money-laundering operation? A drug dealer's den? A hooker's haven?"

The guy didn't flinch. "We, sir, are an economical lodging option that serves a loyal clientele, with friendly, responsive service. I'm sure you do the same at the Fairfax Manor Inn. Not that I've ever heard of it, mind you."

So much for diplomacy. "I noticed a guest in the last unit. Is he one of your loyal clientele?"

The dude's grin grew large and smarmy. "I'm afraid I can't answer that. We respect the confidentiality of all our guests."

I felt myself going on tilt. I raised my voice. "Is he a drug dealer? A pimp? Is he meeting someone? Guy driving a car like that seems a bit out of place here."

"No comment, sir."

I slapped the registration counter, and a jar of petrified jellybeans rattled. "I think I'm going to call the cops. Alert them to illegal activities here. As a fellow motel operator, I feel a certain responsibility to your guests to provide a safe environment."

He lifted a landline phone onto the counter and pushed it in front of me. "Feel free to call the local police. My uncle is one of the deputies."

I pushed the phone back at him. "I should have guessed that."

He nodded a couple of times, then hit me with that infuriating smile again. "Well, now that I've answered all your questions, would you like a room? If not, have a truly blessed day."

I wanted to tell him to shove his blessed day up his rear end, but that wouldn't have been very hospitable.

Back in the car, Vell must have sensed my futility, because he started laughing. "Lemme guess. The manager wasn't interested in befriending a fellow motel proprietor."

"Something like that."

"Proves he's up to something shady."

"How do you figure?"

"Because a guy on the up-and-up would have succumbed to your charms."

"Funny." I jutted my chin at Thorpe's car. "Anything happening?"

"Nope. Nobody in, nobody out. Maybe he's just in there, chilling. Away from the paparazzi."

"You really believe that?"

"Not in a million years," Vell said.

"Maybe he met someone already there."

He shrugged. "Maybe."

"Let's see what develops." We slipped into a comfortable silence as we watched the goings-on at the Clamshell. Or we would have if there were any goings-on. Once, a car turned in, but it was simply using the lot to turn around.

Thirty minutes passed. An hour.

"Maybe he's planning to spend the night," Vell said.

"Here? This guy is loaded. If I wanted to spend the night away from home, I'd be at the Four Seasons."

"Motel man knows his lodgings," Vell said. "So, we keep waiting?"

"We keep waiting."

And we kept waiting. Another hour rolled by. Vell dozed off a couple of times, and I let him sleep, content to let my mind wander. What was going on with Finn? He said he returned to the area, intent on getting his act together. He got a menial job delivering pizzas, and according to his boss, he was always on time and reliable. How did that fit with breaking into Thorpe's house? How did it fit with lying to me? I knew trying to evaluate someone who'd been through what Finn had—living on the streets, drugs, not knowing if you would be alive next week—was difficult. I had no context, no frame of reference.

But I couldn't help but think back to when we were kids. Finn was always so caring and loyal, loyal, loyal.

When I was about sixteen, I got caught drinking beer in our back yard. My parents were supposed to go sailing all day, but Mom got sick, and they came home early. Needless to say, they weren't happy, and I got grounded for a couple of weeks. Ordinarily, I wouldn't have been too angry, but there was this party I wanted to go to the following Saturday. I begged and pleaded and tried to negotiate with my parents; they held firm.

I seriously thought about sneaking out, but if they'd caught me, I'd probably get grounded until I went to college. Finn hadn't been involved in the beer-drinking incident—not that he wouldn't have wanted to, but he was at some piano recital or something. Nevertheless, he bagged the party, came over that Saturday night, and parked himself right below my bedroom window, there in the bushes, talking to me for hours, trying to cheer me up. He didn't, not really, because I was dying to go to that party. But I would never forget his compassion.

My reverie was interrupted by Thorpe's motel room door opening. "Vell, wake up."

"Huh? Yeah. Awake." Vell glanced across the street. "Action."

Thorpe left the room and closed the door behind him. He took a couple of steps, then the door opened, and he turned around.

"Do you see anything?" Vell asked.

"Just Thorpe. You?"

"Nope."

Thorpe reversed course and took a step inside. Two arms engulfed his body in a hug. We couldn't see anything more of the hugger. The two arms caressed Thorpe as they kissed. Whoever it was, wasn't Alluree. She was out of town on a photo shoot.

Looked like Vell was right. Side action. Which, I guess, in retrospect, made the Clamshell the perfect place. No paparazzi here. Nobody much here at all. And a tight-lipped desk clerk. I wondered if Thorpe paid extra to ensure his secrecy. Of course, Thorpe himself hadn't checked in. His paramour had. Made even more sense.

After a few moments, they broke off their embrace. Thorpe said something, then turned and walked out to his car and climbed in.

The motel door closed.

Thorpe started his car.

I had been planning to confront Thorpe to see if he knew about Alluree's affair with Claypool, but what we'd just seen threw that plan out the window. I still would like to talk to him and ask about *his* affair, but I didn't think that would be a very successful endeavor. A celebrity like him would know all the ways of dodging questions and giving nebulous answers. But there might be a better way.

"He's leaving. Don't you want to follow him?" Vell asked.

"Naw. We know where he lives." I faced Vell. "I think we should talk to his friend, instead."

"I like how you think," Vell said. "Maybe we should get closer."

"Good idea." I started the engine and drove across the street. Parked near the room Thorpe had occupied—but not right outside. Didn't want to spook his mistress.

"What if she's a pro? And Thorpe was just one of her many daily appointments?"

I'd considered that. "He stayed for quite some time. And the kiss at the end? Seemed more personal than business."

"Yeah, I guess you're right. Want me to knock on the door?" Vell asked.

I glanced at the registration office at the other end of the motel. Last thing I wanted was for Mr. Friendly to call the cops, upholding his guests' confidentiality. "Let's give it a few minutes."

It only took about ninety seconds. Then the motel door opened, and the object of Thorpe's desires walked out.

Finn.

Chapter Twenty

Next to me, Vell gasped and said something, but it didn't register. *Finn.* Coming out of Thorpe's room. *Finn.* Kissing Thorpe goodbye, the way a lover does. *Finn.* Spending a couple of hours with Headstomper Thorpe in a no-tell motel twenty miles from civilization.

Finn looked our way, then turned his head back, then did one of the most spectacular double-takes I'd ever seen. At first, his eyes threatened to leave their orbits and bounce along the asphalt, and then he glanced away, looking for an escape route, if I had to guess.

But we'd seen him, and he knew we'd seen him, and he also must have known there was no way in the world we wouldn't ask him what the hell was going on. So he simply stood there, shoulders slumped, staring at the ground.

Under his breath, Vell kept repeating the words *Holy Smokes*, over and over again.

Holy smokes, indeed.

"Wait here, will you?" I got out of the car and walked over to Finn. He still hadn't looked at me, so I gently put my arm around his shoulders and guided him back toward the room.

"Let's go in and talk, okay?" I used the same quiet voice I used when trying to calm my nieces after we watched a scary movie we shouldn't have.

"Okay." Finn's voice was barely perceptible. He handed me the key, and I opened the door. Led him in. The sheets were a mess, and I searched for someplace to sit. Anyplace but the bed. There was only a single chair, so I let Finn take it, and I leaned against the wall. This place was older than the

Inn, and the furniture was dated, if solid. The generic artwork over the bed, however, was dated and ugly. The room smelled of cigarette smoke, mildew, sweat, and sex.

"You want to tell me what's going on?" Although it was mighty obvious—unbelievable, but obvious—I figured I'd give Finn a chance to explain.

"It's not what it looks like." His features had turned to Play-Doh, and he looked as if he might vomit.

"Okay."

Finn was silent for the longest time, head in his hands. Then he lifted up and stared me square in the eye. "Actually, it's *exactly* what it looks like."

I stated the obvious. "You and Thorpe are having an affair."

"Yes."

"Thorpe is gay?" The ramifications of an MMA fighter being gay hit me. Not because there was anything wrong with that, but because when I thought of a typical MMA fan, someone who loved brutality and the macho machinations that went along with it, I didn't picture someone who was very progressive socially. I pictured beer-guzzling Neanderthals. Misogynistic. Homophobic. Cretins. Maybe my own biases were showing.

"Yes."

"How long has this been going on?"

Finn looked up at me, eyes moist and red. "We met the very night I got back in town, actually. At a bar. We talked for a while—I had no idea who he was, of course—then one thing led to another. He's really a very sensitive guy, not at all like his public persona. We share a common bond. Both having lived on the streets, overcoming adversity. We just clicked, you know. That's what he said, anyway. It'll probably run its course. They all do, right? But at the moment, it's wonderful."

I tried to get my head around this. I didn't have a hard time believing Headstomper Thorpe was gay. I did have a difficult time, however, believing Thorpe, an MMA celebrity, wealthy and good-looking and a man about town, was attracted to Finn. My cousin, Finn. He wasn't a bad-looking guy, but he was…Finn. Love was crazy, and all that, but this was absolutely bonkers. "I don't know what to say, Finn."

"You can't tell anybody about this. It will destroy Tim, and if he finds out I had something to do with this, he'll…he'll…"

I wanted to finish Finn's sentence with "kill me," but I kept quiet.

Pleading eyes met mine. "Please. Promise me you won't tell anybody."

I stared at him. I had no desire to out someone, nor did I want to wreck anyone's relationship. I tried to operate under the notion that people's private business was their own private business. Live and let live. But if Thorpe had anything to do with Claypool's murder, then all the rest didn't matter. "That's why you were at Thorpe's house and saw the murder. You were with him, and you couldn't come out and say that."

"Yes and no. I was at Thorpe's house, but he wasn't there. In fact, he doesn't know I was there."

"Not sure I understand." A queasy feeling burrowed into my gut.

"I was there. He wasn't."

Would I ever get used to Finn's evasiveness? "Help me out here, Finn. Did you break in?"

"Not exactly. I had a key."

"Thorpe gave you a key?"

"Not exactly."

"Damn it, tell me what happened, exactly."

He scratched the side of his nose while he thought of his response, exactly like Uncle Phil did when he was stalling. Nature or nurture? Finn sighed. "I was there the night before. With him. I found a spare key and borrowed it. I also watched him punch in the alarm code, so I deactivated the system, too. I knew he and his wife were going to be out of town the next night, and I wanted to spend the night in luxury. No offense, but your place isn't nearly as nice as Tim's. I mean, did you see that hot tub and media room?"

"So Thorpe doesn't know you were there? What you saw?"

"No. No. And please, please, please don't tell him. I wasn't trying to cause any harm or anything. I only wanted to enjoy some of the finer things in life, for a change. That's no crime, is it?"

Entering someone's house without permission actually *was* a crime. "Maybe you should tell him."

"He'll break it off; I know he will. Trust is important to him and, well…" Finn raised his hands, palms up.

"If you don't tell him, and he finds out what you did on his own, he'll break it off for sure. That might not be all he breaks off."

Panic bloomed on Finn's face. "You can't tell him. You just can't."

"He's going to find out eventually. He may not like it, but it will be better if it comes from you." I smoothed out my voice. "You know I'm right."

"I do. On some level. But I'm afraid of what he'll do."

I straightened. "Do you think he'll hurt you physically?"

"What? No, of course not. Tim's a sweetheart. He only seems ferocious."

I'd seen plenty of clips from his fights, and he seemed more like a Braveheart than a sweetheart. I remembered why we'd been following Thorpe in the first place. The secret I'd discovered seemed to change the calculus, but it's still possible he killed Claypool after he found out about Alluree's affair with him. Something about not coveting your neighbor's wife and upholding male honor. "Do you think he had anything whatsoever to do with Claypool's murder?"

"No way. Absolutely not."

"Did he know about his wife's affair?"

"Tim and Alluree have an arrangement. She knows about his extracurriculars, and he knows about hers. Theirs is a celebrity marriage, all the way. Just for show. Tabloids and charity galas. Of course, if word got out about Tim's lifestyle, her career would take a hit, too."

Maybe jealousy wasn't Thorpe's motive. Maybe silencing someone who had information that would ruin his career was the motive. Maybe during some pillow talk, Alluree spilled her guts about Thorpe to Claypool. Protecting one's multi-million-dollar career might inspire some people to kill.

Of course, I could apply the same logic to Alluree. If Claypool knew Thorpe's secret and threatened to go public with it, she might want to silence Claypool, too, for the same reason. Self-preservation was a strong primal force.

Which brought us full circle back to Finn's predicament. He witnessed two men kill Claypool, and he feared they were hellbent to silence *him*.

Finn slumped in the chair, sobbing. Even though he'd gotten himself into this situation—having an affair with a married guy, sneaking into his house without permission, choosing not to go to the police with what he saw—I felt sorry for him, I really did. He didn't ask to witness a murder, after all. It was funny how one bad decision led to another, which led to another.

"How did you get here, Finn?"

"To this motel? Uber."

"All the way out here?"

"Tim is very generous."

I sighed. "C'mon, we'll give you a ride back. Vell's with me."

Finn snuffled in a few more tears, then wiped his face with the back of his hands. "Please respect my privacy. Don't tell anybody about this. Especially not your reporter girlfriend."

If there was one person who could help Finn get out of his jam in some way, it was Lia. And she'd be in a lot better position to work her magic if she had all the details. "She can keep what you tell her confidential. She's got a lot of contacts, she knows what's going on in the police investigation, and she can probably help keep you out of serious trouble. You need to trust her, however."

"I don't trust her. I don't trust anybody."

"Not even me?" I asked.

"I don't have much choice, do I?"

I tried not to take that personally, figured it came from a place of fear. "Look, you don't want my help, say the word. But you're family, and I'm here for you. You *should* trust me, but I get that you've been through a lot of stuff, and trust might be hard to achieve. As for keeping this a secret, I can't make any promises. Somebody got murdered, Finn, and you could be next on the hit list. If I need to mention this to someone in order to catch this guy, then I will. But I won't unless I have to, okay?"

Finn stared at me.

"Finn, this is the moment of truth. I want to help you. I do. But either you trust me, or I'll leave you to fend for yourself. Your choice." I hated to give him an ultimatum, but without his buy-in, my chain would get yanked at every corner.

Finn exhaled. "Okay. I trust you."

"How about a hug?"

His lower lip quivered, and he blinked several times. Then he got up, and we embraced. It was awkward—the last time we'd hugged, we were probably in elementary school. Beneath his shirt, his body shivered, and I fought back tears. Why couldn't he have come back home years ago? Sought help from those who loved him? How had his life descended into such a tragic situation? Why hadn't I done more to help him?

We separated, and I sensed a change in his mood. Not exactly hopeful, but maybe a little more optimistic. Or maybe I was simply projecting.

"How does my relationship with Tim have anything to do with Claypool's murder, and why those guys are after me?"

Seriously? Funny how myopic some people were, especially about their own situations. "You were at his house when you witnessed the murder. They may try to get to you through Thorpe or Alluree. I don't know the particulars, but if you think it's not all wrapped up in the same enchilada, you're not thinking clearly. I'm still not sure Thorpe didn't kill Claypool because he was sleeping with his wife." I raised my voice, and Finn shrank back. "Sorry. But how about we get out of here, calm down, and think this through, okay?"

"Okay."

On the way back, Finn sat in the back with his eyes closed and didn't say a word.

Thankfully, Vell was silent, too.

Chapter Twenty-One

That night, Lia and I lay in bed, spent. She squeezed my hand. "What are you thinking about?"

"Besides the fact that I should buy a queen-sized bed?" I hadn't upgraded anything in my room since I moved into the motel about a year ago.

"Yes, besides that."

"Relationships," I said.

"Oh? Ours?"

"No. Families, I guess."

She turned on her hip toward me, beautiful face about ten inches from mine. "Family is very important to you, isn't it?"

"Yeah."

"And yet, your parents aren't what I call involved in your life, and your uncle is *too* involved."

"Hard to explain, I guess. What about you? You've never told me much about your family?"

She sighed, and I squeezed *her* hand. "My dad left us when I was a kid. My mom raised me and my sister all alone, and she did a good job, but I got the feeling—when I was older—that she was bitter about it. Maybe resentful is a better word. Like Jen and I were keeping her from going on exotic foreign adventures and meeting the true love of her life."

"That sucks."

"Looking back, maybe, but at the time, my sister and I felt special. Two princesses being raised by the queen. We were solidly middle class, so we had what we needed, but we never did go on any exotic adventures."

"When will I get a chance to meet your mom?"

"She lives in Silicon Valley. Mountain View. Works for a tech firm doing marketing communications. I see her once or twice a year. She's remarried to a guy named Roderick."

"Do you like him?"

"He's fine. Not exactly the Prince Charming she was looking for, but he makes her happy, I guess."

"Sometimes, that's plenty."

Lia stroked my shoulder. "What's the deal with Finn?"

"What do you mean?" Alarm bells went off. Had I blurted out details about his secret affair with Thorpe in the throes of passion?

"All I know is that he ran away six years ago, lived on the streets, then came back. Why now? Did something change?"

A good question, and all I knew was what Finn told me. "I think he finally saw the light. Said he worked hard to get clean so he could hold his head high when he came home to his family." My stomach knotted. If I didn't tell her the truth now, then I'd get so much crap when—or if—I did. I mean, now was the perfect opportunity.

"I can't even imagine how terrible his life must have been. Takes a lot of courage to come back home and basically admit you've made a mess of your life, don't you think?"

I tried to come up with a response, some sort of half-truth or vague nebulosity, but I decided to give *honesty is the best policy* a whirl. "Okay, listen, I need to tell you something. And you won't believe it, but I saw it with my own two eyes."

Lia shifted position, getting up onto one elbow, and an intensity had crept onto her face. "What won't I believe?"

I swallowed. No turning back now. "Like we agreed, I was trying to find out if Thorpe could have been involved in Claypool's murder." I stopped, trying to make sure I phrased this properly.

"Yeah?" Her gaze bored into me.

"Vell and I followed Thorpe to some pay-by-the-hour fleabag motel, way out in the boonies."

"Oh my god, Thorpe's having an affair, too? Shoulda figured. Good for the goose, good for the gander. Something about that couple didn't seem right."

"Yeah, well, that's not the entire picture."

Lia poked me. "Okay, then, spill."

"Thorpe's having an affair with Finn." I carefully watched her expression change after I dropped the bombshell. First, confusion. Then, her eyes dilated with amazement. Then they squinched up, as if she'd misheard me. A few seconds later, she broke out into a wide grin, and the scar on her chin seemed to smile, too.

"You're joking, right?"

I shook my head.

"C'mon, you've got to be joking."

"Nope. Saw them both in the motel room. Big goodbye hug and smooch when they parted ways."

Lia maneuvered into a fully seated position. "Headstomper is gay? And having a secret affair with someone who, until recently, was a street hustler—no offense to your cousin, of course? That is unbelievable." She hit me with a semi-lethal side-eye. "You sure you're not pranking me?"

"I saw it. Vell saw it. Finn confirmed it."

She got a faraway look as she processed the news. And, presumably, the ramifications. "People will not believe this."

"You can't tell *anyone*. This could wreck Thorpe's career. I don't know how the MMA crowd feels about in-the-closet athletes, but I'm guessing it's not the image *Headstomper* Thorpe wishes to convey."

Her features sharpened again, and storm clouds gathered. Lia was usually even-tempered, but every once in a while—usually when I'd screwed up somehow—she'd let loose with a tirade. "I would never out anyone just for kicks. Who do you think I am, anyway? But this situation might be germane to a murder investigation. The police might want to know this information. The general public might want to know this information. It's my duty as a member of the press to inform the public about things that could affect their safety."

"Don't you think you're going a little overboard?"

"Overboard? The press is one of the bedrock institutions that help keep our democracy strong. It's a check on the powers of government. A vital source of unbiased information. Haven't you been paying attention the last ten years?"

"Still not sure how Thorpe's sexual orientation has anything to do with the public's safety."

"I don't know. It may not. But it certainly may."

"I really don't see how."

Lia's nostrils flared. "Sometimes you're so naïve. Some of the neighbors believe Claypool's murderer is a random killer, and they're probably on edge, worried he might strike them next. But suppose they know Claypool was targeted because he was having an affair or because of some shady real estate deal or whatever. Don't you think they'd feel safer knowing this?"

"Sure, but..."

"Look, Thorpe's neighbor was murdered. The same neighbor who was having an affair with his wife. And Thorpe's lover claims to have witnessed the murder." She paused, and I could practically see the lightbulb go off over her head. "That's why he's acting so squirrelly about going to the cops with what he saw. He wasn't delivering pizza, was he? He was there on *personal business*."

"Yeah."

"And Finn offered up that bogus story as some kind of warped way to protect Thorpe, didn't he?"

I shrugged, and Lia gave me a disgusted look.

"I'd say Thorpe is likely involved in this, at the very least by harboring a witness and refusing to go to the police with what he knew. He probably encouraged Finn the whole way to protect his precious image. So I suppose it's not his sexual orientation that's the issue, it's the fact he wants to keep it under wraps that may factor into things."

"Finn says that Thorpe doesn't even know he witnessed the murder."

"Oh, well, if that's what Finn said." Lia got out of bed, started getting dressed.

"What are you doing?"

"I think it's obvious. I'm getting dressed."

"I can see that. But why?"

"Haven't we been over this? Don't you see the position you've put me in? You want me to keep this quiet, but it may be directly pertinent to the murder and my story investigating the murder. This is my job we're talking about here. My career. And you're mucking around in it, with your erratic cousin, as if it's some kind of family dust-up. A man's been killed!"

"I know this is serious. And I'm not trying to interfere with your reporting at all." I didn't feel like I was doing a good job expressing myself, but I often didn't do well with confrontations.

"In situations like this, when things are a bit murky, I have one simple strategy. I go with my gut. And my gut is telling me that the public deserves to know that truth, no matter where it might lead."

"You're right," I said, voice small. Lia wasn't wrong, on any count.

Lia kept at me. "Are you going to go to the police? Tell them about Thorpe's affair?"

I hadn't planned on it. If I did, that news was bound to leak. A person's personal business was just that—personal. Unless I found out Thorpe was involved somehow. Then I'd tell the cops everything. "Are you planning to tell them about Alluree's affair with Claypool?"

"Once I get confirmation, yes. It opens up some motives." Lia started putting on her shoes. "Listen, Mess. I thought you respected what I do. That you truly believed in a free press. But now I'm beginning to see the truth. You think what I do is just some stupid hobby."

"That's not true at all." I did value and respect the work Lia did. I admired her, and I was proud of what she'd been able to accomplish in a relatively short time. Obviously, I had a crappy way of showing it. I'd let my feelings for Finn obscure my feelings about Lia and her career. "Really. I think what you do is vital."

"Uh-huh." She grabbed her purse and headed for the door.

"It's past midnight. You don't have to leave," I said.

"Yes, actually, I do." She opened the door and disappeared into the darkness.

Chapter Twenty-Two

When I woke up the next morning, I debated texting Lia. Obviously upset, but I didn't have a good read on exactly how upset she was. After a short review of the pros and cons, I decided the cons outweighed the pros by a significant margin. I hoped she would calm down with time and realize I really did care about her and her career and that I was in a tough situation with Finn. He was my blood, and that ran thick. For my part, I vowed to find a better way to balance my loyalty to Finn with my loyalty to Lia. And to be a much, much better communicator.

Next, I debated following up with Finn. After we'd come back from the Clamshell Motor Lodge yesterday afternoon, he retreated to his room. That had become his modus operandi, and while, at first, he kept claiming he wasn't feeling well, he'd dropped that pretense. I imagined he was getting caught up on his network daytime TV shows or watching cat videos on the internet. Our motel didn't offer cable, and I didn't think Finn had the money to sign up for any streaming services. But who knew? Finn was full of surprises, most of them unpleasant.

What would I say, anyway? The killers were still after him. He still wouldn't go to the police, and from his perspective, I could see why. Undoubtedly, they'd ask him a bunch of questions, and his story about delivering pizza would hold up about as well as a dollar-store umbrella in a hurricane. Finn genuinely cared about Thorpe, and there was no way he was going to—potentially—destroy Thorpe's career by outing him. As I've always believed, Finn was an extremely loyal guy. And I loved him like a brother, despite all the shenanigans he brought with him.

Before I could decide my course of action, my phone buzzed with a text from Cesar.

Come to the office now, please.

I was about to respond, but it was just as easy to walk across the parking lot to see what he wanted.

When I got there, Aunt Vera popped out of a chair. "So nice to see you, Mess." She enveloped me in a hug that was fifty percent her, fifty percent perfume. I'd be smelling like I just walked through Macy's for a week. Over her shoulder, I noticed Cesar at the counter, pretending to be enthralled by something on his computer. He glanced at me, and I winked back. After waiting an appropriate amount of time, I extricated myself from the embrace.

"Nice to see you, too." I glanced around, waiting for Uncle Phil to come springing out of the shadows, scowling and snarling. No sign of him. "What, uh, what are you doing here?" The last time she came by the Inn, I was probably in high school.

"I think you know why I'm here."

I thought I did, actually. I wondered why she hadn't been by sooner, in fact. "I'm glad you came. I'm sure Finn will be very, very happy to see you."

"I hope so. I understand his interaction with Phil didn't go so well." Aunt Vera was usually reserved, accustomed to living in Uncle Phil's considerable—and loud—orbit. Theirs was a traditional old-time marriage, where the man wore the pants, and the wife followed along, several paces behind, keeping her thoughts to herself. Very old-time. I knew it must have taken some effort to drive in from McLean on her own. "Which, while I'm heartbroken about, isn't too surprising, is it?" She smiled at me, but it was full of sadness. "Phil and I have had our differences. More now, than before, and getting worse. I'm sure it hasn't escaped you how often I'm away visiting my sisters. But at our age, it's a lot simpler to stay together than to break apart. On some level, I still love him. He can be a royal son-of-a-bitch, though, can't he?"

I wasn't sure how to answer that, so I nodded vaguely.

"He really does love Finn, despite his very destructive way of showing it." Her voice caught. "When I heard he was alive, and back home, no less, I almost fainted. And I'm not proud of this, but I didn't know what to do. Rush to him? Give him his space? I mean, he ran away from us and *stayed* away for six long years. You have to hate someone a lot to do something like that. So, I've been fretting these past few days, dying to see him but not wanting to say or do anything that might drive him away again. Finn needs his freedom, always has. Needs to make his own decisions. I figured if he wanted to see his mother, then he'd make the effort. Obviously, he hasn't. But I couldn't wait a minute longer." She licked her lips and looked past me through the windows of the registration office to the row of rooms.

"I know he wants to see you. It's just that, well, he's in the middle of some stuff…and, well…you should talk to him. He's in Room Six. I can walk you over, if you'd like."

"That's okay. I think I'd prefer to do this on my own." Aunt Vera fumbled with the clasp of her purse as she tried to open it. Finally, she managed to get it undone, and she removed a small hankie. She wiped her nose with it, then replaced it, closed the latch on her purse, and put the purse on her shoulder with a certain amount of determination. "Thank you, Mess. I hope we don't wait this long to see each other in the future. We'll have to have you over for dinner soon. Now," she said. "If you'll excuse me."

I nodded, and she marched out of the office, headed for Finn's room. As much as I wanted to be there for the emotional reunion, I didn't tag along. Some things needed to be private, after all.

"It is good she finally came," Cesar said, tearing himself away from the computer. "Although Finn is a grown man, he could use some time with his mother."

"True."

Cesar cleared his throat. "Speaking of people's mothers. Norma Rae is complaining."

I sighed. "About what?"

"About everything. The linens smell bad. The room is dirty. She's too hot. She's too cold. The TV doesn't work. The bottles of shampoo are too small, and the bars of soap are too big. I think it's time you speak to her."

"She's not the one I need to speak to. Rosie is."

"Sounds like a plan of action," Cesar said.

"A good plan, you think?"

Cesar's eyes twinkled. "Perhaps this is one problem Mess Hopkins cannot solve."

"Then what do you suggest I do?"

Cesar shrugged. "I'm only the manager. *You're* the owner."

I left Cesar in the registration office and trudged back to my room. I'd already failed once to reunite Norma Rae with her daughter. What made me think I could succeed this time? I'd been unable to make any headway with Finn as far as getting him to report what he saw to the police, and now that I knew about his involvement with Thorpe, I realized that would probably never happen. And Lia had stormed off, believing I didn't respect her. I wasn't doing too well.

My phone rang as I walked into my room. Lia.

"Hi, Lia. What's—"

"Please come down to my office, Mess." Urgency punctuated her words. "And hurry. I'll explain when you get here."

* * *

The Fairfax Observer had its offices in a building in the Old Town section of the City of Fairfax, near the City Hall, a few blocks from Paolo's Pies. I found a spot in an adjacent parking garage and hustled into the newspaper's lobby. I signed in, the attendant called Lia, and he gave me a clip-on visitor's badge. "She'll be right out," he said.

In less than a minute, she appeared. Her eyes were red and moist. She didn't say anything, just hugged me. After a moment, she stepped back, a smattering of tears on her cheeks.

"You okay?"

"Actually, no." She took my hand. "Come on."

She led me through a maze of cubicles to hers, along the side wall. Several people stood around her desk, speaking in hushed tones. "Okay, everybody, time to get back to work," she said.

The people drifted off to their own desks. Lia dragged over a chair from an unoccupied cubicle. "Have a seat."

I looked around the office. No obvious drama going on. But I hadn't seen Lia this upset before. "What happened?"

"Someone broke into my desk."

I gave it the once-over. Everything seemed normal, except for the bottom left drawer, which had a dent in it. Some of the gray paint near the dent had been scratched.

"When?"

"Evidently, last night, someone snuck into the office and jimmied open my desk drawer." Lia shook her head. "The security guard works till about midnight. Then he clears the office—kicking everyone out—and locks up. The break-in must have happened after that."

"Did they take anything?"

"My reporter's notebook is missing. Usually, I keep it with me, but I was with you last night, so I didn't figure I'd be doing any research. I locked it up in my desk."

"What about your laptop?"

"I had it with me, in the car. Not too wise to leave valuables around here. But who would swipe a notebook?"

I glanced around. A few people whispered and pointed at us. Hadn't they ever seen a broken desk drawer before? "Is there someplace we can go to talk privately?"

"Sure." Lia escorted me to an empty conference room and shut the door behind us. Glass windows looked out onto the newsroom floor, and the same people who were scoping out Lia's desk were now scoping us out. I felt like a lizard in a terrarium.

She sniffled. "I know it's only my notebook, but I feel violated. Somebody was in my personal space."

I wanted to hug her and console her and tell her everything would be all right. But not under the watchful eyes of her officemates. I walked over to the conference room window and twisted the plastic rod that closed the blinds.

Then, I gave her another giant hug. "I'm so sorry, Lia."

She didn't say anything, just buried her head in my shoulder.

"It's terrible what happened, but I have to say, I'm glad you called me. A little surprised, even, given how you left last night."

She stepped back but grabbed my hand. Gave it a squeeze. "Things might be a little bumpy between us at the moment, but you're still the person I turn to. I think we have that connection, don't you?"

"I'd like to think so. And about the bumpiness, I'm sorry about that, too. With everything that's going on with Finn, I'm afraid I haven't been around for you. He's just so…needy."

"Finn's your cousin. I understand, at least intellectually. If I'm being honest, I've let this Claypool story take over my life, too. This is my first big solo story, and I'm stressed. I think maybe I've taken it out on you. I'm really sorry. That's not fair."

I leaned over and kissed her on the cheek. "Safe to say that we're each under some stress right now."

Lia smiled, just a hair. "Maybe we can try to be a little more understanding of each other's situation?"

"Sounds like a plan. An *excellent* plan."

Her smile grew. "I knew we were a good team."

A moment of silence passed between us.

I cleared my throat. Time to get back to the unpleasantness. "What about the break-in? Any idea who did it?"

"Whoever stole my notebook targeted me specifically," Lia said.

A bad feeling grew in my gut.

"My desk was the only one broken into."

The bad feeling got worse.

"What was in the notebook?" I asked, but I was pretty sure I already knew.

"I use a new one for every story. My old notebooks are still there. They took the current one. The one I was using to take notes on Claypool's murder."

I thought a moment. "There's good news here."

"Getting my notebook stolen is good news?"

"No, of course not. But did you have a chance to transcribe your notes into your computer?"

"Yes. Virtually all of them, anyway."

"They must have known that. Which means they weren't trying to prevent you from writing your story."

Lia dabbed her nose with a tissue. "Still waiting for the good news."

"They must think you're on to something. That you've uncovered a clue, or clues, pointing to Claypool's murderer. They want to know what you know. They're afraid of you."

"Do you think I'm in any danger?" Lia asked.

"I don't think so. They have to assume you've told your editor what you've learned so far."

The color drained from Lia's face, and her lips parted slightly. I thought she might say something, but she just stared into the distance.

"What is it?"

"I may not be in danger, but somebody else might be." She focused on me, worry in her big brown eyes. "I write everything about the stories in my notebooks. Some are facts; other things are opinions or theories or musings. I brainstorm there, too. What-if scenarios. Stuff like that."

"And?"

"And Finn's name was in there as a possible witness. Whoever took my notebook knows that Finn Hopkins claims to have seen the two men who killed Claypool."

Oh shit! "Did you write down where he was staying?"

"Not explicitly, but the Fairfax Manor Inn is mentioned, I think. Whenever I have a conversation or interview or whatever, I note the time, day, place, details like that. I'd say they'd be able to put two and two together and at least check it out. And as soon as they find out who's running the motel, last name Hopkins, it will become even clearer."

My thoughts raced. The killers knew Finn's name. They'd killed Claypool, so obviously, killing people wasn't against their beliefs. We needed to alert Finn, and fast. I sprang out of the chair. "Okay, we need to tell my cousin."

"Should we tell the police, too?" Lia asked.

"Oh, we definitely should. But as much as it pains me to say it, we should let Finn make that call. If we don't, we'll never see him again. I'll go talk to him and do my best to persuade him to tell the cops himself."

Chapter Twenty-Three

Lia went back to work, and I went straight to Finn's room at the motel. When he opened the door and saw me, his face dropped. "Oh, it's you." He tried to close the door, but I stuck my foot in the way.

"It's me." I pushed the door inward, and he didn't even mount any token pressure, just stepped back. "Where's your mother?"

"She left. She did her duty, visited her loser of a son, stayed the minimum amount of time dictated by etiquette, then bounced. Of course, she told me she loved me."

"She does, Finn. So does your father. They just have a tough time showing it sometimes. You put them through a lot over the past six years, you know. You're not without blame here."

"I knew I should never have come back. I shoulda stayed living in a cardboard box under some highway overpass." He leaped into his bed and turned on his side to face the wall.

I didn't know if Finn was being literal. I shuddered to think so. "I have something to tell you, and you're not going to like it."

"Then I don't want to hear it." He kept staring at the wall.

I sharpened my tone. "You might want to hear this."

"I doubt it," Finn said to the wall.

"Can you please act like an adult and turn around?" I was getting fed up with Finn's petulance. I knew he'd been through a lot, but still…

Slowly, with an abundance of sighing, Finn maneuvered to face me. He was still lying down, head on the pillow, and he looked as if someone had just run over his dog. I supposed that's what he was going for: sympathy. I could have insisted he sit up, but figured this might be as good as I was going to get. "Unfortunately, someone broke into Lia's office and took her reporter's notebook. You, by name, are mentioned in that notebook as being a possible witness to Claypool's murder."

There was a long pause, then Finn said, "I was right to begin with. I didn't want to hear that."

"We have to assume the killers took the notebook, so they now know your name. And it's quite possible they also know where you're holed up."

"Maybe I should run. I'm good at running."

"I thought you said you were done with that," I said.

"I want to be."

"If you run, the cops will think you're guilty. Besides, if you stay, I can help protect you. If you bolt, there's no telling what might happen. Do you really want to be looking over your shoulder the rest of your life? This is murder we're talking about, not shoplifting. There's no statute of limitations, you know."

Finn covered his face with his pillow, exactly how I pictured a nine-year-old acting. I knew some people regressed when they returned home, but this was ridiculous. I took a deep breath and tried to center myself. If Finn's life wasn't at stake here, I'd probably walk right out the door and let him fend for himself. "Come on, man. You can't hide from this. But I'm here to help you. Why don't we have a conversation and figure out what we're going to do?"

Finn didn't move.

"Okay, tell you what. I'm going to see if Griff is around. If he is, I'll bring him into the discussion. I'll be right back."

Griff was in his cave, so I asked him to join us in a strategy session. He agreed readily, and I got the impression he was happy to help with something, anything, that would get him off his ass and out of his monotony. When we got back to Finn's room, Finn still had his head covered with a pillow.

As far as I knew, Griff hadn't met Finn yet. "Finn, I want to introduce you to Griff. He handles security for us."

"Nice to meet you." Griff's voice was deep and gravelly, and it fit exactly with his enormous bulk.

"Nice to meet you, too," came Finn's voice, muffled by the pillow.

"I'm going to ask Griff to watch over you, like your own personal bodyguard, until we get this thing settled. How's that sound?"

"Okay."

"Cool," Griff said. "But I kinda need to see what you look like." Griff was plenty odd, but he seemed to be able to act like a fairly regular human when the need arose.

Finn lowered the pillow; slowly sat up. Ran a hand through his hair. "Hey."

"I'll keep you safe, don't worry."

"What, me worry?" Finn said, exactly like the guy from *Mad Magazine*, which Finn and I used to read as kids.

Griff laughed like it was the funniest thing he ever heard.

* * *

With Griff installed as Finn's bodyguard, I felt a bit better, so I drove out to talk with Uncle Phil. There were a lot of people named Hopkins in the DMV, but I figured I owed him a heads-up on the very off, off chance that two murderers knocked on his door looking for Finn.

When I got to his mini-mansion in McLean, Phil answered the door promptly. The surprise on his face told me he was probably expecting someone else. Today's preppy outfit consisted of a pink polo shirt and yellow slacks, as if he was about to rush off for his tee time. "Hello, Benjamin. To what do I owe this lovely visit?" Sarcasm practically dripped down his chin.

"I need to talk to you."

"Let's retire to the den, shall we?" Every time I came over to talk to Phil, we *retired to the den*. I'm sure he thought it was his most intimidating room. Paneled in dark wood with heavy club chairs, it smelled of old books and cigars. It was a man's room. Furnished by a man, intended for a man. I wouldn't be surprised if Vera never set foot in here.

I crossed the threshold, and Phil headed directly to the bar. "What can I get you, Benjamin?"

"Nothing, thanks," I said. Whenever we had our little business meetings at his place, Phil nursed a scotch no matter what time of day, while I either declined or drank water. Not because I liked water so much, but because I liked being a contrarian, especially when it came to my uncle. I never knew why Phil always insisted on going through the charade of offering me a drink. Must be some kind of archaic notion of hospitality—trying to force something down the throat of your adversary.

"Suit yourself." He gestured to a chair. "Take a load off."

I sat. Phil made his drink, then he joined me. He made a big show of taking a sip of the amber liquid, then savoring the aftertaste, as if he was somehow rubbing my face in it. I looked on, making sure I hit him with the most bored expression I could muster. He wasn't fazed. "What's so important you had to drive out and tell me in person? Decided to leave the hospitality industry?"

I smiled. "You'd like that, wouldn't you?"

"I just want you to be happy. That's all."

Uncle Phil was full of crap. I knew it, and he knew it. "I'm happy running the motel. That's not why I'm here."

He nodded knowingly. "This is about Finn, isn't it? He sent you to talk to me, didn't he?"

"It's about Finn, but he didn't send me. I need to tell—"

Phil held up his hand. "Look, I appreciate what you're trying to do, really. But don't you think Finn needs to man up to me directly, rather than send some intermediary, no offense? I mean, I'm his father, and he's my son, and this is a conversation that has to happen between the two of us." He stood and headed for the doorway. "Tell him I'm here for him, whenever he decides the time is right."

Everything always had to be on Phil's terms. I didn't get up, although Phil was halfway out of the room. He finally noticed I wasn't following. "Is there something else, Benjamin?"

"Actually, the reason I came over."

Phil stood there, looking at me expectantly. A moment passed. Then another. "Well?"

"Maybe you should have a seat."

He all but harrumphed as he returned to his chair. "Okay. What?"

I'd debated how much to tell him, keeping in mind that Finn himself didn't want to tell anyone what was going on. But I felt I owed Phil and Vera, so I settled on something vague but ominous. "I can't tell you all the details, because frankly, I don't know all the details. But there may be some people who are looking for Finn."

"What people?"

"Some bad people."

"What do they want with Finn?"

I swallowed. "I'm not sure, exactly, but they may come looking for him *here*. And if they do, you don't want to mess with them."

Uncle Phil gave me a hairy eyeball. "I don't know what you're trying to accomplish, but if I'm supposed to be scared, I'm not."

"It's probably nothing, but you might want to check into a hotel—a good one—for the next few days. No sense taking any chances."

He peered at me over his drink. "You're serious about this."

I nodded. "None of this is Finn's fault. He was in the wrong place at the wrong time and saw the wrong thing."

"If you want me to take this threat seriously, I'm going to need more details."

"Trust me, Uncle Phil. I know we've had our minor differences now and then, but I'm dead serious now, and even if the likelihood of something bad happening is slim, why take that chance?"

"And what about Finn? Are you saying he's in danger?"

"Finn is laying low, and he's not alone."

Phil pursed his lips, noodling things through. "You've got that Bigfoot character watching him, don't you?"

"If you mean Griff, then yes. And we're not positive these men know where Finn is."

Uncle Phil rose, drink in hand. He began pacing quickly, back and forth, and I was impressed his drink didn't even slosh around. All that practice,

I guessed. He stopped and pointed at me. "Maybe we should get Finn to come home and circle the wagons."

I was pretty sure Finn wouldn't go for that. "I'll ask him. But I have a feeling Finn wants to try to stay under the radar. Bringing him here amid a show of strength might just alert these men to Finn's whereabouts."

"Sometimes a show of strength is exactly what's needed when dealing with cowards."

When Uncle Phil started to launch into a series of inspirational quotes, it was time for me to go. I stood. "Just wanted to give you a heads up. If you decide to stay in a hotel or, better yet, take a little vacation, please let me know in case Finn asks about you. I know he'd want you to be safe."

"Tell Finn to call me, and we can discuss this entire thing."

I didn't take orders from Phil as much as he liked to believe I did. "I'll pass along your request." I didn't add, *but don't hold your breath.* "Goodbye, Uncle Phil. Please don't take this lightly."

As I walked out, I felt his judgmental eyes burning two holes in my back.

Chapter Twenty-Four

I'd just stretched out on my bed back at the motel when my phone rang. *Ostervale.* "Hello. Are you calling about my car's warranty? Or is there a virus in my computer?"

"Always the clown, Mess. Sometimes, you're even funny. Now is not that time."

"They can't all be winners," I said.

"I'd settle for twenty percent. Believe it or not, I'm calling for an actual reason."

"Hit me."

"I'm hearing some stuff on the street, and I thought you might know something about it."

"Good stuff or bad stuff?"

"Bad stuff. When I hear good stuff, I generally don't think you're involved."

"Touché, detective." I paused. "What stuff have you heard?"

"I heard there are a couple of low-lifes asking around about a guy named Hopkins."

I sat up. "My name is Hopkins."

"Fancy that. They weren't asking around about you, though. They're trying to locate a guy named *Finn* Hopkins," Ostervale said.

Oh crap! A dozen things to say flitted through my mind, some witty, some insightful. Instead, I said, "Oh?"

"Oh? That's all you got?"

"Oh, detective?" Various thoughts ricocheted inside my brain as I tried to figure out how to play this. I didn't like lying to my buddy, and I didn't like lying to the police, either.

"Cut the crap, Mess. If I recall correctly, you have a cousin named Finn Hopkins. If he's in trouble, I wish you'd let me know."

The spinning decision wheel in my head finally landed on *partial-truth*. "As a matter of fact, I do have a cousin by that name. And he's being hounded by a couple of guys. I suppose it's the same two. How about if I send you a photo of them?"

"Why?"

"Why should I send a photo?" I said as innocently as I could.

"No, why is Finn being hounded?"

"Some things are not mine to say." I waited for Ostervale to call bullshit, but he just sighed.

"It's always the same with you, isn't it? You want me to do favors for you, but when I ask for information, you're always playing games. Some day, that might catch up with you. Send me the photos of the men, and I'll look into it. But I'm warning you, Mess. If this is just a ruse to get information out of me to help Finn with some illicit scheme, you will be sorry." He disconnected.

I didn't even get a chance to remind him that *he* called *me*. I texted him a picture of the two guys at the campaign event, but not before I cropped out Jimbo Young and Webster Claypool. Ostervale would probably connect the dots on his own somehow—he was a smart guy—but I didn't have to make it easy for him, at least not until I could persuade Finn to go to the police with what he saw.

I couldn't help but get the feeling things would come to a head very soon.

As much as I wanted to simply rest for a few minutes—talking with Uncle Phil exhausted me, and my conversation with Ostervale had only made things worse—I figured I should probably go check on Finn to see how he was getting along with Griff. I walked down to his room and gave his door three quick knocks.

A moment later, the door swung open, and Griff was standing there, looking intimidating, which, to be honest, was his standard appearance. "Hey, boss. Come in."

I entered, and Finn was in his customary position, in bed and watching

TV. "How's it going?"

"Terrible," Finn said. "TV sucks, and I'm afraid if I go outside, someone will kill me. How are you doing today?"

I could see Finn was still in his pissy-mopey mood. "Fine. I think we should talk again about going to the police. If you tell them what you saw, they can catch these guys." I thought about the photo I'd sent to Ostervale. All I had to do was tell him that Finn had seen those two kill Claypool, and this whole ordeal could very well be over. As it stood now, I'm sure identifying those two wasn't high on Ostervale's priority list.

"In my experience, the police don't trust people like me, and even if they did, they're not so great at nabbing criminals. Plus, even if they caught them, some fancy lawyer would just be able to get them out of jail. At which time, they'd hunt me down and snuff me out so I couldn't testify, and without the prosecution's star witness, they'd walk. The system is rigged against guys like me, from top to bottom."

He had a decent point. "Sometimes you just have to trust somebody."

"Trust is important," Finn said. "How do you think Tim would feel if I betrayed his trust and blabbed to the cops? Because you know that will all come to light. I'll not only have ruined my life, but his as well."

"Wow, I'm impressed. You've got everything all figured out. So, Mr. Future Seer, what happens if you continue the way you're going and don't tell the cops what you saw? Am I looking at it? You're going to be hiding in motel rooms the rest of your life watching bad TV?"

"Better than most of the places I've been."

"You need to stop feeling sorry for yourself." Since his return, I'd alternated between coddling Finn and trying tough love. Neither had been successful. Right now, I seemed to be his only real advocate, but he was definitely trying my patience. Part of me wanted to wash my hands of the Finn problem. I should probably haul his ass into therapy—maybe that would help. Then, I'd feel less guilty if things didn't go well. I bet I could get Uncle Phil to pick up the tab, too. Spending money made him feel like a big shot.

"I'm tired, Mess. So unless you've got some other good idea, I think I'm going to take a nap."

I wanted to leap across the room and slap Finn silly. Slap him into seeing the obvious, namely that we're going to need help to resolve this situation and that the best form of help would be the police. Instead of resorting to physical violence, however, I turned and walked out of Finn's room, again not sure if letting him slide was the best course of action.

* * *

I sat on a bench in the entrance plaza outside Government Center. Lia sat next to me, and the Chair of the Fairfax County Board of Supervisors, Jimbo Young himself, sat next to her. It was a pleasant afternoon, and Young thought meeting outside and getting some fresh air would be a good idea. I think he did it because it gave him the opportunity to eat his way through a brown paper lunch bag of peanuts in the shell.

We were fortunate Lia had managed to snag a spot on his busy schedule. Knowing her, I'm sure she emphasized the notion that a "did not agree to be interviewed" line in a story about the murder of a local celebrity businessman didn't look good.

Young wore a crisp navy pinstripe suit, a tie loosened at the neck the only indication that the workday was almost over. Of course, he probably had a dinner engagement followed by late-night meetings. *If* the stories about Young being a wheeler-dealer were accurate.

He dug into his bag, pulled out a peanut, and shelled it, then popped the edible pieces into his mouth, tossing the bits of shell over his shoulder. The way he was motoring through the bag, I figured at some point he'd get mixed up and eat some shells by accident. "Okay, then, Ms. Katsaros, what would you like to know?" He glanced down at Lia's phone, which sat on her lap. He probably didn't like having his words recorded because it made denying his comments much more difficult.

"I know your time is valuable, so I'll try not to waste it. I understand your relationship with Webster Claypool had soured recently, and he was planning to throw his support—financial, endorsement, whatever—behind your opponent, Ike Garrity. Is that correct?"

Young smiled—not a genuine reflection of happiness, but more a politician's reflex to a question they don't like. "I can't speak to exactly what was going through Webster Claypool's mind, but I can say we were in discussions about his positions concerning growth in the county."

"Could you be more specific?"

He fished into his bag for another peanut and shelled it while he spoke. "Certainly. Over the past ten years or so, this county has seen tremendous growth. Businesses have moved their headquarters here. Retail has expanded. Housing has boomed. Which has all been great for those entities, but especially for my constituents. The standard of living, while already high, has risen further. We've really undergone a boom that we haven't seen for a long time, if ever. And Claypool was a prime beneficiary, too. Our growth made him a very, very wealthy man." Young tossed the detritus over his shoulder. I guessed he could fix any littering citation he received. "But we've reached a point where we need to reconsider our policies. Put brakes on our rapid growth. Think *smart* growth. I think you'd probably agree with that, wouldn't you? Our county can only sustain so much."

Once again, I was there as the photographer, so I kept my mouth shut. Which was fine because the local political scene wasn't my jam; I had enough trouble trying to keep the permits for the Inn up-to-date.

"And Claypool didn't agree?" Lia asked.

Young laughed. "No. He did not. He just wanted more, more, more. When he backed my first campaign, he was more reasonable, and our goals were more or less coincident. But as he grew larger and richer, he seemed to lose perspective. I guess our divergence wasn't really a surprise, at least not to me. I had to do what I thought best for the county and its residents. Webster Claypool only did what was best for Webster Claypool."

"Are you saying there was animosity between you two?"

Another peanut, more shells on the ground. I imagined a huge pile after our conversation was finished. "Not on my part. We'll be fine without his support. The voters know me now, and I have an incredible track record. So I'm not worried about that."

Lia pressed him. "But was Claypool angry about the new direction you're taking? Slower growth?"

"Probably. But he and his company would have been fine. They *will* be fine. Danielle Sakai is as sharp as they come, and I'm sure she'll lead them capably for the next decade and beyond."

"Maybe she'll donate to your campaign."

"Ha, maybe she will. But I won't hold my breath."

Lia chuckled politely. "Can you tell me who these two men are?" She stuck her hand out to me, and I gave her my phone with the picture of the two guys Finn had seen already queued up. She handed the phone to Young.

He glanced at the picture on my phone briefly, then handed it back. "Don't know their names, but they worked for Claypool. Not very pleasant, if I recall. Why?"

"I'd like to ask them a few questions. Do you know what they did for him?"

"Security, I think. I can't afford people like that on my civil servant salary."

"Do you know why he needed two security men? Had he been threatened?" Lia asked.

Young's eyebrows pinched. "Not to my knowledge."

"Did you ever meet these guys?"

He pursed his lips. "I might have. I meet with a lot of people. If I did, I'm sure it wasn't anything important. Just logistics or something to coordinate with Claypool."

According to Steve, his aide, Young had met with these men recently, but his answer was anything but definitive. I could see why Young excelled in politics.

Lia's tone changed, tilted even more serious. "What would you say to those people who might think eliminating a supporter of your opponent is a motive for murder?"

"What? Who says that? Who?" Young's face took on a deep red hue almost immediately. For a moment, I thought he'd toss aside his bag of peanuts and throttle Lia.

"I'm speaking hypothetically. A big donor goes from supporting you to supporting your opponent. Some people are going to wonder if you had anything to do with his murder."

"Some people? Name one person, besides you, who thinks that. Or is this some ploy to have me explode on camera, providing you with clickbait?" Young took a trio of deep breaths, but his face still blazed. "I'm disgusted and offended by your insinuation. I've served this county for more than two decades, and there's never been a whiff of scandal. How dare you try to start something." He stood, bag of peanuts in hand. "This interview is over, Ms. Katsaros. I know your editor, and if he wouldn't think I was somehow trying to influence what might appear in his newspaper, I'd call to complain about your baseless accusation. For now, though, I'll let karma take its course. Goodbye."

Young stalked off, and I waited until he had entered the building, fifty yards away, before speaking. "That went well."

"Dammit, Mess. I may have crossed a line there." She gave me a distressed look.

This was where a boyfriend's calming words were needed. "It was a fair question because, despite what he thinks, there will be some who might come to that conclusion. You gave him an opportunity to refute the accusation, and he just went off, feigning indignation."

"You think he was faking it?"

"He's a politician. He's accused of being a scumbag every other day. They're all used to it, trust me. If you pretend to be offended, you get out of having to answer the question. It's the oldest trick in the book."

"You think?"

I shrugged. "Don't know, really. But I *do* know he never flat-out denied being involved somehow, did he?"

Chapter Twenty-Five

I think the break-in at Lia's office, followed by the intense interview with Jimbo Young, had diverted Lia's anger at me. But I was pretty sure she was still quite miffed—with good reason—so I wasn't surprised when she declined my offer of dinner. Instead, I went back to the motel and dropped in on Finn and Griff.

They were playing backgammon, so I left them alone and went back to my room to catch up on all the things I'd neglected over the past few days. Hours later, I'd barely made a dent in my to-do pile, but I was saved from the drudgery by a call from Ostervale.

"Hello, Detective. Aren't you up a bit late tonight?" I asked.

"It's ten minutes past nine o'clock."

"Precisely."

"You missed your calling as a stand-up comic. With your talent, you could easily have made as much as you do running your fleabag," he said.

"I don't make anything running this joint."

Silence.

I smiled to myself. Ostervale was a fun sparring partner. "Why are you calling?"

"Besides the fact that I miss hearing your voice?"

"Yes."

"The photo you sent me of those two guys? We IDed them, and they are officially persons of interest. Kyle Long and Nubs Porter."

"Nubs?"

"Nickname."

"I figured. What kind of parents would name their baby Nubs?"

Ostervale ignored my rhetorical question. "I don't suppose you've uncovered any more information about them?"

"Only that two different sources said they worked for Claypool."

"Yeah, I called over there," Ostervale said. "Talked to their second-in-charge, Danielle Sakai. Hadn't heard of them." He sounded tired or, more likely, frustrated. Being a detective had to be ninety-eight percent frustration, tempered by being a hero maybe two percent of the time.

"If they were working for him, it was off the books. Personal bodyguards, or something like that," I said. "Of course, that brings up the question: why would Claypool need two bodyguards? And, I might add, two bodyguards who aren't very good, considering what happened."

"Not only did you miss your calling of being a stand-up comic, you missed your calling of being a detective."

"Is it too late?" I asked.

"For you, yes. Yes, it is." Ostervale clicked off.

* * *

First thing on my agenda the next morning: taking care of Norma Rae Williams. She'd been up in the middle of the night crooning again, and I'd had enough. I often housed drug addicts, drunks, and other unsavory characters, but I drew the line at three a.m. off-key karaoke.

Somehow, between Norma Rae's wild rants, aimless tangents, and virtually incoherent ramblings, I'd managed to get her daughter Rosie's address. She lived about fifteen minutes away in a quiet residential area, where all the houses were very small and very similar. One of those neighborhoods where you probably knew most of your neighbors and liked about half of them.

Typical middle-class suburbia.

I hadn't called ahead, not wanting to give Rosie the opportunity to come up with an excuse or to suddenly realize she needed to run a bunch of errands.

I parked at the curb and walked across the brown-ish lawn to the brown-ish front door. Poked the doorbell. A dog barked inside; then a voice told the dog to pipe down. A moment later, Rosie opened the door. I assumed she didn't peep through the peephole because she seemed momentarily surprised. Then she placed me. "Oh, what do you want?" She glared at me, then softened. "Mom okay?"

I couldn't lie and say she was fine. "She's the same. Unhappy that you asked her to leave. Can I come in so we can discuss this?"

Rosie hit me with the loudest sigh I'd heard in a long time. "Fine. But I've got some errands to run soon, so make it quick."

I entered her house, and a shaggy brown-ish dog ambled up to me, gave me a sniff, then ambled away. Evidently, my aroma wasn't very interesting. "Come on, don't mind her." Rosie pointed to a room off the small foyer. "We can talk in here."

She led me into a jumble of a room. A TV balanced precariously on a card table, and dozens of needlepoint masterpieces occupied virtually every available bit of wall space. There was a brown-ish couch along one wall—I think it was a couch—covered in balls of yarn and all sorts of other needlepoint and macrame and knitting paraphernalia. I think so, anyway. I wasn't really up on the knitting arts.

"Hang on a sec." Rosie shoveled an armful of stuff off the couch and dumped it on the floor, and she did the same to a nearby chair. I knew that move well; I used it in my room and office back at the motel frequently. Looked like Rosie and I had something in common.

Rosie crossed her arms. "Let me guess. You want me to take Mom back."

I resisted the temptation to cross my arms in response, not wanting to cause some kind of non-verbal stand-off. I clasped my hands on my lap instead. "Yes, I do. That would be the best thing for everyone involved."

"Don't you think I want to take her back? She's my mother." Rosie blinked rapidly. "But I don't think I can live with her anymore. She's too…too…well, you've seen her."

"I have. And I've also spoken with her. She's a proud woman, and she thinks she can take care of herself."

Rosie snorted. "Yeah, right."

"Look." I sat back and smiled, trying to project good ol' common sense.

"We both know she *can't* take care of herself, not completely. And maybe, deep down, she knows she can't either. But you're the only one who can help her. Unless you put her in a facility, that is."

Rosie spread her arms wide. "Does it look like I can afford a facility? At least one that's good enough for Mom?"

"Many people are in your situation. It's hard, but they figure something out. There are day-programs providing elder care, many are affordable."

"She says she won't go to those. Too many old people."

"Maybe social services can send someone over a few hours a week. Maybe there's a neighbor who wouldn't mind coming over once in a while to sit with your mother. These things add up."

"I dunno. Mom can be very picky. And ornery, too, if you hadn't noticed."

I'd noticed. "Well, she's going to have to compromise, I guess." I spotted a needlepoint canvas on the wall with the words, *Forgiveness is Divine*. I nodded at it. "Maybe if you forgive each other for past incidents and concentrate on working together as you move forward, you can make it work. Don't let her think she's a burden. Make her feel needed. You both want what's best, and I think you know that's having her here. One day, you might be in her shoes, and I'm sure you'd appreciate being appreciated. You have children, don't you?"

"Three. Two boys and a girl. None are local." Rosie uncrossed her arms and picked up an unfinished needlepoint canvas. "Do you mind? I think better when my hands are busy."

"Not at all." Another thing I had in common with Rosie. One person's needlepoint was another person's Nerf basketball.

Her hands got busy, threading the needle through the tiny squares and drawing the thread along. "I do miss her."

"And she misses you. How about if I bring her home, and we lay out some ground rules, including she must try out one of the elder care programs?"

"That could work." Rosie nodded as she needlepointed. "Oh, Mess. What is it about families? How some of the people you're closest to in the world drive you so incredibly crazy?"

I thought of me and my parents, of me and Uncle Phil, and of Uncle Phil and Finn. Families *were* messed up, and I couldn't name more than a handful that weren't dysfunctional, at least to some degree. Yet one more thing I had in common with Rosie—along with about ninety percent of the population. "Between you and me, I think she's tired of living at the motel." I had no idea if this was true, but I was certainly tired of hearing Cesar's complaints about her living at the motel.

Rosie met my eyes. Nodded definitively. "Okay. Yes. Let's do that. Bring her home, lay out some guidelines, forgive each other."

"And live happily ever after," I added.

Rosie snorted again. "Let's not push our luck."

* * *

I was trying to get caught up with my emails—only one-hundred-twenty-two to go—when Cesar texted me. *Please come to the office, stat.*

I knew better than to ignore a stat request from Cesar, and besides, I was desperate for an excuse not to have to plow through any more old emails.

I crossed the parking lot and opened the registration office door to the familiar jingling bell. Cesar greeted me, but without his usual fake smile. Instead, a scowl. "Hello, Mess."

"What's up, *stat*?" I asked.

"It appears there is a man sitting in a car in Sandy's parking lot."

"So? I've been inside Sandy's, and eating in your car isn't the worst idea I've ever heard."

"He does not appear to be eating."

A picture of a dead man, throat slashed, sitting in his car flashed through my mind. "What does he appear to be doing?"

"He appears to be watching the Inn."

I turned around and peered out the window. From our office, you could see Hole Lotta Love and about half of their parking lot. There was indeed a car there. "Black sedan?"

"Yes." Cesar came out from behind the desk to join me at the window. "Griff saw it there and alerted me. I then alerted you."

"How long has it been there?"

"Griff did not say, but he called me about half an hour ago, and I kept an eye on it. I believe Griff is worried it has something to do with Finn."

"I assume Griff is with Finn."

"Yes, in his room," Cesar said. "What are you going to do about it?"

Why did everything always fall to me? Because I was supposedly in charge around here? "Let me think about it a minute, okay?"

"Take all the time you need." Cesar stepped around me and returned to his post at the computer behind the counter.

I ran through some possibilities in my head, and none of them sounded very good. I was leaning toward doing nothing and hoping he'd simply move on after a while. He wasn't breaking any laws that I could tell. He wasn't on our property. He didn't pose any obvious threat. And if Finn didn't have people chasing him, I most likely wouldn't have done a thing.

But I was in charge around here, and it was up to me to do something. Something decisive.

"I'm going to talk to Griff," I said to Cesar, who, give him credit, didn't roll his eyes.

A minute later, I knocked on Finn's door. "It's Mess."

Griff let me in. Finn was watching TV, seemingly oblivious to the man in the car.

"Did Cesar tell you?" Griff asked.

"Yes." I turned sideways and motioned for Griff to lean over. Whispered, "Does Finn know?"

"Yes, Finn knows about the guy in the car. That's why Finn is spending his remaining time on earth watching Family Feud reruns," Finn said from his bed.

"Yeah, he knows," said Griff.

"How long has he been there?"

"Not sure. I noticed him an hour and a half ago. Watched him for a while, then called Cesar."

"Was Finn able to tell if that's one of the guys who was after him?"

"No, he wasn't," said Finn, eyes still glued to Steve Harvey hamming it up on TV. "Too much reflection off the windshield. But who else would it be?"

Indeed.

"What are you going to do?" Griff asked. "Want me to go talk to him?"

I was pretty sure Griff's definition of talking differed than most people's. "No. He could be dangerous."

"I'm not afraid." Griff issued some sort of guttural noise.

"I know. Give me a moment to think, okay?"

"Sure."

I was doing a lot of thinking without much to show for it. "Okay. I've decided. I'm going to call Ostervale. Report a suspicious person. That's the safest thing to do."

Griff's face deflated. "If you say so."

"I do." Much to Griff's disappointment, I pulled out my phone and called my buddy. He picked up quickly.

"What?" Ostervale snapped.

I cut right to it. "There's a guy in a dark sedan sitting in Sandy's parking lot, staring this way. Been there for a couple of hours, at least."

"And?" he said.

"And it could be one of the guys after Finn. Long or that Nubs guy."

"Does he look like a Nubs?"

"Now who's the comedian?" I said. "I suppose it could just be a man reading the newspaper in his car after lunch. But I don't think so."

"Well, I have nothing better to do." Ostervale paused, and I didn't take the bait. After a few seconds, he went on. "I'll be right over. You stay put and let me handle this. We'll do this quietly."

Ten minutes later, Detective Ostervale rolled up in an unmarked car and parked next to the registration office. He got out and glanced in our vague direction—where Griff and I were peeking out the window between the curtains. He made some kind of gesture I took to mean what he'd said on the phone, *stay put*, and then he strolled down the sidewalk in the direction of Sandy's.

I noticed his blazer was unbuttoned, and his right hand was tensed at his side—but I might have been imagining the part about his hand.

Physically, he was a little taller than average, a little more muscular than average, a little better looking than average. Mentally, though, was where he had the edge on most people. Whip-smart, with a chameleon-like ability to fit in with whomever he was dealing with. He could converse in the language on the street, and he could talk to college professors with equal ease.

One of the things I liked most about him was his ability to think outside of the proverbial box and to employ his good judgment when necessary. Many of the other cops I'd dealt with over the years looked at things in terms of, well, black and white. Ostervale appreciated shades of gray, as well as chartreuse, mauve, and tangerine. Ostervale also was sensitive to the rainbow, as it were, which, again, meant he was more accepting and progressive than many of his police brethren.

He was a shining star in the department, but he was as down-to-earth as they came.

We had a good friendship, started in high school, but we didn't hang out a lot anymore. He was married with two young kids, and he spent whatever free time he had with them. I figured we'd hang out again in fifteen years or so.

Ostervale moseyed along, and when he got about thirty feet away from the car, the driver's door opened, and the guy climbed out.

Chapter Twenty-Six

From this distance, he didn't look familiar. But the man waved to Ostervale, and Ostervale waved back. Ostervale seemed less tense—his arm had returned to his side like a normal human being's—and he walked right over to the guy.

What the hell?

"Stay here," I told Griff, then left Finn's room and jogged across the parking lot to where Ostervale was chatting with the guy from the car.

"I thought I told you to stay put," Ostervale said. He jutted his chin at the man. "This is Lanny Rickert. He was on the job with me for a few years, before getting out to go indie."

Rickert stuck out his hand. "Nice to meet you."

I looked from Ostervale to Rickert back to Ostervale. "What's up?"

Rickert looked to Ostervale, who nodded. "Go ahead, tell him."

Rickert shrugged. "I was hired to keep an eye on Finn Hopkins. He's in Room Six, right?"

This smelled funny. "Who hired you?"

Rickert slowly shook his head. "I'm private now, and if word gets around I've got loose lips, it'll be bad for business."

"Mess deserves to know," Ostervale said to Rickert. Then, to me, "Finn's father hired him."

Uncle Phil hired a bodyguard? Without telling me or Finn? I was surprised but not shocked. Throwing money at the problem was usually Phil's preferred way of handling things. Better than having to deal honestly and emotionally with his son. What a jackass!

A shadow seemed to fall over me. I turned around, and Griff stood there. For a giant of a man, he could move quietly when he wanted. "Everything okay here, boss?" he asked me.

"Hello, Griff," Ostervale said. "Haven't seen you around in a while."

Griff didn't always do well with authority figures, especially law enforcement authority figures, but he'd had enough decent dealings with Ostervale to trust him. I wasn't sure how he'd react to Rickert. Even though he was no longer on the force, he probably still gave off law enforcer vibes. Ostervale must have picked up on it, too, because he didn't introduce Griff to Rickert.

"Detective," Griff said, forcing half a smile. "What's going on?"

I interjected. "Everything's fine. This guy was hired by Uncle Phil to keep an eye on Finn."

Griff's face clouded. "That's my job."

"I'm sure you're doing great, too," said Rickert, sizing up Griff and realizing he should probably try to placate the big dude. "Name's Rickert, and I'm just here for back-up. Phil's very concerned about Finn's well-being, that's all."

"I don't think I need back-up," Griff said.

I detected a slight edge to his voice, but only because I'd known him a while.

I turned to Rickert. "Maybe you should tell Phil we have this under control."

Rickert made a face as if he'd sucked on a lemon. "Phil was quite insistent. And I like to do right by my clients. I'm sure you understand. I handle a lot of important corporate customers—in fact, that's how I got referred to Mr. Hopkins—and they don't have any complaints about my services."

Stand-off. Having an extra bodyguard would make things easier. But it might also serve as a flashing light: *Finn is here, Finn is here.* "Are you anywhere close to finding these two guys?" I asked Ostervale.

"We've put out the word, but so far, nada."

"So this could drag on for a while?"

"Look, Mess. I'm a pretty good detective, and it's obvious Finn knows something about these guys being involved in Claypool's death. If he identifies them as such, then we can act accordingly. Otherwise, they remain as *persons of interest.*"

"He's not positive the guys in the photo are the same guys," I said.

"Well, it's hard for me to persuade people to expend our valuable resources for *persons of interest.* Murder suspects? A whole 'nother level of mobilization."

I sighed. Time to put the full-court press on Finn. "Come on, let's go change his mind."

The four of us—me, Griff, Ostervale, and Rickert—traipsed across the parking lot to Finn's room. I knocked once, then pushed the door open. "Finn. You've got visitors."

He wasn't in bed watching TV. I checked the bathroom. Empty. "Finn?" I called out, although it was obvious. Finn had given us all the slip while we were having a circle jerk in Sandy's parking lot.

"Hold on, everybody." I left them and jogged over to the registration office. Cesar was at the window.

"What's going on?"

"Have you seen Finn?"

Cesar raised an eyebrow. "No."

"Crap. He's gone."

"Who was that man in the car?"

"Phil hired a bodyguard to watch Finn."

"Finn will hate that."

"Well, he might not have the chance to hate it. He's gone. Ran off while we were jawing over at Sandy's." I exhaled. "You sure you didn't see him leave?"

"I was watching all of you. Sorry."

"It's not your fault."

"No, it is not." Cesar met my gaze. "I do not think Phil will be happy about this."

Ya think?

* * *

Ostervale took off, back to "real police work," as he called it. Rickert searched the surrounding area on foot, clearly embarrassed that he'd already lost track of the person he was supposed to be watching. I knew it was futile; Finn had become a master of disappearance over the past six years. If there was an opportunity to run, Finn would seize it.

I gave Griff a short pep talk, told him it wasn't his fault that Finn slipped out. We both knew, though, that it kinda was, especially since I told him to stay put. But I can't really blame the big guy for coming out to our impromptu meeting to make sure I was okay. It was reassuring that he had my back.

I returned to my room to think. I was concerned about Finn in more ways than one. There were guys out to silence him, and they were not to be toyed with. But I was also concerned about Finn's mental state. The last couple of days, he'd seemed even more depressed than he had when he showed up. He had a lot on his plate, and I could only imagine what it felt like to deal with all of that, in addition to handling the stress Uncle Phil was heaping on him.

I didn't want to lose Finn again, and I didn't want Morose Finn. I wanted Good Ol' Finn, from before. What chance did I have of getting that version of my cousin?

Zero, if he never came back, that was for sure. Priority one had to be finding him, and fast. Before the killers found him. Before he did something to himself—made a terrible, desperate choice that put him in an even more tenuous situation. Or worse.

I needed to get the word out to those on the street. Naturally, I texted Vell: *I need to talk.*

A moment later. *Sure. I'm at Mama's. Helping her move furniture around. Come on over lol.*

It was the least I could do. *Be right there.*

* * *

I found them downstairs. Vell was sitting on the floor, drinking a soda, and Mama was leaning against the wall. In between them was a gigantic armoire kind of thing positioned five feet away from the wall and at a weird angle in relation to the rest of the furniture in the room.

"I like what you've done with the place," I said.

"Always the wise guy." Mama grabbed me for a hug and squeezed until I couldn't breathe. Then she let go and pushed me away from her so she could size me up. As if I'd somehow changed since the last time I'd seen her, two days ago. "How you been, sweetie?"

"Good. Always good."

"Now, that probably isn't true, but it's nice you don't want to burden me with your problems." She pointed at me. "But, Mess, that's why I'm here. To help people with their problems."

Mama had been a nurse for a long time, and now she helped people with their problems as a seer-fortune teller-clairvoyant. She had the biggest heart of anyone I'd ever met. "Thanks. I know I can always count on you."

Vell piped up. "Right now, we need to count on you to help move this beast of a monstrosity. I think there's a car somewhere inside. Least it feels like one."

This wasn't the first time I'd helped Vell move furniture around at Mama's. "Did you take out everything inside of it?"

Vell slapped his forehead. "Now, why didn't I think of that?"

I stepped over and opened the doors. Empty. "Oh."

"It looks like it's made of wood, but it's really made of lead," Vell said.

"That's my grandmother's. Back then, they made things to last," Mama said.

"Uh-huh." Vell put down his soda. "Okay, Mess, let's do it." He took one side, and I took the other. "One. Two. Three."

We grunted and heaved and really put our backs into it for what seemed like five minutes. "Okay, break."

The armoire might have moved three inches. "I think I need to hit the gym," I said.

"Maybe I should help," Mama said.

"That's okay," Vell said. "We got it." He turned to me. "Right?"

"Right. Now that we're warmed up, should be a piece of cake."

More grunting. More heaving. Some mild cussing. Finally, we had it where Mama wanted it.

"Thank you so much, Mess," Mama said. "I don't know what we would have done without you." She eyed Vell pointedly.

He didn't respond to being poked, instead flopping on a nearby chair. "What do you want to talk about?"

"Yeah, Mess, what do you want to talk about?" Mama was all ears, too.

"Finn."

"Oh, for a change," Vell said. "What now?"

"He's gone."

"Hold on, hold on." The concern was evident on Mama's face. "This your cousin? He's gone? Didn't he just come back from being gone for years?"

"Yep. Now he's gone again." I filled them in on the latest developments in Finn's saga.

"Nobody should have to endure what that poor boy's been through," Mama said. "Do you think he's run off for good?"

"I don't. That's why I'm here. I was hoping you could put out the word to your network. If anyone spots him, please let me know. He's not in a good place mentally, and I'm afraid he'll do something reckless. He was always a bit of a risk taker."

Mama took my hand in hers. "I'll start contacting people right away." She turned her gaze toward Vell. "*We'll* start contacting people. We'll have Finn located and back with you before you know it."

"Yeah, what she said." As if Vell had any choice. When Mama said something, it was *said*.

"Thanks, guys. I really appreciate it."

"Oh, honey. You're family, and where I come from, family looks out for one another."

Chapter Twenty-Seven

I left Vell and Mama to jostle their network while I played a hunch. I went online, first to Thorpe's website and social media to see where he happened to be. He had something local scheduled tomorrow night—an appearance at a high school fundraiser—so he was likely to be in town. Then, I checked Alluree's social media and discovered she was in San Francisco on a fashion shoot.

It was amazing how you could track an individual's whereabouts through their social media, and I wasn't sure if, on balance, that was a good thing or a bad thing. For me, right now, I was hoping it was a good thing.

When I pulled up at Thorpe's home, describing the street as quiet would be a colossal understatement. There was *absolutely nothing* going on. No mail carrier, nobody walking their dog, not even a car driving around. Almost certainly, this didn't mean a thing, but it had me a little creeped out.

Worse, the gate in front of Thorpe's house was closed, which *was* expected. I just hoped that if Finn was indeed hiding out here, Thorpe would let me in.

I got out of my car and pressed the tiny button on the intercom mounted on the metal stalk right near the gate. As I waited, I imagined Thorpe's neighbors staring at me through slits in their blinds, wondering who the hell I was and what I wanted. I stood up straighter and smoothed out a few wrinkles in my shirt.

A couple of minutes later, as I was about to get back in my car, a disembodied voice said, "Who is it?"

"Mess Hopkins." I explained I was the photographer who'd accompanied

Lia during her interview with him.

"What do you want? Is this a follow-up to the interview?"

"If you have a minute, I'd love to clear something up." I tried to sound upbeat.

"Now's not really a good—"

"I'm looking for Finn," I said.

There was a buzz, and the gate swung inward.

I walked up the driveway, right up to the door, as if I belonged. I hoped the neighbors were still watching.

Thorpe opened the door before I knocked. "Come in."

This time, we skipped the solarium and went to the kitchen. "Thirsty? I'm having a protein shake, but I've got beer, soda?"

"I'll take a Coke if you have one." A pink-red smoothie was sitting in front of a stool at the high counter. I wondered what was in there. It looked a lot tastier than one of those concoctions full of kale and chia seeds. Athletes all seemed to have their own favorite healthy potions.

I slid into a seat next to Thorpe's. He set down a bottle—not a can, a bottle—of Coke in front of me, cap already off.

"Want a glass?"

"No, I'm good." I took a sip, and it definitely tasted better than Coke in a can. I looked around. "Where's Finn?"

Thorpe didn't answer. He sat and took a long sip of his drink. Set it down. Wiped off his mouth. Looked at me. Finally, he spoke. "Why are you looking for this Finn person?"

He seemed very calm and collected, but it was quite obvious he was fishing to see what I knew about his relationship with Finn. And since I showed up mentioning Finn, he had to know that I knew. Thorpe wasn't stupid. "He disappeared rather abruptly, and I'm worried about him."

"And you think he's here? Why would that be?" Thorpe took another sip of his smoothie.

I exhaled slowly, keenly aware Thorpe could break me in half if he so chose. I softened my tone. "As you might have guessed, I'm not following up on the interview. I'm here on a personal matter. Finn's my cousin. He didn't tell me, but I know about your relationship with him. I saw you two together at the Clamshell Motor Lodge."

Thorpe's eyes dilated, then snapped back to normal size. He took a very long sip of his smoothie as he decided how to play it.

I waited. I imagined that me knowing his secret—*anyone* knowing his secret—posed a dire threat to his career and to his life. He didn't know, yet, that I had no desire to wreck his life. For all he knew, I was here to put the squeeze on him. I thought about him ripping me to shreds and burying the pieces in the back yard. I tried to maintain my cool as I waited.

Finally, he spoke. "Does Finn know you saw us?"

"Yes."

"He didn't mention it." Thorpe eyed me, and I couldn't tell if he was disappointed that Finn didn't confide in him, or if he was pissed I knew the score. Maybe a dash of both.

"Is he here?"

"No. Haven't seen him since…"

"Since the Clamshell?"

"Yes." Thorpe pushed the smoothie away from him on the counter. "What do you want?"

There it was. "I want Finn to be safe."

"And why wouldn't he be? You think I'm going to hurt him?"

It was obvious Finn also hadn't told Thorpe what he'd witnessed. This was going to be another unpleasant discussion. But I was through keeping Finn's secrets. He'd dragged me into this, and I was going to handle things as I saw fit from now on. "What I'm going to tell you is sensitive, but I trust you won't start blabbing it around town. It concerns Finn, Claypool, and to a lesser extent, you, I guess."

Thorpe stared at me. "Go on."

I explained the entire story to Thorpe. He stopped me with a few questions here and there, but I managed to get it all out, with as little judgment as possible and with a minimum of editorializing. Just the facts, at least as I knew them. When I finished, I downed the rest of my Coke while he processed everything.

"You're not putting me on here, right?"

"Nope."

He ran a hand along his closely cropped hair. "I wish Finn had confided in me. I know he has trust issues. And for the record, if he *had* asked, I would have let him stay here—he didn't have to break in." He nodded at me. "I know what you must be thinking. Finn and I don't seem to go together at all. A celebrity and a guy off the streets. But we both had similar experiences in life, profound experiences which will stay with us, no matter what happens going forward."

"If it's any consolation, Finn hasn't been exactly forthcoming with me, either."

"I should be clear. This thing with Finn isn't long-term or anything. Just a moment in time where two needy souls got together. I mean, I care about him, but…" Thorpe held his hands out, palms up. "He deserves some TLC after what he's been through, but I've worked too hard to get where I am to jeopardize everything for something I'm not a thousand percent invested in."

"Does Finn understand that?" I asked.

"That's a good question. I hope so, but I guess I'll have to be very clear with him, too."

"I hope you'll get that chance. Nobody knows where he is."

"You thought he'd be here, huh? Makes sense, but like I said, I haven't seen him—or heard from him, for that matter—since the Clamshell. If there's something I can do to help find him, please let me know."

"Thanks." I got up to leave. "I'll ask him to call you when he turns up."

Thorpe nodded. "One more thing. My relationship with Finn is personal, as is my relationship with my wife, and my personal life and everything else that isn't MMA stuff. You seem like a stand-up guy, so I probably don't need to threaten you." Thorpe's eyes bored into mine. "But I will do anything to protect my interests, if it requires lawsuits, gag orders, or anything else. In other words, if I read about any of my personal business in your newspaper, I will not be happy. Do you understand?"

I swallowed. "I do. And you don't have to worry. All I'm trying to do is find my cousin."

I let myself out.

* * *

When I got back to the motel, Phil was sitting on a molded plastic chair outside of my room. We'd picked up a dozen of the cheap chairs from a nearby bowling alley when they'd remodeled. They were supremely uncomfortable, but they were practically indestructible.

Phil didn't look happy, and I didn't think it was from sitting in the chair. On the plus side, he didn't appear inebriated.

"What can I do for you, Uncle Phil?"

He labored to his feet. Today, he wore lime green slacks and a yellow v-neck sweater. "Do you know where Finn is?"

"I do not. I assume, then, that he did not go home."

Phil glowered at me. "You do know where he is, but you're not telling me, right?"

"I have no idea where he went, and I resent the implication that I'm lying to you."

He stared at me for a beat. "Okay, fine. Any idea where he might have gone?"

Movement to my left caught my attention. Rickert was walking our way. I turned to watch him approach, trying to determine if having your charge disappear under your nose caused you to walk funny.

Rickert joined us. "Mr. Hopkins?"

"Yes?" Uncle Phil and I said, simultaneously.

"I think he's addressing me, Benjamin," Phil said. Then he snapped at Rickert, "What?"

"We've talked to our contacts. Nothing to report."

"Well, I was paying you to keep an eye on him; now I guess I'm paying you to find him. So, go. Find him." Phil waved him away, as if he was a stray dog. Then he turned back to me. "How can we work together to find him?"

"Together?"

"Yes, together. We may not always see eye-to-eye on things, but I think we're in agreement here. We both want Finn to remain safe and sound. If he's floating around somewhere, his safety is a lot more difficult to ensure." He reached out and grasped my forearm. "Please, Benjamin. Let's put aside our differences and focus on our objective. Finn needs us."

"Sure, Phil. Let's concentrate on getting Finn back, safe and sound."

A memory flitted through my mind. I was at a family event years ago—I must have been about ten years old. Finn and I were sitting on the floor, in front of Uncle Phil, who sat in a chair performing magic tricks for us. Pulling quarters from behind our ears, then making them disappear from his hands. Doing something with a deck of cards. All of a sudden, Finn puked. Uncle Phil leaped up, scooped up Finn, and carried him to a couch. Cleaned him up, sat next to him holding a cold compress on his forehead for what seemed like an hour.

To that point in my life, I didn't recall ever seeing an adult man show as much care and compassion as Phil had. The look of gratitude on Uncle Phil's face now reminded me of that day.

"Great. I'm going to ask my guy to check out any places Finn might have frequented, but I'm afraid I really don't know what those places might be. Can you assist him?"

I didn't really know where Finn would go, except for the one place I'd already been—Thorpe's. Did Phil think there were designated spots for gay runaways to flee to? "I'll talk to Rickert, but I don't know how much help I'll be."

"You know him best, Benjamin." Phil pulled out his phone and started scrolling. I was dismissed.

I wandered over to where Rickert leaned against his car. He had a small notebook out and a pen at the ready. He pointed his pen at me. "So, got any idea where Finn might have gone?" His tone was clipped, and it was obvious he was pissed at being given the slip by Finn. Being treated dismissively by Phil probably hadn't helped his mood, either.

"Nope. I imagine he's gotten very good at staying hidden if he wants to be. Living on the streets will do that."

Rickert slapped his notebook closed. "Fine. If you think of something, call me." He got in his car and started it up.

I took my time getting out of his way, then watched as he drove off in search of Finn. I had no idea where he was going, but I had a strong feeling he didn't either.

Chapter Twenty-Eight

I went back to my room and called Vell. "You find any leads?"

"Nope. Mama neither. Kinda hard to track somebody down who nobody knows. Finn's been gone for six years." Vell whistled. "Six years. I can barely go six hours without contacting Mama before she starts to get anxious. I don't care what was going on, what Finn did to his parents—and to you, too, my friend—just wasn't cool. And now he's doing it again."

Vell made an excellent point, and I could definitely see why Finn wasn't his favorite person. "Well, I appreciate your efforts. Let me know if you find anything, no matter how small, okay?"

"Yep." Vell disconnected.

Next call on my list: Lia. She picked right up. "How did you know I was ready for a break?"

Pure luck? "I'm tuned in to your wavelength, I guess."

"What's going on?"

"Finn's gone."

"Gone? Like, see you in another six years gone?"

"I sure hope not. It's unclear where he is, or why he went."

Silence on her end. Finally, "He never went to the police, did he? They'd protect him if he did, you know."

"I tried, I really did. I hope his stubbornness doesn't kill him. I don't suppose you've heard anything about where he might be?"

"How would I?"

"Ostervale told me that he heard a couple of guys were beating the bushes looking for him. I thought maybe you'd heard something from your network of sources."

"Actually. I did. Danielle Sakai from Claypool Development called. Said she had it on good authority—some kind of internal investigation—that Jimbo Young hired, or wanted to hire, details murky, those two guys to infiltrate their operation. So they could spy on Claypool and feed information back to Young about how he could discredit them. Either the company or Claypool individually."

"Wow. I wondered why Young was so evasive when we asked him if he knew those men."

"Sakai went on to suggest that maybe Young was involved with Claypool's murder. To prevent him from supporting Young's opponent, Garrity, in the upcoming election. She didn't have any evidence, of course. She said if anything came to light, she'd let me know. I still need to figure out if Sakai is using me somehow to spread misinformation, but I'll verify everything before it'll go to press."

I supposed people had been killed for much more trivial reasons, although Young had a squeaky-clean reputation. "Once again, you're right in the middle of all the action. You really are an excellent reporter. You know how to work your sources."

"Oh, now you think I do something valuable?"

I thought about engaging in a long discussion trying to clarify my remarks from the other night but figured that needed to be face-to-face. I went for something simple instead. "I think what you do is quite valuable. And that you are terrific at it."

"Well, thank you. But don't think that's getting you off the hook. When we have time, we'll discuss this whole thing properly. I gotta run, but if I hear anything, I'll let you know. Talk to you later."

I set my phone down. Closed my eyes. Tried to absorb the latest scuttlebutt from Danielle Sakai. Was it true? Or something she wanted to float in the court of public opinion in some kind of political battle? Beyond my pay grade, really.

My thoughts drifted back to something more personal. What was going through Finn's mind? Where had he gone? His father was pissed at him, and his mother wouldn't stand up to his father, so he wasn't going home. He couldn't go to Izzy's because Russell would rat him out. He couldn't return to the motel because Uncle Phil and his hired bodyguard would find out.

He couldn't go back to Thorpe's without jeopardizing Thorpe's career.

Hole up at the Clamshell? Hit the road again?

I'd failed him, and I felt awful.

When I was a kid, and I felt awful, I'd sometimes go down to the creek. And on more than one occasion, Finn would find me there and comfort me. Not really the kind of comfort a parent might give—Finn wasn't hugging and reassuring me or anything. But he'd show me through his actions that someone besides me knew what I was going through.

In trying times, people often sought the comfort they'd once known. Worth a try.

The creek ran through a section of a regional park, which was located only a few blocks from the house I grew up in. Uncle Phil had a house on the other side of the park, maybe half a mile away.

I guessed the two brothers wanted to live close to each other. Of course, Phil's home was in a slightly better development. Finn and I could each walk to the park, and we would often meet there.

On one side of the park were all the ballfields and tennis courts. A disc golf course wound through the entire property, crisscrossing some kind of fitness trail—where every hundred yards, there was a chin-up bar or other exercise contraption. Half a dozen pavilions occupied another section of the park, and on nice weekend days, you could smell grilled meat if you were downwind.

I entered the park through the main entrance and drove to the back corner of the parking lot, the side closest to the trail down to the creek. It wasn't an official county trail or anything. Just a path through the trees that had been trampled down by thousands of kids' feet throughout the decades.

I tromped my way through the woods. As a kid, I didn't usually drive to the park and approach the creek from this direction, but if I remembered correctly, the path intersected the creek about half a mile in. As I went along, I searched for signs that someone had been down this path recently, as if I were an expert wilderness tracker. Frankly, I didn't think I'd be able to tell if anything smaller than an elephant had used this path.

Careful not to let any branches *thwack* across my face, I continued along the narrow trail. The hike brought back memories, some good, some bad. In addition to using this place as a sanctuary of sorts, Finn and I had a lot of fun here. Playing explorers, we always managed to survive, even if most of our adventures ended when someone got too aggressive during our tree-branch swordfights.

I heard the gurgle of the stream before I saw it and felt the temperature drop several degrees. I wasn't sure if the air was actually cooler, or if my mind recalled the cold water those times when our feet would slip, and we'd get wet.

I turned a corner, and there was Finn, lying on the same wide, flat rock we'd both lounged on many times twenty years ago. Weird how part of me felt like a ten-year-old again.

"I guess I shouldn't be surprised." Finn shielded his eyes from the sun when he gazed at me. Although the tree canopy was thick, some rays of sunlight carved their way through.

"What are you doing here?" I asked.

"Thinking. Chilling. If my days are numbered, then I'd like to go out peacefully."

"Your days are not numbered." I gestured to the rock. "May I?"

Finn slid over, and I settled down next to him. The rock protruding from the creek's bank angled so our feet were below our heads. If we scooted down a foot or so, we could dip our toes into the water. As kids, this rock seemed as large as an aircraft carrier, which we pretended it was on many occasions.

"Remember all the time we spent down here?" Finn asked. "How about the time we caught all those tadpoles in the pickle jar and took it to my house? And somehow, it ended up in the fridge? Two days later, I heard this shriek. Mom never bought pickles again!"

That had cracked me up then, and it was just as funny now—if not more so. Aunt Vera was always skittish about gross boy stuff. "She forbade you to come back here. How long did that last, two days?"

"I don't know if you noticed, but I wasn't much of a rule follower." Finn picked up a stone and chucked it at a tree on the bank. It hit the trunk with a tiny thud.

"I noticed." We sat in silence for a while, listening to the water gurgle over the rocks and the buzz of the crickets. If I closed my eyes, I was ten again, thinking of tadpoles and aircraft carriers and battles on pirate ships. The innocence of youth. Much preferable to the fears of adulthood.

Finn's sneeze broke the silence. I waited for him to sneeze a second time—all the Hopkins men sneezed in pairs—before I said, "You can't run from this, Finn. Better to face it head-on. You've got support, you know."

"Are you talking about the two guys trying to kill me? Or are you talking about my father, who's trying to do something just as bad."

"I was speaking about the guys after you."

"Solving that problem would be great, of course, but that still leaves me with a larger one. What is it about families, huh? Fathers, specifically? I'm tired of his judgment, tired of his need to control every single thing that goes on in his life, or in mine. I'm sick of the lofty expectations. Go to college. Get good grades. Get a good job." Finn picked up another rock and tossed it into the creek. "Get married—to a woman—and have a family. Whatever happened to unconditional love?"

"People show their love in different ways." My turn for target practice. I tossed a smooth river rock and hit the branch I was aiming at. "He did hire a PI to find you. He hired a bodyguard to protect you. He cares about you."

"All I want is for him to accept me for who I am. Is that so difficult?"

"For some people, it's a definite challenge." I felt the cool slab beneath my shirt. "Remember Grandpa?"

"Sure. He was an SOB. I mean, who's nasty to their grandkids?" Finn laughed.

He laughed now, but it was disconcerting getting yelled at by someone who we were always told loved us. He wasn't mean all the time—I remembered spending some quality time with him, reading books and playing checkers—but he wasn't your typical grandfather. He'd been a successful businessman and didn't have a sense of humor. I guessed he didn't know how to deal with all the tomfoolery and shenanigans—his words—that Finn and I bombarded him with.

"Couldn't you see, though, how he could raise our fathers to be judgmental and demanding, just like he was? They learned it from a master, all right. All their baggage runs in the family," I said.

"We'll break the chain, huh?" Finn said. "Well, you will. I doubt if I'll ever have kids. I'd be afraid I'd mess them up, but good. Besides, I'll be dead soon."

"Will you stop talking like that?"

"The truth is painful sometimes."

Self-pity never sat well with me, my own, or someone else's. "You do have some influence over your future, you know."

"I'm more the fatalist type," Finn said.

"I think you're full of crap. You came back home to face up to things. You realized your life was going in one direction—down—and you gathered your courage and decided it was now or never. You got clean, Finn. Huge accomplishment. So don't blow it now. There are some times in everyone's life where they are tested, really tested. This is one of those times for you. You can either rise to the challenge or shrink away in shame." As I said these words, I wondered where they came from. Were they mine, or was I parroting some Little League coach trying to fire up the team? Didn't matter, I guessed. I believed what I said was true, regardless. "You make your own destiny, Finn. Don't sit back and let things happen to you."

Finn didn't respond. He picked up a twig and scratched it into the face of the rock, as if he was leaving some kind of message. Like when we were kids and we pretended to write with invisible ink. I found it amazing that in times of stress, we often regressed to our childhood, when things were simpler and we—usually—had parents to protect us from all the harsh realities of the world.

I elbowed him in the side. "I know that you know that I know that you know I'm right."

That brought a tiny smile to Finn's lips.

He opened his mouth to say something, then closed it abruptly. Voices from the trail floated to us on the breeze. Sounded like two people. Men, not kids. Finn's eyes filled with panic.

I held up a finger to my mouth, then motioned Finn to slide off the rock onto the other side of the creek. I quickly followed. We ducked behind some brush, keeping as still as we could.

Most likely, it was just a couple of hikers. Maybe two guys—unfamiliar with the creek—who thought there might be fishing. It didn't sound like a father and son, but we couldn't really tell, and there was no sense taking chances.

We waited and watched through the leaves as the voices came closer.

The men rounded the bend, and I'd seen them before.

Kyle Long and Nubs Porter. The two killers after Finn.

Chapter Twenty-Nine

Next to me, I sensed Finn tense. I put my hand on his forearm and gave him a reassuring squeeze.

They paused on the trail, on the opposite side of the creek from us. The taller one mopped his brow. I didn't know which was Kyle and which was Nubs. Honestly, they both looked like they could have been called Nubs. They weren't exactly dressed in hiking clothes, and they were both sweating pretty good. "You sure he went this way?"

"I saw what you saw."

"And you're sure he's going to lead us to Finn?"

"I'm not sure about anything. Except we need to find that joker and eliminate him from the picture. Unless *we* want to get eliminated."

I gripped Finn's forearm a little tighter.

"I knew I should have been an insurance salesman."

The shorter guy laughed. "That's exactly what we're doing. Providing insurance to our employer. Now, let's keep going."

It was what we'd been afraid of. They'd connected Finn to me, and they'd followed me here, figuring I'd lead them to him. And I had. I definitely needed to be more careful.

They continued along the trail. I leaned forward to watch their progress, but the branch I was leaning against gave way, and I slipped down the muddy bank a few feet, sending a mini-avalanche of rocks splashing into the creek. I might have let out an audible yelp, too.

"What was that?" one of them said.

We didn't wait around to hear the answer. "Come on," I yelled to Finn.

"Run!"

We took off, sprinting away from them, on our side of the creek.

"Hey, hold up," one of them yelled.

I glanced over my shoulder, and they were coming after us. One of them was on the rock, and the other was right behind. We knew these woods better than they did, and we had a head start, and they looked more like football players than track stars. But I figured they had guns, and we couldn't outrun bullets.

"We need to lose them," I said to Finn. He was keeping pace, and I'm sure he was as scared as I was, if not more. Those guys made it clear they were out to eliminate Finn. I had no doubt that if I was in the way, though, figuratively or literally, they'd eliminate me, too, without giving it a second thought.

We tore through the woods, following a fainter trail. I ventured a glance behind me again, and I didn't spot them, but I was pretty sure I heard them cussing to themselves. Or to each other, I couldn't be sure.

"They're still behind us," I called to Finn, who'd opened up a lead on me. I knew if we continued straight, we'd hit the fence that bordered the entire park. We'd be trapped. I also knew if we veered right, we'd come to an open field which, in turn, led to a neighboring housing development.

I hit the jets and caught up with Finn. "Let's cross back over the creek. They'll never find us." I pointed to a spot up ahead. "There."

After another glance behind to make sure they couldn't see us, we ducked into the foliage on our left and plowed through the underbrush. The creek was wider here, but we were able to pick our way across a series of stepping stones. One teeter-tottered when my foot landed on it, and I almost lost my balance, but my momentum carried me forward to the next stone.

Then we were across and racing for the parking lot. I didn't think the two goons were still behind us, but they could have cut through the woods and crossed the creek at a number of different spots. I wondered if they were smart enough to use their phones' GPS apps to help guide them, but I had no idea how well those apps worked in the semi-wilderness.

The parking lot came into view and not a moment too soon. I was breathing hard, and my left ankle throbbed. Finn's labored breathing matched mine.

We kept going, slower and with more grunting, but we finally made it to the car. We hopped in, and I roared off, eyes glued to the rearview mirror, searching for any sign of our pursuers.

Nowhere to be found.

I drove out of the park, but a realization hit me like a branch in the face. Those guys had followed me to the park, and they must have picked me up at the motel. Which meant they had not only connected me with Finn, but they knew where I lived—and presumably where Finn was staying, too.

We couldn't go back there. So where?

* * *

I knew Mama would take Finn in, no questions asked. I'd parked people who needed refuge with her in other situations, but this time felt different. More dangerous. And there was no way I was dragging someone else into this quagmire.

I was friends—maybe acquainted colleagues was a better description— with Harry Utley, the owner of a nearby motel, The Sleeptight Inn. We had a loose arrangement to provide rooms to each other, if the need arose. But he also didn't deserve to be put in harm's way.

We could go to some random motel—Finn was already familiar with the Clamshell—but again, was that being fair? Of course, the odds that the two guys after Finn would find us there were very small, but I didn't really know the extent of their contact network or how deep their pockets were. Or how long they'd been following me.

We could go on a camping trip to the Shenandoah, but running from the problem wouldn't get us any closer to solving the mystery and extricating Finn from the entire sordid situation.

We'd been driving aimlessly for a while, putting distance between us and the two killers, when I pulled into a grocery store parking lot. It was time for The Talk.

"What are we doing?" Finn had been staring out his window quietly as we'd been cruising, no doubt as lost in his thoughts as I had been in mine.

"We need to have a discussion."

"I'm not much in the talking mood."

I forced—absolutely forced—a smile on my face. I'd reached my limit with Finn, and we were either going to come up with a plan he and I could live with—literally—or I was going to toss him out of the car right there and leave him to his own self-destructive ways. "We're going to have a conversation now, so I suggest you get in the mood." I hit the button to roll down the windows. Maybe some fresh air would help put Finn in the proper frame of mind.

Outside the car, a man wrestled with a shopping cart, trying to maneuver it into a corral. He banged the cart back and forth, and we couldn't help but watch the spectacle for a few seconds. Finally, he succeeded, then slapped it once and returned to his car. Finn swiveled in his seat to face me.

"Okay, Mess. Let's talk."

"We can't keep doing this. Eventually, these guys are going to find you. And if you run, they'll hunt you down. You witnessed them murder someone. They don't strike me as the types of guys to let it slide."

"Interesting perspective. You've obviously spent a lot of time thinking about this. What do you suggest? Invite them to tea and have a discussion?"

"Don't be a smartass. I know you've spent a lot of time thinking about this, too. No more games."

Finn nodded slowly, then faster and faster. "Okay. You're right. I've been hoping this whole thing would just blow over, but that's not going to happen, is it?"

"'Fraid not."

"Okay. Running is out. I don't suppose we can barricade ourselves at the motel."

"This isn't the Old West. No barricades. No showdowns at noon."

"What, then?"

"Go to the police. Tell them what you saw." I couldn't believe I had to spell it out for him. This is what he should have done the night of the incident.

That would have eliminated a lot of this unnecessary drama, stress, and fear.

"What other options do I have?"

"Realistically? None. And unless you do, I'm outta here. You're on your own."

"You'd abandon me?" Finn whined.

"Sometimes you need to trust someone. I'm that guy. You're lucky I'm a level-headed guy with your best interest in mind."

"I do know that I'm lucky to have you on my side, Mess. I really do. But it's just a lot, you know?"

I knew. Of course, I knew. I'd have to be an idiot not to empathize with what Finn was going through. But someone had to be the adult here, and I'd been waiting for Finn to rise to the challenge. It was painfully obvious he was unable to on his own. "We're going to the police. It's the only way forward that has a good chance to succeed. We'll talk to my buddy, Detective Ostervale, okay? He'll make sure you get treated well." I knew Finn's prior dealings with the cops had not been pleasant, to say the least. Ostervale will make sure he got a fair shake.

A few tears dribbled down Finn's cheek. "Okay, Mess. I trust you."

"I know this is difficult. And it might get more difficult. But ultimately, you really have no other choice. You realize that, don't you?"

In the most pitiful, tiniest voice, Finn said, "Yes." A beat. "And thanks."

* * *

We arranged to meet Detective Ostervale in the far reaches of a Home Depot parking lot. He wanted to bring in the detectives actually working the case, but Finn wouldn't have any of that, at least not before talking to Ostervale.

I gestured to the vast empty—paved—expanse. "Nice place for a get-together."

"You didn't want to come down to the station. You didn't want to meet in a place with a lot of people. You didn't want to meet in a restaurant or bar. So, Home Depot it is. Besides, I need to run in and pick up some paint when we're done. Got a little home fix-up project in the works." Ostervale was nothing if not efficient.

I introduced Finn.

Ostervale shook his hand. "Actually, I remember you. We met at some Hopkins family function. Fourth of July picnic, or something. Of course, we were teenagers."

"Sure, sure," Finn said, although I was certain he didn't remember that at all.

"Go ahead, Finn. Tell the detective what you saw."

Finn launched into an account of what he did and saw the night of Claypool's murder. It matched what he'd told me—several times—and he delivered it with emotion appropriate for each step of the way. He went on to tell Ostervale about the events that had transpired since, too. The two guys staking-out the pizzamobile at the mall all the way up to Long and Porter chasing us at the park an hour ago. I noted that Finn left out the details about why he'd been at Thorpe's that night.

Ostervale, who'd kept quiet the entire time Finn had been talking, nodded sagely. "I have some questions. That okay?"

Finn glanced at me, and I gave him a nod.

"Sure."

"Mess showed me a photo of the two guys—although he didn't say exactly why he thought they might be involved." Ostervale shot me a pointed look. "Are you positive these are the two men you saw kill Claypool?"

"Yes," Finn said. "Kinda positive."

"Kinda?"

"Mostly positive? I didn't get a look at them for long, and I was scared, so…"

"Okay. But these are the same two you saw sitting in their car at the mall?"

"Yes. Pretty sure. I think so."

Another look from Ostervale. "And the same two guys today at the park?"

"Yes. It was them. Ninety percent. You don't think it's different sets of guys after me, do you?"

"I don't know what to think. I'm trying to figure that out. Okay, let's assume the two guys you saw kill Claypool are the two guys after you. You believe they want to kill you, so you can't identify them as the murderers?"

"Yes. Why else? Do you think they want to tell me I've won the lottery?" Finn's frustration was obvious. And I could identify with him. But I knew Ostervale was thorough and wanted to make sure he knew exactly what the score was before he acted.

"Let's move on. To that night. Why were you at Thorpe's house?"

Finn glanced around the parking lot nervously. "I was there. I saw the murder. Then I ran, and they chased me. I explained that."

Ostervale gazed off into the distance for a moment, then refocused on us. "Look, Finn. It's important that you tell me *exactly* what happened and not leave anything out. If one part of your account isn't accurate, then whoever—the prosecutor, the defense counsel, the other detectives—will tend to look at the rest of your account with some skepticism. So even if you think what you did or saw isn't relevant, you still need to be truthful. And being truthful means you can't leave things out."

Finn's lower lip trembled. "Tim didn't know I was there that night. He was out of town, and his wife was, too. I borrowed a key the night before and let myself in to enjoy the hot tub and big-screen TV and living in luxury. It had been a while since I'd lived in luxury, even for one night. I didn't think it would do any harm."

"And Thorpe didn't know you let yourself in, as you said."

"No."

"Okay. What is your relationship with Thorpe?"

Finn sighed. "We're lovers."

Chapter Thirty

To his credit, Ostervale didn't change expression. In his line of work, he'd seen and heard it all. "How long have you two been seeing each other?"

A shrug. "A month. Six weeks."

"How did you meet?"

"We met at a bar, and something clicked between us. From the very first moment," Finn said. "I've been around a bit, but he's different than the rest. Caring. Smart. Generous."

"So it was more than a one-night stand?"

"Yes."

"Does Thorpe think this is an ongoing thing?" Ostervale asked.

I kept quiet, knowing what Thorpe actually thought. Across the lot, a truck's backup beeper sounded.

"I hope so," Finn said. "But after this whole episode? I doubt it."

"Okay. Does his wife know about your relationship with him?"

Finn shook his head. "Not specifically, I don't think. She knows about who he really is. They've come to an understanding."

Ostervale exhaled. "Anything else to add?"

"Not that I can think of," Finn said.

"Okay, if you think of anything else, let me know." Ostervale waved a mosquito away. "For your information, as a favor to our friend Mess here, I've asked to be put on the case, and the higher-ups have okayed my request. I'll pass along this information to the team."

"What are you going to do to protect him?" I asked. I mean, that was one of the carrots I used to persuade Finn to come forth.

Ostervale spoke to Finn. "First, I suggest you apologize to Rickert for running out on him. He's in the best position to keep you safe. Second, let me know where you're at, and I'll have some patrol cars come around every so often."

"That's it?" I wasn't sure what I expected from the county police, but I expected something more.

"If there's trouble, we can be there in three minutes. Rickert used to be on the force, before he left for greener—and more lucrative—pastures in the private sector. I'm sure he remembers what he learned." Ostervale reached out and gently touched Finn on his shoulder. "We're going to catch these guys, don't worry. Just keep your head down until we do, okay?"

Finn nodded, but he didn't seem convinced.

* * *

We still weren't sure where to go, but Finn wanted to stop by the motel to pick up his stuff so he'd have it wherever we ended up. I figured if we parked in the rear and made sure nobody was lurking, we'd be okay, but before we even drove around the motel, we spotted Uncle Phil waiting for us. Along with Rickert, who leaned against his car ten yards away, watching us.

"Oh, shit," Finn said when he saw who was there.

"Just be cool, Finn. You're doing the right thing now, remember? And the right thing here is to be polite and talk to your father."

"Oh, shit," he said again.

Mercifully, Phil waited until we were out of the car before he started in on us. He walked right past me so he could stand toe-to-toe with Finn. Each man stared into the other's face, no one moving or saying a word.

Then Phil stepped forward and embraced Finn as tightly and as warmly as I'd ever seen him hug anyone.

After about ten seconds, my eyes were so watery, it was all just a blur. I had to look away.

When I heard clapping on the back, I turned back. I wasn't the only one with wet eyes.

Phil turned and greeted me with a quick nod and a terse, "Benjamin."

"Hello, Uncle Phil. I see you've brought your henchman."

He glared at me. "I hired the best money can buy. And nothing is too good for my boy." He smiled at Finn. "Now, I think it's time to circle the wagons. Hunker down until these killers are apprehended." He took a couple of steps to the side, then waved Rickert over to join us.

"You know everybody, right?" Phil asked him.

"Sure do."

"Okay. We're going to take your advice and bunker in at the house," Phil said.

I had the distinct impression that our input—Finn's or mine—was not going to be considered. Was it worth arguing about? Uncle Phil and Finn had made up, at least for now, and although it might have only been because things had gotten desperate, I was okay with that. Baby steps. If Phil wanted to take the reins in his quest to protect his son, I was doubly okay with that, too.

It solved our problem of where to go, and not having to babysit Finn would free me up to help Lia investigate.

"Sounds like a plan." I jutted my chin at Finn. "You okay with this? Seems like a good idea to me. Like Ostervale said, the cops can be there in minutes, if needed."

Rickert let a small smile crack his marble façade. "I'll take care of everything. Don't worry."

For some reason, I'd feel better if people stopped telling me not to worry.

* * *

The three of them—Finn, Uncle Phil, and Rickert—piled into Rickert's car and took off, headed out to Phil's home in McLean. I called Lia and Vell, requesting—hoping—that we could get together to discuss a few things. More than anything, I wanted this situation resolved. I wasn't sure how long Finn could survive living under the same roof as his father. That might turn out to be more dangerous than facing two murderers.

As it happened, both could break away from what they were doing. Vell was shooting hoops—in other words, hustling high school basketball stars who thought they could take the older guy. And Lia was working late on a story about Claypool Development, but she welcomed the break.

Instead of cramming into my motel room, we sat around the picnic bench outside. Dusk had fallen.

"Lotta bugs, I gotta tell you." Vell slapped at his neck for the tenth time in the last minute.

"They're not bothering me," I said.

"That's because you're sour, and I'm sweet. Irresistible. Delectable." Vell swatted his forearm.

"I think it's because I used bug spray." I held up a bottle. "Want some?"

"Nah, I'm good. All these bugs lining up for a taste makes me feel wanted."

"Guys, do you think we can get to it now?" Lia flashed a fake smile. "Unless you have more insectalia to discuss?"

I looked at Vell. "I'm done."

"Me, too," Vell said.

"Okay, then." I cleared my throat to signal it was time to get serious. "Finn is safe now. Uncle Phil and the bodyguard he hired whisked Finn off to McLean, where they'll protect him. And more importantly, Finn told Ostervale what he saw, so the cops are up to speed, too."

"He didn't provide any kind of protective custody?" Lia asked.

"Ostervale's going to send around a patrol car periodically to keep watch. Plus, the bodyguard used to be on the force, so he's probably fully capable." A car with a broken muffler roared by on Route 50, and I paused a few seconds rather than get drowned out by the noise. "Anyway, having Finn out of here is a load off my mind. Now I can focus on getting to the bottom of this." I exhaled. "Lia, what's going on with you?"

"I've been trying to discover a motive for Claypool's death. Digging into his past, professional and personal. I gotta tell you there are a lot of people who probably are not unhappy Claypool is out of the picture. He made a lot of enemies over the years."

"Are you speaking about professionally or personally?" I asked.

"Yes."

"Rich guys always rub somebody the wrong way," Vell said.

"Enough to drive someone to kill you?" I asked.

"That's the question, isn't it." Lia brushed some hair off her face. "He has at least four ex-partners, three of whom sued him over the years. And three who are still in the area. There are numerous other business executives he's dealt with who have publicly criticized him for the way he conducted business. Called him sleazy and unprofessional and a crook. On the personal side, he has two ex-wives, and both divorces were high-profile and very contentious. Each ex-wife claims Claypool's high-priced lawyers screwed them out of millions. *Tens* of millions."

"Yikes." Vell swatted his forearm.

"You sure you don't want some bug spray?"

"Nope."

I glared at him. "Did anyone ever tell you that you're stubborn?"

"That's how Mama greets me every other day." Vell held his hand out. "Pass it over, just to get you off my back."

I handed Vell the bug spray, and he doused himself.

"Any closer to coming up with a short list of possible suspects?" I asked Lia.

"Short list? No. So far, I've got eighteen on my list of suspects and another two dozen names of people who flat-out hate him."

"Including Thorpe?"

"Yeah. He's on there. Alluree, too."

I'd discussed that possibility with Lia previously, and she agreed with me. She'd taken it one step further and suggested that maybe they'd worked together to kill Claypool. A couples project.

"Do you think the cops have the same list?" Vell asked.

"I'm sure they have a list. But we have different sources, and some people who wouldn't give the police the time of day have no trouble at all talking to the sweet local newspaper reporter." Lia batted her eyelashes. "My source in the PD says they know about the two guys Finn IDed, but there's no concrete evidence connecting them to anything. There wasn't much forensic evidence, period, at the scene. They think the murderer or murderers wore gloves."

"If they're truly freelance muscle, who are they working for?" Sometimes I had a bad tendency to ask the obvious.

"Highest bidder?" Vell asked.

"We've got Danielle Sakai saying that they were spying on Claypool for Jimbo Young, and we've got Jimbo Young's aide saying they worked for Claypool, but then he saw them talking to Young," I said.

"And that doesn't even consider that someone might be lying," Lia said.

We all pondered that for a moment. I voiced my thoughts. "Young had to be pissed Claypool was not backing him and double-pissed Claypool was going to throw a lot of money and support at Ike Garrity. Seems like high enough stakes for murder, doesn't it? And if they can finger the two guys as being spies or as part of some palace takeover, then all the better."

"What do the cops say about them?" Vell asked.

"Both have lengthy records. Assault, battery, general mayhem. Intimidation. Nasty men all around. And dangerous. If we come across them, up close and personal, I think it's best we steer clear. Very clear." More stating of the obvious from me, but I wanted to be sure everyone knew the score.

"I don't think Supervisor Young would agree to another interview, especially how the last one ended," Lia said.

A thought struck me. "Why don't you try to talk to his aide, Steve? He had loose lips, and I bet the sweet, attractive local newspaper reporter would be able to get some valuable information from him. Especially after a few drinks."

Lia raised an eyebrow.

"His drinks, not yours." I considered things for a second. "Maybe I should come, too. He already knows me, and if I'm there, maybe he'll be able to concentrate more on what he's saying."

Chapter Thirty-One

I woke up early the next morning, and for a split second, I felt refreshed, not a care in the world. Then I remembered the crisis I was currently embroiled in.

Then I remembered Finn wasn't my responsibility at the moment and breathed a tiny sigh of relief. But only a tiny one—his problems hadn't gotten any better. Two guys were still trying to kill him.

But with Finn not around, I felt freer. I still wanted desperately to help him out of his jam, but I didn't have to worry about his minute-by-minute moods. Or his whereabouts. Finn had proven to be a slippery one. Let Rickert keep a protective eye on Finn.

Maybe I should have been more worried about my own safety, but Long and Porter wanted Finn, not me, and I had Griff on alert, so I figured I was okay.

Next to me, Lia still slept. She'd spent the night, and I took it as one step—a big one—toward her forgiving me for not taking her job as seriously as I should. Her hair covered one eye, and her lips were slightly parted, and she looked so peaceful. I wondered why the awake versions of people couldn't be as peaceful as they appeared when they were sleeping.

* * *

Lia arranged for us to meet Steve at Van Dyck Park in the City of Fairfax. It was near the Sherwood Community Center, and it boasted a basketball court, a hiking trail, a playground, and tennis courts. It also featured a skateboard park, which was where we sat on some low-rise metal bleachers.

It was also out of the way, so Steve wouldn't have to worry about being seen talking to a reporter. Clandestine meetings were becoming my specialty, it seemed.

Lia and I had arrived first, and we watched a twenty-something skateboarder—wearing a royally scuffed-up helmet—work on some of his fancy moves. There was a lot more falling down than skating, but I had to give him credit; he was persistent. Maybe in another few years, we'd see him riding the half-pipe in the Olympics.

A few minutes later, Steve strode toward us. Shiny burgundy shoes poked out from under an open beige trench coat, although there wasn't a cloud in the sky or a drop of rain in the forecast. Underneath, a smart, too-tight-for-my-tastes blue suit with a red striped tie. Decked out like a true Young Politician. The look was almost as important as the ideology. I bet he did okay with all the Young Female Politicians at their happy hours.

He saw us and raised a hand in greeting.

When he got to the bleachers, he settled in right next to Lia. A little too close for my tastes. "Good morning," he said.

I sat forward so I could see him better.

"Morning. Thanks for meeting with us," Lia said. "I'm Lia Katsaros from the Fairfax Observer, and you already know Mess."

"Nice to meet you," Steve said. "And good to see you again." He looked back and forth between me and Lia, and I got the feeling he was trying to determine if we were a thing, or if he had a chance with Lia. I hoped he thought he had a chance; it would make him more open with his answers. "Okay, what would you like to know?"

"This will be on the record," Lia began. "If that's a problem, just say so and, depending, we can go off the record."

Steve smiled, and it reminded me of a crocodile. "Is there really such a thing with reporters as off the record?"

He thought he was being cute, and I wanted to smack that smile off his face, but I kept quiet and let Lia answer.

"Of course. If you want something off the record, I will honor that. Not all reporters are the sleazeballs you sometimes see in movies."

"Okay. Yeah. Sure. I didn't mean anything by that."

Lia smiled back, bigger and brighter than anything Steve could ever muster. "Of course not. No offense taken."

Steve shifted in his seat. I felt sorry for him, about to be eviscerated by a pro. But only a little.

"How long have you worked for Supervisor Young?"

"Almost three years."

"He comes across as a nice guy. That accurate?" Lia kept her smile in place.

"Yeah, he's pretty cool." Steve was about to say more but closed his mouth.

"Well, I'm sure he's not cool all the time, right?" Lia asked. "I mean, a guy who's trying to please all his constituents is bound to get pulled in different directions some of the time. Bound to be some high-pressure situations."

"Yeah, I guess." Steve glanced around. Nobody there, except for the skateboarding dude.

"What do you do for him?"

"Whatever he asks. Work on policy, mostly. Translate what the citizens say they need into proposals that are feasible. A lot of people want a lot of things, and there's only so much money to go around."

"Are you involved with campaign funding?"

"Sometimes. We're a small staff, so everyone is involved in everything to some extent at some time."

"I understand Webster Claypool told Supervisor Young that he would no longer be supporting him. Is that correct?"

Steve squirmed. "Yes. That's no secret. Claypool was frustrated Young wanted to pump the brakes a little on development. There are a limited number of resources in the county, so something had to be done. I mean, you've seen the traffic, right? Crazy." Steve let loose with a nervous chuckle, but he was the only one laughing.

The skateboarder's wheels grinding against the concrete provided a monotonous background soundtrack.

"Whose idea was that? To slow development?" Lia asked.

"Everyone's, I guess. The county has undergone tremendous growth over the past ten years. Unsustainable at that rate. Common sense dictated that—"

Lia held up her hand. "Yes, I've heard the stump speech. Is there any truth that Supervisor Young is positioning himself to make a run for the governor's seat?"

Steve almost did a spit-take. "I, uh, where did you hear that?"

"I have my sources. Is it true?"

Steve licked his lips, glanced around. I wondered if he thought he'd been followed or something, as if some low-level aide had something that important to divulge. "I don't think it's going out on a limb to say that anyone in such a vital position as Supervisor Young might have designs on higher office. He's been a beloved figure in county politics for years, and it's only logical to consider statewide office as a next step."

"We'll take that as a yes," I said, inserting myself into the conversation. "If Young lost the upcoming *local* election, that might hinder those chances. So exactly how far would he go to ensure that he won?"

"I'm not sure I follow," Steve said.

"With Claypool backing Garrity, Young's reelection would be in jeopardy. But without Claypool's support, Garrity wouldn't have as much of a chance. So…" I let it hang.

Steve tilted his head and narrowed his eyes. "If you're suggesting that Supervisor Young had anything whatsoever to do with Webster Claypool's death, then you don't know him at all."

"People have done worse things in the name of politics," I said. "You said yourself that those two mysterious men were seen talking to Young a few weeks ago."

"If he was plotting with those guys—which is ridiculous, by the way—do you think he would have done it in the Government Center cafeteria?" Steve's complexion had turned a little red.

I shrugged. "Some politicians think they are bulletproof. Invincible. Young strikes me like that."

"Okay, okay." Lia tried to take control again, and I felt bad derailing things, but I couldn't just sit back and listen to Young's operative spin the facts his way without even a bit of pushback.

"I thought you wanted to ask me some questions to help catch whoever's responsible, not to accuse Supervisor Young."

Steve had a point.

"That's *exactly* why I wanted to speak with you. Forgive my friend here. He gets carried away." Lia fake glared at me.

I thought we did a very good rendition of good cop-bad cop. Out of the corner of my eye, I saw the skateboarder complete an impressive maneuver, then let loose with an enthusiastic fist pump. Nice to celebrate the small victories in life.

"Can you tell me anything more about these two guys?" Lia softened her tone.

The color of Steve's face returned to normal. "Well, I'm afraid I don't know too much. They appeared at a joint press conference, and they stood in the background. I thought they were two of Claypool's bodymen. I was assigned to Supervisor Young's personal team that day, so I asked them a couple of questions, and from what I can recall, they answered as if they were working for Claypool."

"What kind of questions?"

"I don't remember exactly. Probably something to do with the timing of their statements, or who was going to speak first, or how they wanted the photo ops staged. Fairly meaningless stuff like that. Maybe I should have asked them if they were planning to kill anyone soon, huh?" Steve smiled, but neither Lia, or I returned it. *Just another jerk in a trenchcoat.*

"Was that the only time you saw them?"

"Later, like I said, I saw them in the cafeteria talking to Supervisor Young."

I thought it was cute how every time he referred to Young, he called him Supervisor Young, and I imagined Young holding training sessions where that was requirement number one to work for him.

"Do you have any idea what they were talking about?" Lia asked.

"No. In fact, I asked Supervisor Young what it was all about, figuring I might be asked to liaise with them again on an appearance or something, and he told me not to worry about it. After that meeting, though, I figured they might not actually be on Claypool's payroll anymore. I think this was after Claypool split with Supervisor Young, so I did wonder what was going on. Maybe they were jumping ship and looking for a job? Honestly, I didn't give it much thought. Our office is very busy, so it was on to the next thing, you know?"

"How much interaction did you have with Webster Claypool?"

"Believe it or not, I only met him once. I was at plenty of functions with him, but Supervisor Young preferred his junior staff to keep behind the scenes for the most part."

"You must have heard lots of stories, though, about his many dealings."

Something lit up behind Steve's eyes. "Sure. But it's hard to know which things were true and which things weren't."

"Like what kind of things?" Lia smiled, and I recognized it as the one she used to elicit more information from those she was interviewing.

"I think we should go off the record now, okay?"

"Sure. If that would make you more comfortable."

"It would." Steve glanced around, then leaned in. "He was a player. At least, he thought he was. I guess when you're that loaded, you can do whatever you want, huh? He didn't treat his business partners well, and he was a terror in negotiations. Our office got plenty of complaints about him personally and about corners being cut on his development projects. And I guess it's fair to say nobody liked him. Not his ex-wives, not his business associates, not the general public."

"What about Supervisor Young?" Lia asked.

Steve snorted. "Supervisor Young hated the guy's guts." He pointed at Lia. "That is *definitely* off the record. I'd be toast if Supervisor Young found out I said that."

Lia pointed right back at Steve. "I won't tell a soul."

"Good."

"So even though Supervisor Young hated Claypool, and Claypool had a terrible reputation, he had no problem appearing with Claypool at events and having Claypool as a supporter."

Steve rubbed two fingers together. "This is politics. Money talks. Ethics balk. Constituents squawk."

Catchy. My turn to play bad cop. "Was Young happy when he found out Claypool had been killed?"

"Happy? I don't think Supervisor Young is happy when anyone gets murdered." Steve was back to pushing the party line.

"Was he distraught?"

"Look, I know you want to somehow paint Supervisor Young as being involved in this, but I can assure you he isn't. And as Chairman of the Board of Supervisors, he is doing everything he can to capture the perpetrators of this heinous act and bring them to justice."

"Exactly what is he doing along those lines?" Lia asked.

"Cooperating with local law enforcement. Directing them to employ sufficient resources to solve this case rapidly. The safety and well-being of the residents of this county is his number one priority. Then, now, and tomorrow."

Politicians made me sick to the stomach.

* * *

Lia dropped me off at the motel, and she returned to the salt mines, or whatever those in the know called the newspaper offices. Griff accosted me before I could even get the door open to get inside my room.

"Hey, boss."

I craned my neck to look up at him. "How's it going?"

"Not too good. I had things under control, and then Phil comes around and snatches Finn. I don't think he and Finn get along too good. And I know Phil hates my guts."

"He doesn't hate you." I patted Griff on the arm, and it was like patting a block of granite. "He doesn't think the Inn needs full-time security, and he doesn't think you are worth what we pay you."

"You let me stay here, but you don't pay me anything."

"Listen, Griff. You're a valuable part of the team here, and I'm glad you're here, every single day. As long as I'm running things—and you continue to serve us well—you have a home for as long as you need, okay? Forget Phil taking Finn away. He doesn't always make good decisions."

Griff nodded, and he seemed to be mollified, at least for the moment.

"Is Norma Rae causing any trouble?"

"Is she back?" he asked.

I stared at him. I honestly lost track. "Well, if we haven't heard anything from her, I guess maybe she isn't." With that wise pronouncement, I said goodbye to Griff and went inside my room.

I kicked off my shoes and texted Finn. *How're things going?*

Almost immediately, Finn responded: *What made me think this was a good idea?*

C'mon, family is great.

Maybe your family, not sure about mine.

Same family.

Finn texted: *Different relationships. Your parents are thousands of miles away. Mine are breathing down my neck.*

Hang in there. Easy for me to say, I realized.

I hope they catch those guys soon.

Amen. Later. I set my phone down. Finn had only been back under his parents' roof for less than a day, and I wondered how long he could last without going crazy. Aunt Vera was no problem, but my limit was only about half an hour with Uncle Phil.

Not three minutes later, my phone buzzed with a text from Vell. *Be there in five. We're going to meet a friend for some info.*

Sounded like Vell had come through again.

Chapter Thirty-Two

Vell's *friend* was a street snitch named Pudding, and he worked in a secondhand store in Dunn Loring doing who knew what. When we arrived, he was arranging throw rugs in one corner of the cavernous store, and he told us to have a seat on a stack of Persians. Vell and I did what we were told, and he perched on a nearby metal step stool. Smudges dotted his chin. Food, if I had to guess. Pudding came by his nickname honestly.

"D'Marvellus Jackson, my man. Always good to see you." Pudding smiled, and a gold tooth glinted. He was one of the few people who pronounced Vell's given name properly, with the emphasis on *Vell*. "How's Mama getting along?"

"She's fine."

"Fine, she is. And dandy. Fine and dandy." Pudding chuckled, but it turned quickly into a cough. "'Scuse me. Something done crawled down my throat." He coughed some more, then dragged a sleeve across his mouth. I noticed plenty of food smudges on his sleeve, too.

"Maybe you ought to see someone about that," Vell said.

"I'll see what my health insurance can provide. Think they'll foot the bill for a trip to the May-go Clinic? As in, you got money, you *may go*." Pudding turned to me. "Nice to see you again. Max, was it?"

"Mess."

He laughed, then coughed, then kept on laughing and coughing. "Max, Mess, close enough. I bet I'm not the first cat to call you Max, am I?"

I couldn't remember anyone else. "Nope. Happens every so often."

Pudding turned serious. "Vell outlined things in broad strokes, but tell me exactly how I can assist you guys."

Vell and I had talked to Pudding a few months back when I was helping a woman and her son escape from a bad domestic situation. He seemed to have his pulse on a lot of stuff that took place under the radar.

"Show him the picture." Vell nodded at me.

I pulled out my phone and called up the photo of the two killers. "Know where we can find these guys?"

Pudding took the phone from me, squinted at the photo. "Yep. Yep, yep, yep."

"You know where they are?" I asked.

"I know something about them."

I remembered the last time we'd dealt with Pudding, which was why we stopped at an ATM on the way over. I reached into my wallet and pulled out a twenty. Handed it over. Before I could blink, Pudding had folded it up and slipped it into the pocket of his jeans.

"Excuse me," a woman said from behind. "Do you work here?"

"Yes, ma'am, I do. What can I help you with?" Pudding said.

"Where are the vacuum cleaners?"

Pudding pointed. "Down this aisle about two-thirds of the way. Right-hand side. If you need to try one, just let me know. I'd be happy to dump some dirt on the floor so you can test it out."

"Thank you so much." The lady set off, following Pudding's direction. I noticed *she* didn't have to grease his palm to get the information she wanted.

Pudding refocused his attention on us. "Those two guys are bad men. Avoid them if you can. That's my advice."

Vell and I exchanged glances. "I thought you knew where I could find them."

"You get what you pay for." Pudding smiled, and the gold tooth seemed to be mocking me.

I gave him another twenty and watched this one disappear even quicker. "Vell, I wish you'd tell your friend to listen to my advice. He'll be healthier in the long run. No broken bones or worse."

"I try to talk sense into him every chance I get, but he's a stubborn one. Go ahead, tell him what he wants to know."

Pudding shrugged as if to say, *okay, but it'll be your fault when something terrible happens to your friend.* "I don't know where they are. But I know where they're heading."

I supposed that was just as good. "I'm listening."

"They're heading for you."

A chill rippled through me. "Huh?"

"These two guys been asking around about your friend, Flynn. Seem to know all about him: Works at a pizza place. Staying at your motel. Got a rich father."

Oh, crap. This wasn't good. "His name is Finn. Did you hear why they're after him?"

Pudding canted his head. ""Finn. Flynn. Flim-flam. Whatever. According to my peeps, they want to make him vanish. And not like some magician assistant. Vanish like you vanish a cockroach. Seems your boy saw something he shouldn't have. And then he gone done and start blabbing to the five-oh about it. These two guys are not happy. Maybe put your cousin on a plane to Tasmania. That's a real place, right?" Pudding scratched his chin theatrically. "He is your cousin, right? See, they seem to know all about you, too. And your motel. Which, my friend of a friend, is not a good thing. Not at all."

"My name came up?"

"Max Hopkins, yes, sir. I'm sure they think they can get to him through you." Pudding got up, and the stepstool squeaked in relief. "I need to demonstrate some vacuum cleaners. But I urge you to reconsider your involvement with these gentlemen and leave it to the professionals. Maybe join your cousin in Tanzania. Your orthopedic surgeon—or mortician—will thank you."

* * *

This changed everything. I probably shouldn't have been surprised—Long and Porter have been after Finn since the murder, and it wouldn't have been difficult for them to figure out I was Finn's cousin. And they had been chasing us at the park. But for some reason, up until now, I felt at least slightly removed from their direct attention. And to think I held the illusion that the motel provided safety…

How stupid that idea was.

These guys were killers. They didn't play by the rules, they didn't hew to any moral code, they wouldn't think twice about harming anyone else—impersonally labeled collateral damage—as long as they achieved their goal of erasing Finn. The thought of Finn being killed and me being collateral damage sent another ripple through me.

"What's the plan?" Vell asked when we reached the car.

Could you call wanting to hide in a closet until it all blew over a plan? I didn't think so. "We need to alert Uncle Phil and Finn. Let them know what's going on."

"This is all coming to a head, isn't it?" Vell asked.

"Yeah. One way or another, this will all be over soon."

* * *

I'd gone out to Uncle Phil's in person to deliver the news that the killers had learned Finn's identity from Lia's notebook, and this seemed even more urgent, so Vell and I hightailed it to his mansion in McLean. I also wanted to get a firsthand picture of how Phil and Finn were coexisting. When we got there, we were blocked from entering the driveway by Rickert's car.

When our car pulled up, he got out of his and walked over toward us.

I got out, too, and met him.

Rickert spoke first. "What's up?"

"Got some information you all need to hear. And we need to call Ostervale, too."

"We do?" A bulge was evident on Rickert's hip underneath a windbreaker.

"Can you please move your car and let us in?"

He pointed at Vell through the windshield. "Who's that with you?"

"My buddy, Vell."

"I don't know your buddy, Vell."

I was getting annoyed. "When you let us in, I'll introduce you."

Rickert stared at me. I stared back.

"I'm simply following security protocols," Rickert said.

I kept staring at him. "I need to talk to my uncle. This is his house, as I recall. He's paying you, as I recall. If you need to get approval from the man footing your bill, I suggest you call him. And my information is time critical, so I suggest you stop screwing around and get on with it."

Rickert stared at me a beat longer, then got in his car and moved it aside. Very slowly.

I got back in my car and rolled down the window. As we drove by, I called out. "If you want to hear what I have to say, you might want to come to the house." Then I rolled my window up without waiting for any kind of response.

"Seems like a nice fella," Vell said.

"Uncle Phil only hires the best." I drove and parked in the shadow of an ostentatious fountain in the middle of the circle in front of his house.

Phil lived on about two acres, and his property was surrounded by a high wrought iron fence, painted black. All the posts had pointy things on top. Inside the fence, around the entire perimeter, was a tall, thick hedge. On the other side of the fence were other mansions, all similarly landscaped.

In the back yard, Phil had a good-sized pool, although I don't think he or Aunt Vera had gone swimming more than a handful of times in the past ten years. Probably only when they invited Izzy and the girls over.

Right now, the only thing that mattered was how secure the place was. It wouldn't be easy for Long and Porter to get past Rickert. But it wouldn't be impossible, especially if they came bolstered with additional firepower.

I didn't envision a full-on attack. Too obvious, too blatant, too dangerous. I'd guess it would be some kind of surgical strike. Something quiet and clever and surprising.

I caught myself thinking in war terms and was utterly dismayed by where we'd gotten to.

Vell and I went inside, and after I introduced Vell to Aunt Vera, she told us to go back to the kitchen. There, we found Phil sitting at the kitchen table, staring out the window into the back yard. A glass with about two fingers of scotch rested on the table, not far from his hand. He didn't even turn around when we entered, although I'm sure he heard us.

"Uncle Phil?"

He didn't move.

"Uncle Phil? You remember Vell, right?"

Slowly, agonizingly slowly, Phil turned to face us. Bags under his eyes, sallow skin. I'd just seen him last night, and he hadn't looked like Death warmed over. Did spending time with Finn bring forth some dormant disease? Or was it all-consuming stress? "Good to see you again, Vell." He tipped his chin at me. "Benjamin."

"Where's Finn?"

"In his room. Some things never change, do they?"

I wasn't exactly sure what Phil was referring to, Finn hiding out in his room or some age-old disagreement that had perpetuated. "I saw Rickert out front. Seems kind of exposed."

Phil waved his hand in the air. "I don't tell him how to do his job, you know."

Actually, I'd bet Phil *did* try to tell him how to do his job. "Do you feel safe here?"

"Safer than at the motel, anyway. I'm thinking about hiring a couple more guys."

Vell and I exchanged glances.

"Really?" Having an escalation in arms might lead to an escalation in arms on the other side, too. The idea of an all-out firefight in the McLean suburbs was terrifying. "I don't think these guys will be bringing an army."

Phil stared at me through rheumy eyes. The bottle of booze on the table was a third empty, and I wondered if he'd just opened it. "Can't be too careful."

I'd say bringing more weapons into the situation was care*less*, but it wasn't my child being hunted. "Hopefully, they'll catch these guys before anything really bad happens."

"You've always been an optimist, Benjamin. That's been a big part of your problem. Things are going to shit, and the quicker you realize that, the better you can plan for it."

I didn't need one of Uncle Phil's anti-pep talks right now. I filled him in on what Pudding said. He simply shrugged.

"We're going to talk to Finn, if that's okay."

Uncle Phil's gaze returned to the back lawn. He picked up his glass with one hand and waved the other in the air, over his shoulder, dismissing us.

Vell and I left Phil to wallow while we went to see Finn. Through the kitchen and butler's pantry, through the formal dining room, to a rear staircase. This one was normal, could have been in any old house, while the staircase in the foyer was one of those double curvy ones that met at the top, like from *Gone With the Wind*. I'm sure it had a distinct name, but I sure didn't know it.

"Servant's stairs," Vell said. "Classy."

"This house was built about thirty years ago," I said.

"Even better." Vell had a way of making his point with a scalpel, which I admired greatly.

We found Finn in his childhood bedroom, lying on his bed, watching something on his tablet. Just like I usually found him back at the motel. I guessed when you didn't have any friends in town and two guys were trying to kill you, there weren't a lot of options. At least he lowered the tablet when we entered his room. "Hey." Listless, but not quite as bad as his father.

His room looked the same as it did the last time I was there, probably about ten years ago. Even the plastic ping-pong tournament trophy was still on his bookshelf. "How are you holding up?" I asked.

"I just wish it would end, one way or the other. I'm sick of being a prisoner."

"I can only imagine." I stepped over to the window, looked out. It was the same view of the back yard Phil had, only from a higher vantage point. "Maybe you could sit outside, get some sun and fresh air."

"They said I'd be too vulnerable. As if there are snipers just waiting to pluck me off." Finn snorted.

CHAPTER THIRTY-TWO

"Actually…we, uh…" My voice vibrated, and I trailed off.

Finn sat up, as I'm sure he heard alarm bells go off in my tone. "What?"

"Go ahead, Vell. Tell him."

Vell shot me a look, then cleared his throat. "Don't know why I have to be the bearer of bad news, but okay. We talked to a guy I know. A guy who's plugged in. Says these two guys know your name. Where you work. Almost certainly know where your father lives, where you are now. And they're coming for you."

Vell didn't mince any words.

"Of course, they are. I figured it was just a matter of time," Finn said. "It'll be like the shootout at the OK Corral. I forget, who won that? The good guys or the bad guys?"

I didn't remember, either. "There's not going to be any shooting. This is merely a precaution. To ensure your safety."

"My mother is packing her bags and going to visit her sister in Miami. I think she's got the right idea."

"We've been through this. These guys won't give up looking for you just because you leave the zip code. And here, you're protected."

Finn nodded. "I know. I know. I know. They'll only give up looking for me after they've found and disposed of me. If anyone wants to know, I'm a size eleven in cement overshoes. I understand they usually run a little big."

"I'd tell you to cheer up, but I know you won't. At least not until this is over. I do want you to know that Vell and I—and Lia—are doing what we can to help catch these guys. You're not alone in this, okay?"

"If you know what's best for you, you'll both leave me alone and never come around again. I'm bad news, bad luck, and bad company." He picked up his tablet again. "I love you, Mess. Take care, okay?"

On our way out, we said goodbye to Uncle Phil, who didn't even acknowledge us, and then we passed Aunt Vera in the driveway as she was getting into a Town Car on the way to Dulles Airport. "Goodbye, Mess. Goodbye, Vell. Take care of my two guys, okay?"

I assured her we would, not because I thought we stood a decent chance, but because comforting her with what she wanted to hear was the right thing to do. She was family, after all.

It wasn't hard to see where Finn picked up his habit of running from trouble.

Chapter Thirty-Three

The next morning, I woke up early. Alone. And sad. And hungry.

When I'd gotten home last night, I wanted some companionship, so I'd called Lia and invited her over. She was too tired. Then I thought about Finn's situation, and that bummed me out, but when I went to the mini-fridge to try to boost my spirits with some Ho-Ho's, I was plum out.

Six hours of sleep hadn't made me any less lonely, sad, or hungry.

I got dressed and trudged over to Sandy's to address the easiest malady to cure. She was opening up her place just as I got there.

"Hey, Mess. Haven't seen you in a couple of days. Everything going all right?" Sandy said, as she pushed open the front door and flipped the CLOSED sign to OPEN.

"What's the polar opposite of all right?" I asked.

"This have to do with Finn?"

"Yep."

"Come on back and talk to me while I get things set up."

I followed her back into the kitchen. Spotless. Everything in its place and not a crumb to be seen. Exactly what I'd expect from a Navy vet.

She slipped on an apron and tucked her hair inside a baseball cap with the Navy insignia on it. "I remember when you two would come in here. Coupla twenty-somethings with ferocious hangovers, the kind you can only have when you're young like that. Still managed to devour plenty of pancakes. You both liked to act tough, but underneath you were marshmallows." Sandy went to the fridge and started pulling things out as she spoke. "That was not long before Finn took off. I knew he was gay, and I knew Phil wouldn't approve."

"You knew?"

"I did. Pretty obvious, if you were paying attention. Not that I blame you for not knowing; you were just a kid, too. At the time, I thought changing venues wasn't such a bad idea. Move someplace else, find yourself, mature, then come back all grown up. Seems like Finn had a little trouble with everything but the moving someplace else part. But you know what? He's still the same guy underneath all those bad experiences, and you're doing the right thing, sticking by him and helping like you are. You're a good man, Mess Hopkins. Yes, you are."

"If this is how you treat all your customers, I bet you get a lot of great tips."

"I only treat the ones I love like this." Sandy stopped fussing with her feed prep for a moment and faced me. "Let me know what I can do to help, okay?"

"I appreciate that, I really do. Right now, I need some food. I'll take a bagel with peanut butter. And put it in on my tab, okay?"

"Coming right up." Sandy winked at me. "I'll give myself a good tip, too."

I took the food back to my room, and when I was done, my hunger was satiated, but I was still lonely and sad. I thought about ditching all my self-directed responsibility and asking Sandy if she wanted to play hooky. Get Crystal to mind the restaurant for the day. Go downtown and walk along the Mall. Check out a Smithsonian museum. Maybe stroll through an art gallery or two.

But my sense of duty was too strong. I cared for my family's welfare, even if they annoyed the hell out of me at times. Most times, even. Right now, Finn had few advocates, and he'd been forced, basically, to return to the nest. The same nest he felt the need to escape from six years ago.

Six years.

Six years of living on the streets. Hustling. Often not knowing where your next meal was coming from. Finn hadn't offered up any details, and I didn't feel like it was my right to ask. Surely, there must have been stretches where he'd had a job, rented an apartment, existed as a functional member of society. Hopefully, those times had encompassed the vast majority of those six years.

But I'd been led to believe by Finn himself that for some portion of that time, he'd been living on the streets, literally. Under highway bridges, using cardboard appliance boxes for shelter. Eating out of dumpsters, strung out on who knew what.

Every time I thought about living like that—existing, to be more accurate— my stomach twisted into knots, and I felt nauseated. And every time I thought about what Finn's been through, I admired his perseverance as much as I hated his inability to seek his family out—seek me out—to help him in his dire moments. If he would have called, I would have been on the next plane out to wherever he was, no questions asked. Why were people so self-destructive?

* * *

Most of the people I offered rooms to stayed for a night or two, then moved on, never to be heard from again, at least not by me. A few thanked me, but more often than not, they were too preoccupied with whatever terrible situation sent them my way. And I was fine with that. I understood, and I certainly hadn't embarked on my mission with the goal of getting thanked. Knowing I'd helped in whatever way I could was thanks enough.

Once in a while, though, I would hear from someone who had managed to overcome their situation. A text. An email. A phone call saying they'd landed a job or found an apartment or made the break from a bad relationship. Those happy updates reminded me that I did make a difference in people's lives, and being human, that buoyed my spirits.

I decided to take a drive.

I pulled up in front of Rosie's house about ten minutes later. She and Norma Rae happened to be sitting on the front porch. When they saw me, they waved me up.

Norma Rae tipped her head at me and mumbled something, but her mouth was full, and I couldn't quite make it out. She had a muffin the size of a grapefruit on her plate and a lot of crumbs on her blouse.

"Hello, Mess," Rosie said. "What brings you this way?"

"Just thought I'd come by to see how things were going."

"Have a seat." Rosie pointed to a beach chair out on the front lawn. "Can I get you some tea? Something to eat?"

"No, thanks. I can't stay." I glanced around the neighborhood, the complete opposite of Webster Claypool's. The houses were small and close together, and from where I stood, I could see half a dozen people, puttering in their yards or walking their dogs. The cars in the driveways—no garages here— were old and utilitarian. But overall, I didn't think the people here were markedly less happy than those in Oakton, just had different challenges to contend with.

"Well, we're doing fine, aren't we, Mom?" Rosie said.

Norma Rae swallowed a mouthful of muffin. "Yes, we are. Thank you, Mess, for what you did for me. For us."

"You're welcome," I said.

"We seem to be getting along, thanks to your suggestions. Got Mom signed up for some day programs next week, in fact," Rosie said.

"I think I changed my mind about that, hon," Norma Rae said.

"What? Since when?" Rosie said. "I asked if you wanted to go, and you said yes. I already registered you and paid the money, so you can't back out now."

"I can do what I please," Norma Rae said.

"Ladies, please," I smiled, trying to exude as much peace and love as I could. "Why don't you give it a try, Norma Rae? I'm sure you'll like it. Besides, we're remodeling your room at the motel, so you can't come back. At least not for about six months."

Norma Rae frowned, and Rosie mouthed the words, *thank you*, to me. I winked back at her.

"I've got to run, but I'm glad to see things are working out. Take care and remember, be nice to each other."

"We will," they said.

As I walked to my car, I got a text from Izzy. *Need you at Phil's. ASAP.*

I started to text her back to ask what was going on, but it didn't matter. If Izzy said I was needed, I was needed. And if I didn't know the details, my ride out to McLean wouldn't be as stressful. Being needed at Uncle Phil's, ASAP, was *never* a good thing. I simply texted *ok* and ran to my car.

* * *

This time, when I got to Phil's, Rickert wasn't guarding the driveway. I drove up to the house, parked, and ran inside. Uncle Phil was in the same exact spot in the kitchen, although today, there was no booze on the table. Izzy sat across from him, worry evident on her face.

Rickert was there, too, leaning against the counter at the far side of the kitchen, near the butler's pantry. Scrolling through his phone. He nodded at me but didn't say a word.

"What's going on? Is everything okay? Something happen with Finn?" I blurted out, although I knew they'd tell me as soon as I shut up.

"Have a seat, Benjamin." Uncle Phil looked even worse than he had yesterday, and that was saying a lot. The bags under his eyes had gotten bigger and darker, the effect only exacerbated by the growing paleness of his skin. Had he eaten anything since yesterday, or had all his calories come from a bottle?

I sat.

Phil spoke loudly. "Rickert, can you give us the room?"

One of Rickert's eyebrows went up. "Sure. I've got some calls to make. I'll be out front."

He walked past us and flashed me a look I couldn't quite interpret.

After we heard the front door close, Phil stared at me blankly. "Finn's gone. Again. He snuck out sometime last night. My man didn't spot him. And neither did the cops in the patrol car. Can't rely on anybody these days."

I remembered when he would sneak out as a teenager, mostly from his stories, but there were one or two nights I accompanied him on some midnight adolescent adventures. "I guess he didn't leave a note."

"Why should he tell me where he's going? I'm only his father." Phil hiccupped. "You know, he had good credentials."

"Who did? Rickert?"

"Yes, Rickert. I put the word out on my business executive listserv. Figured they could recommend someone. Good credentials, law enforcement experience, even knew your buddy. Turned out to be worthless. Disappointing, like everyone else."

Izzy glanced my way, and she seemed terrified. She hadn't seen Uncle Phil yesterday, so she wasn't the least bit prepared for the person who sat before us now. Growing up, Phil was always the strong one. The decisive one. Sometimes bordering on being a bully, but he was never so...beaten down. So listless. So depressed. Even in those first few months after Finn ran away, he wasn't despondent. Pissed, yeah. Feeling betrayed, sure. But he was resolute. Determined to do whatever he could to find—and presumably help—Finn.

He maintained his edge, too, through the entire time Finn had been gone, and I often wondered if he treated me like a surrogate son as he nagged me to conform to his notions about running the motel. That he was transferring his anger at Finn to me. I wasn't a psychologist, but I didn't think I was too far off the mark.

I remembered the first Thanksgiving after Finn had left. The entire family had gathered here, in this very house, and we were all walking on eggshells. Uncle Phil and Aunt Vera started the meal off by trying to act as if everything was normal, like Finn was simply on a vacation somewhere, but right about the time the pumpkin pie was being served—and after a lot of wine had been consumed, Phil spouted off. Carrying on about how ungrateful Finn was, about what a terrible son he'd been, and about how he'd been a coward by running from the problem rather than facing it head-on.

Phil had been dead right on one count: Finn was certainly a runner. He'd taken off again.

"We'll track him down, Uncle Phil," I said, wholly unsure that we actually would. I'd been playing a game of Whack-A-Mole with Finn. He'd disappear, and I'd look for him, and then he'd pop up someplace, rinse and repeat. Part of me wished he had taken off for parts unknown, parts far away, for safety, but based on his mood, I think he was just tired of living on the streets. If I had to guess, I think Finn wanted to end this, one way or another.

He was too young to give up on life without a fight, especially after he'd already endured the worst of times.

"I don't know. That boy can do quite a good job of hiding when he wants to." Uncle Phil put his head down on the table, braced by his arms. My worry about him increased, if that was possible. I thought about calling Aunt Vera to come back, but although she loved him, she'd learned to cope with Finn's disappearance by escaping, and she'd never displayed the strength it took to stand up and face the darkness. Plus, I was afraid she'd say no in Phil's time of need, and that would be devastating for all involved. A spouse not having their mate's back was a form of betrayal right there, at least in my book.

Izzy pulled me aside, whispered, "What are we going to do?"

"I'm going to find Finn." I didn't want Izzy and Phil to stay here, in case the goons showed up. "Can you take him to your place? Maybe feed him?"

"I can do that, but where do you think Finn went?"

"Damned if I know. I know he's fed up with all this. And people at the end of their ropes make bad decisions. What did Rickert say before I got here?"

"Nothing. Was on his phone mostly. From what I overheard, he was telling people to let him know if Finn shows up. He does seem to be doing a bang-up job."

I always loved my sister's sarcasm. I returned to Uncle Phil. He'd closed his eyes, and I hated to disturb him, but I gently jostled his shoulder. "I'm going to talk to Rickert and then go look for Finn. Izzy's going to take you to her house, get you some food, okay?"

Phil's eyes opened slowly. "Not hungry." His eyes closed again, and he continued to talk, although most of the words were indecipherable mumbles, but I could make out a few "Rickerts" with some cuss words thrown in. I didn't blame him for his assessment of Rickert's performance.

Maybe Rickert had an idea where Finn might have gone.

I thanked Izzy—and wished her luck—then went to talk to him. He was leaning against my car, talking on the phone. I approached and stopped nearby.

Seeing me, he ended his call. "Yeah?" he snapped.

I recoiled, and he softened his tone. "Sorry. I hate screwing up. I shouldn't take it out on you." Clearly, he was pissed at himself for botching his assignment, and rightfully so. I didn't think he'd be getting a referral from Phil for his services.

"Don't worry about it. Do you have any idea where he might have gone?"

Rickert shook his head. "No. You?"

"Nope. Any idea when he snuck out?" Obviously, Rickert had fallen asleep at the wheel. I knew Finn was slippery, but this guy was supposed to be good. What was Phil getting overcharged for exactly?

"No. He didn't take a car, so he might be wandering around. Who knows? He struck me as a little…" Rickert stopped, as if just realizing this moment that Finn and I were related and had been close at one time. "I've alerted all my contacts. We'll find him and reel him back in."

"I'm going to search for him. I'll let you know if I find him. If you locate him, I trust you'll let me know, right?"

"Sure." Rickert stared at me. "Anything else?"

I knew when the conversation was over. "No. Good luck."

He'd gone back to his phone. I'd been dismissed.

Chapter Thirty-Four

From my car, I called Vell. Told him what had happened.

"Come pick me up. You can use a wingman," he said.

"You got it."

My next call went to Cesar. I told him what happened, too, and asked him to let me know if Finn showed up at the motel. I hoped he didn't, figuring the killers might have it staked out. I didn't think Finn was stupid, but I did know he was erratic and couldn't always be counted on to make rational decisions. "Is Griff around?"

"As far as I know," Cesar said.

"Thanks."

I called Griff, explained the situation, and told him I'd be swinging by after I picked up Vell. I needed him to go to Izzy's and keep an eye on things. There was no reason to think the two killers had connected Izzy to Finn—or Uncle Phil—but I wasn't about to take any chances with my sister and nieces. He asked if he should prepare for trouble, and I said he should always be prepared. He said okay but didn't go into details, and I was grateful. Some things I didn't want to know.

I also called Lia. "Hey, there."

"Hi, Mess. What's up?"

"Finn snuck out of Uncle Phil's house last night, whereabouts unknown. I'm picking up Vell, then we're going to look for him. Hopefully, we'll find him before the bad guys do."

"How can I help?"

I would have loved to have her beside me for moral support, but I had a feeling things might get sticky, or worse, and I didn't want to put her in harm's way. Vell knew what he was signing on for—Lia most likely didn't. Besides, she could help us in a way we couldn't. "Can you plug into your network of contacts? See if they mention anything out of the ordinary. It seems as if things are coming to a resolution."

"Okay. I'll let you know if I hear anything. Good luck, Mess. And stay safe."

She hung up before I could say, *I'll do my best.*

My next call went to Ostervale, and I told him what happened. "I guess your guys didn't see him sneak out, huh?"

"My guys are very good at making sure no bad guys get *in*. Not our job to make sure Finn didn't get *out*." Ostervale sighed. "I'll let my people know he's in the wind. Talk to you later."

I picked up Vell and then drove to the motel. Griff was waiting outside his room for us, a hulking man with a long beard and wild hair, wearing an old olive army fatigue jacket. I was almost positive he'd never been in the service, but with Griff, you never knew exactly what was going on.

There were a couple of noticeable bulges under his jacket. Again, I didn't ask.

He shoehorned himself into the back of my Corolla, and when I looked in the rearview mirror, I noticed he had to tilt his neck to avoid mashing his head against the car's roof. "Comfortable back there?" I asked.

"As comfortable as I get, boss. Don't worry about me."

It was out of the way, but twenty minutes later, we dropped Griff off at my sister's place, and I could cross one stressor off my list.

"Now, where?" Vell turned to face me from the passenger seat.

"I've got two places in mind. We'll start with the closer one."

It took us another twenty minutes to get to Headstomper Thorpe's home. I parked the car two feet from the iron gate and hit the intercom button. Waited for a response.

And waited. And waited.

"Any idea if they're here?" Vell asked.

"Nope. Just hoping I'm right."

I pressed the intercom again, and while I waited, I texted Finn. *I'm outside. Can you open the gate, please?*

As we sat there, I wondered how Thorpe would react to me returning. Had Finn even filled him in on the latest turn of events? That Finn had been identified and was squarely in these killers' crosshairs?

Of course, they might not even be here.

Then the gate buzzed and opened inward.

I drove up the drive and parked on the side so that I didn't block any of the three garage bays. Before we got out, I turned to Vell. "Okay, listen. This guy's a mixed martial artist, and I've gotten the impression that, while he doesn't hate me, he doesn't really like me. Let's just say he tolerates me because he likes Finn. I'm sure he will not be pleased that we, uh, dropped in today, but once I explain the reason for our visit, I'm hoping he'll realize we're here to help and that he'll accept it in the spirit that it's offered. So what I guess I'm trying to say is—"

Vell interrupted me. "You're trying to tell me to be cool and wait for you to let me know what I should do."

I stared at him for a beat. "Yeah. That."

"I think I know the score," Vell said.

"Okay, then. Let's go."

We got out, and when we reached the front door, it opened, as if there had been an electric eye activated when we approached. Thorpe poked his head around the edge of the door. "Come in."

We stepped into the foyer, and Thorpe closed the door behind him.

"Is Finn here this time?"

Thorpe sighed. "He is. But can you do me a favor? Try not to get him riled up, okay? He's been through a lot, and having him more stressed out than he already is won't be good for anyone." He appraised Vell. "Who's your friend?"

I introduced Vell, and Thorpe nodded. "Come on, this way."

Our trio traipsed through Thorpe's home, but instead of winding up in the solarium, he took us to a study even larger than Uncle Phil's. This one seemed clean and bright, whereas Phil's was dark and stodgy. Although they both owned mini-mansions with all the accouterments, Thorpe's seemed a whole lot more inviting. I guessed that wasn't too surprising.

In the middle of the room, Finn sat in a modern, ergonomic chair. What was most shocking was that he was reading a book. Or at least it looked like he had been reading. Right now, he was staring at us.

"Hey," I said. "We were in the neighborhood, so we thought we'd drop in."

Finn smiled at that, and I wondered if Thorpe had given him something to settle him down. "Pull up a chair. We were just about to get started with a read-along."

I didn't know if he was serious—about me pulling up a chair—but I did anyway, dragging over one from across the room. I nodded at Vell and Thorpe. "Do you guys mind if I have a few minutes alone with Finn?"

Vell said sure, but it took several more seconds before Thorpe answered. "Okay. Fine." They left, and I wondered if Thorpe was going to show Vell his trophy room. I mean, I would have if I had any trophies.

"Why did you take off, man? You had a bodyguard protecting you."

"It felt like I was in prison. With an SOB for a warden."

I knew Uncle Phil could be an SOB, but he seemed so weak now. Like an old man. "He was on your case?"

"Of course. Some things don't change. He was criticizing my choices, moaning about how I destroyed his life, and Mom's. As if this was all about him. I'm the one he couldn't accept. I'm his son, and he's ashamed of me. I can't help who I am, you know. In fact, I've got his genes."

"You're not wrong."

"I know that. And you know that. But he is a bitter old man. And I told him so. Told him if I had any other father, I would never have taken off. Told him if he hadn't been an alcoholic, I wouldn't have had my own substance issues." Finn laughed, but it was a thin, hollow sound. "He didn't like that very much."

"I'm sorry, Finn. You didn't deserve the treatment he gave you back then."

"And my mom? I love her to pieces, but she lives in his shadow, runs at the slightest hint of a wisp of a suggestion of unpleasantness. Always did. Maybe if she stuck up for me when I was a teen, he would have realized what a bigoted ass he was."

I doubted that. In my experience, most assholes didn't realize they were assholes. "Unfortunately, we've got more pressing problems now. I was thinking about asking Detective Ostervale to put you in some kind of protective custody, at least until these guys are caught. But I figured I'd clear it with you first. You know, considering how you always seem to disappear."

"I learned that from my mother, I guess." He pondered my suggestion. "I hate being confined, Mess. More than any rational person, I'm sure. I always need to know I have an escape hatch, and I'm afraid that if the cops start guarding me, I won't have that. I'll literally go crazy. No. No cops. I don't trust them."

I doubted Finn would *literally* go crazy, but I didn't debate him. His point was well-taken. Maybe it was better that nobody knew where Finn was. At Uncle Phil's, we figured the killers knew he might be there. If the cops took him to some undisclosed location, the cops would know Finn's location, and leaks were always possible. I think it was a safe bet that there was no way anybody would connect Finn with Thorpe.

The door to the study opened, and Thorpe walked in. "We might have a problem."

"What?"

"The motion detector alarm went off. Back yard. I didn't see anything, but who knows?"

"Maybe an animal?"

"Maybe. But we have the sensitivity set pretty low. It usually ignores squirrels and smaller animals."

"False alarm?" My insides churned.

Thorpe shrugged. "Ordinarily, I'd ignore it, but under the circumstances…"

Finn popped out of his chair and began pacing. "It's them, isn't it. Well, good. Let 'em come. I'm tired of hiding."

I wasn't sure I agreed with the *let 'em come* part. I'd brought Vell in case there was trouble, but now that the two killers—no doubt armed killers—

had possibly showed up, I realized I'd made a giant mistake. My friend and I were no match for assassins with guns.

"Let's get out of here," I said.

"Hang on. Maybe that's what they want," Thorpe said. "Let's sit tight. I asked Vell to watch out the back, and I'm going to see if the system is working properly. We wouldn't want to panic over a short circuit in the alarms."

He rushed off, leaving me and Finn standing there, in the hallway. "Come on. Let's find Vell."

He was in the kitchen, sitting on a stool, staring out the back window. "I guess you heard," he said without turning around.

"Yeah. See anything?"

"Trees. Grass. Top of the neighbor's house. No killers." Vell glanced at us, then whipped his head around to stare out the window. "Probably nothing."

"Yeah. Thorpe went to go check the unit." I clapped him on the back. "Let me know if you need to take a break."

"I'm good," Vell said.

And he was. He could sit there for hours if we needed him to without uttering a single word of complaint.

"Don't worry. It's probably just something wonky with the alarm." However, the longer it took Thorpe to investigate, the more doubtful I got. I mean, it would be a big coincidence for the alarm to malfunction at the exact moment we needed it most, right?

Something beeped, and the power went out.

Chapter Thirty-Five

I stepped out into the hall and flipped a couple of light switches, trying to confirm it was a house-wide outage and not just a tripped circuit breaker. No lights flickered on. The sinking feeling in my gut intensified. Had Thorpe turned off the power to examine the alarm system? Or had something more nefarious occurred? I hoped for the former, but my innards were fixated on the latter.

I returned to the kitchen.

"I can see lights on next door, so it's not a neighborhood outage," Vell said. "Any idea what's going on?"

"Nope."

"Where's Thorpe?" Finn asked.

That was the question. "Not sure." I addressed Finn. "You stick with Vell. I'm going to look for him."

Finn started to complain, but my expression cut him off. I knew those two didn't get along so great, but I didn't want Finn tagging along. He was bound to be more of a drag than a help.

"I'll be back soon."

I left the kitchen and searched for a stairway down to the basement. After opening a few closet doors, I finally found the down staircase. I flipped the light switch out of habit—obviously, nothing happened—then pulled out my phone in case I needed the flashlight. There was a dim glow coming from somewhere, which led me to believe there were windows or perhaps even a walkout.

I debated calling out to Thorpe, but I'd seen plenty of horror movies and didn't want to warn the monster I was coming. I crept down the stairs, gripping the handrail. I didn't have any sort of weapon, so I wasn't sure what I'd do if the killers attacked. Try to blind them with the light from my phone?

I reached the bottom of the stairs without incident. Without hearing any noise or sensing any movement, either. On the other side of the large room, two sets of French doors led out to the pool deck. They provided enough illumination for me to survey the area. A pool table on one side, a ping-pong table on the other. Along one wall stood a row of vintage arcade games. With the power out, their usual bright, motion-packed displays were dead.

I hoped those machines were the only dead things down here.

I remained at the foot of the stairs, trying to determine the location of the utility equipment. There was almost always a separate room for the electrical box, the furnace, hot water heater, and whatever other stuff a fancy mansion like this might need to provide all the latest luxury necessities.

There was a door in the far corner, opposite the French doors. That had to be it, unless there was another room, directly behind the staircase, which I couldn't see from where I stood.

Alarmingly, there was no sign of Thorpe.

I crept along the wall, away from the doors and the light. If someone had infiltrated Thorpe's house, I didn't want to make myself a target. There *was* a door behind the staircase, and since I was right there, I figured I'd give it a try first.

Bracing myself as if someone—or something—might come leaping out, I yanked the door open quickly. I exhaled when nothing sprang my way. Only storage.

I took a deep breath and continued inching along the back wall. Knowing that the alarm system went out, followed by the power, conjured up all kinds of horrible scenarios, and the fact we hadn't heard from Thorpe in at least ten minutes was fueling my fear.

I finally made it to the door, and I flung it open. It was indeed the utility room. And it was dark. "Thorpe? You in here?" I was hesitant to enter—too many places for a bad guy to hide.

Thorpe didn't answer.

I turned my flashlight on and scanned the room. Two hot water heaters. A furnace. A separate air filter. Some kind of water treatment apparatus. A free-standing freezer. Next to the freezer was an electrical box, and next to that were two tall stacks of electronic components housed on a rack system. Probably the alarm and some video equipment, and who knew what else.

I debated my next move. I could stand there, out in the relative open, or I could enter the utility room and take a closer look. If nobody had jumped out at me yet, did that mean nobody would?

I decided to forge ahead. If something happened, I could always scream, and Vell would be down there in less than a minute. I might be severely injured by then, but how long did it take for a person to bleed out, anyway?

Letting my phone light the way, I crossed the room to the electrical box. I wasn't an electrician by any means, but I ran a motel, so we experienced the occasional electrical problem. Cesar usually handled it—frankly, he handled all the important stuff—but I often held the flashlight and did the cussing. From what I could tell here, though, the whole house power switch was ON, and it seemed as if none of the breakers had tripped.

I moved over to the first bank of electronics. One of the chassis covers had been removed, probably Thorpe looking to see if something was awry. I had no idea, of course, what the deal was, and with the power out—and no discernible backup supply functioning—it would be impossible to run even rudimentary diagnostics.

Then a chilling thought struck me. What if an intruder had disabled the alarm system and had hidden down here, waiting for Thorpe to investigate? Had that intruder somehow *disabled* Thorpe, too?

I left the utility room quickly.

But where next? Back upstairs or outside? Obviously, I hadn't passed Thorpe, and unless he'd come upstairs a while ago and not told us—not likely—he must have left the basement through the French doors. Either under his own power or someone else's.

My decision became clear.

Staying in the shadows as much as I could, I edged my way along the wall toward the back door. When I reached it, I peered out at the pool deck and the pool, the green grass of the yard beyond. A gargantuan grill and complete outdoor kitchen occupied the right side of the pool area. A bar counter wrapped around a portion of the kitchen area. Could the intruder be crouched behind it, waiting to attack?

One way to find out.

I eased open the door and slipped through the crack. Tiptoed around the bar and ventured a quick glance behind it. Nothing.

I straightened. No sound. No movement. It was as if I was in some kind of weird dream. On a typical day, the birds and the insects would be chirping and buzzing, but now, everything was eerily silent. All I could hear was my heart thumping in my chest. And boy, was it chugging along.

I tried to think things through. I was still underneath the awning that protected the kitchen area, so I was out of Vell's sight. If he'd seen someone in the back yard, Thorpe or intruder, wouldn't he have come rushing out? Or alerted someone, at the very least?

And the ultimate question: was something really going on? Or had my imagination taken a few relatively harmless facts and spun them into a wild tale of terror?

"Hey," someone whispered at me.

I turned toward the voice and spotted Thorpe behind a large bush about five yards away, motioning me over. He was obviously hiding from someone, and from his orientation, it seemed that person was deeper in the back yard.

I hustled over, and he pulled me down next to him. "Stay quiet, and keep hidden," he whispered as he let go. "I saw one of them back there. In the yard. Pretty sure he knows we're here. A stand-off, I'd say."

"Do you have a gun?" I whispered back.

"Don't need one."

A stand-off? The killer was most likely armed, and we were not. Not sure I liked our odds. "I'm calling the cops," I said, pulling out my phone.

Thorpe covered my hand with his, then slowly pried the phone from my hands. I tried to resist but quickly realized I had no chance, so I relinquished it. He stuffed it into his pocket. "This is *my* home. I'll handle this. You just stay here, okay? And be quiet." He duckwalked away before I could protest.

I looked over my shoulder to see if Vell could spot me out the back window, a story above. Nope. I was clear of the awning, but the angle between my hiding place and the windows was too severe. And I doubted Vell would see Thorpe, because he'd gone right, squeezing between the hedge line and the neighbor's fence.

I did what Thorpe told me to do. I stayed put and kept quiet.

I barely had enough time to worry before I heard shouting. Thorpe's, followed by someone else's. I jutted my head around the bush and saw Thorpe tackle the tall, bald dude, out in the middle of the lawn. They began to wrestle, and even though the killer still had a gun in one hand, I figured he didn't stand a chance in hell against an MMA champ.

I was right. Thorpe grabbed the guy's arm and twisted it until the gun dropped, then kneed him in the gut, bent his arm backward, and tossed the man to the ground. Then Thorpe stomped on the guy's knee. I could *almost* hear the knee crack into pieces from where I stood, but I could *definitely* hear the killer's screams of pain.

Thorpe bent over to pick up the weapon, and a gunshot rang out.

Chapter Thirty-Six

Thorpe yelled and clutched his side, going down into the grass. Five seconds later, another boom echoed.

The tall, bald guy on the ground yelled and then went silent. Lifeless. Someone had shot and killed him.

I glanced back at the house but didn't see anything. Looked back at Thorpe and, thankfully, he had managed to crawl out of the line of fire, seeking cover behind a tree.

It took me a moment to realize what was happening. There were *two* killers hunting Finn, and I think the other one had made his presence known. First trying to kill Thorpe, then trying to nail his buddy, probably to clean things up. So where was he now?

In the house? With Vell and Finn?

I focused on Thorpe. I could see his legs poking out from under the tree, and they weren't moving. I desperately needed to check on Finn, but I couldn't just leave Thorpe, not after he'd been shot.

Of course, there was someone still lurking about with a gun and no hesitation to use it. I took the same route Thorpe had—between the hedge and the fence—toward the back half of the lawn. The passage was tight, and branches clawed at me, but it was better than being a target out in the open.

The hedge thinned out, allowing me to pick up speed. I hit the brakes right before I almost tripped over Thorpe. I dropped to my knees. "You okay?"

"Sure. I've been hurt worse than this in half my matches." The lower third of his shirt had turned red with blood.

"Where's my phone?" I asked.

"Pocket?"

I patted his pocket. Nothing. Patted his other one. No phone. "Not here."

"Must have fallen out."

I gazed out on the lawn but didn't see the phone. I considered crawling out there, figured it wasn't worth the risk. "How bad is it?"

"Pretty bad. But I'll be okay. Who shot us?"

"Don't know."

"Go get help. I'll be fine here." Thorpe kept his hand pressed against his side. I couldn't tell if he was still bleeding; there was so much blood already soaking his clothes.

"You sure you want me to leave you?"

Thorpe forced a smile. "Yeah. I'm not going anywhere."

"Okay. I'll go call 911. Keep pressure on the wound." I felt bad about leaving him, but there wasn't anything I could do for him here. I needed to summon help.

As I started back, I heard another gunshot. Had they found Finn?

I scrambled through the narrow gap between the bushes and the fence as fast as I possibly could, doing my best to ignore the scratches and scrapes. When I emerged near the outdoor kitchen area, I stopped to scan the area, making sure nobody had materialized.

All clear.

I raced into the house, through the lower level, and up the stairs. At the top of the staircase, I almost collided with Vell and Finn.

The cavalry had arrived. Rickert stood next to them. He moved slightly to reveal the body of the second killer on the floor behind him, staring at the ceiling with unblinking eyes.

"What the—"

"Got him before he got Finn," Rickert said.

"Holy shit, are you all right?" I stared at Finn, and except for the look of abject panic on his face, he seemed okay. Physically, anyway.

"We're fine," Rickert barked. "But we need to get Finn out of here."

I took a second, trying to catch my breath. "Yeah, sure. I gotta call 911 first. Thorpe's lying in the back yard. Shot. Bleeding badly."

"Already done. The EMTs should be here any second." Rickert glanced around. "But we need to get going. Right now."

"Why? The killers are both dead."

"You don't think these two morons are acting on their own, do you? Someone else is in charge of this operation. Finn's still in trouble. Even more, really, because we don't know who's after him."

"We can't leave Thorpe alone," I said.

"I'll stay with him," Vell said.

"What if *another* guy with a gun shows up?" I asked.

"Don't worry, I'll be careful," Vell waved his hands. "Get going. They're after Finn, not me."

"Guys, we can have a tea party later," Rickert said. "Right now, let's move."

I bumped fists with Vell. "Be safe."

"Likewise," Vell said.

"Let's go," Rickert said. He ushered Finn and me out of the house, pausing at the front door. "Okay, we make a beeline for my vehicle. You two go first. Keep your heads down and run. I'll bring up the rear and be on the lookout. First one to the end hits the switch to open the gate. Then race for the car and hop in." He drew his gun. "Ready?"

Two nods.

"Let's do it." Rickert flung the door open, and we shot through it. Finn took the lead, but I was right on his heels. I assumed Rickert was behind us, although I was too busy trying not to trip over something as I tore down the driveway. Along with not getting shot, of course.

Finn smacked the switch, and the gate rolled open. We were through the opening in no time, and we piled into Rickert's car, and ten seconds later, we were squealing tires as we rocketed away.

"Everyone okay?" Rickert called out from the driver's seat.

"Okay," I said from the passenger seat.

"Okay," Finn said from the back. The car smelled like someone had been smoking a pack of Marlboros.

"Who shot the first assassin?"

"Must have been his buddy. More money if you don't have to split the contract. Luckily, I came in when I did to take care of him. But *I'm* paid to make sure Finn here stays safe, and there's no way I'm risking sticking around. In case the person behind all the mayhem is lurking about, making sure things get done properly."

"Where are we going now?" I asked.

"Safe house. Not too far."

"Maybe you should take us to the police. Ostervale will make sure nothing happens to us."

Rickert glanced at us in the rearview mirror. "I haven't mentioned this yet, because I don't have any proof. But I think there's a mole in the police department. I feel a whole lot better handling this myself right now. When this is over, I'll go to the cops and explain the shooting. In my years on the force, I never even drew my weapon, and now this. I had no choice, but it still feels awful."

I could only imagine. "I don't know. I think we should get the cops involved sooner rather than later."

"First of all, the cops are probably already at Thorpe's, and Vell and Thorpe can explain what happened. Second of all, your uncle agrees with me, that we should keep Finn safe on our own, without involving the cops at this point."

"You talked to him?"

"Sure. He's the one writing the check; he's the one calling the shots."

Based on how Uncle Phil seemed a few hours ago, I found it hard to believe he was calling any shots. Having a bad apple in the police department would explain some things, like how they were never quite able to catch the two guys. I made a note to bring it up to Ostervale the next time I spoke to him. "What kind of safe house is this?"

"The safe kind. Look, I've been doing this for a while. We go off the grid, let the good cops clean things up, then we can all get back to our lives, okay?"

The fact that Rickert made sense highlighted how crazy our situation was. "Fine. You and Finn go into hiding. I'll connect with Vell and Lia. See if we can figure out who hired those goons."

"I think you've misunderstood slightly," Rickert said. "All three of us are going to the safe house. The killers know you're related to Finn, and they're not above using you to get to him."

"What are you talking about?"

"You're not safe walking around in public. It's possible they'll try to capture you to trade for Finn."

"That's ridiculous."

"Maybe so, but these guys are ruthless. They'll stop at nothing to get what they want. And I don't have to tell you that if they do catch you, they won't be letting you go. Not after you've seen them and can identify them." Rickert paused to let that all sink in. "Relax, with any luck, this will be over in a few hours."

Ten minutes later, Rickert turned off the main drag down a side street, where the houses were farther apart and dumpier. Another several minutes and we were out of the residential neighborhood and into some kind of light industrial district.

We drove through a vast area of warehouses and shuttered manufacturing facilities, riddled with condemned buildings. We didn't see another vehicle. I didn't know if where we were going was safe, but it sure was isolated. Most of the DC area had been built up, but there were still a fair number of pockets that hadn't yet been turned into expensive houses or fancy condos.

I had no doubt this tract of land was on some developer's radar.

We turned into one of the large parking lots and drove to the far end of a row of squat, ugly buildings. Rickert backed into a parking space in front of the last unit and killed the engine.

"This is it? Where's the house?"

"Safe house is just an expression."

"More like a safe *ware*house," I mumbled.

"Come on, get out."

Rickert and I got out. Finn didn't. He remained rooted in the back seat. I waved him out, but he shook his head and turned to look away from me. Having Finn in one of his moods was all we needed. I opened his door.

"Finn? Come on, let's go inside." Rickert had stopped by the unit's door and was staring at us.

Slowly, Finn brought his head around. "Why? So I can wait for the slaughter in some sketchy warehouse? I've been in too many places like this, and I swore I wouldn't ever die in one. At least at Tim's, I could spend my last hours in a hot tub or in his fabulous bed with those fabulous sheets."

"That's not an option anymore, and you know it. Maybe you can get back to it. But staying in the car isn't going to help. It's only going to aggravate Rickert, and right now, he's the one giving the orders. And rightfully so. There are people trying to kill you, or have you forgotten. They shot Thorpe, remember?"

Tears began to drip down Finn's cheeks. "I know, Mess. I know."

"He'll be fine. Rickert called 911 before we left."

"He hates me now. I know it. This is all my fault."

"It's the killers' fault." I reached for his arm. "Come on. You're not going to die here. I mean, look where we are. In the middle of absolute nowhere." I pulled, and after a moment of resistance, he yielded and climbed out of the car. "Now, let's try to make the best of this, okay?"

He didn't answer, just trudged alongside me as we went inside.

Rickert flipped on the lights. One large space with a couple of tiny offices in the back. I don't know what it used to be, but now it was depressing. A makeshift kitchen—mini-fridge, utility sink, microwave—took up one corner. A door at the other end probably led to a bathroom. I put the over/under on us going crazy here at about five hours, if we were lucky.

"This is your home for the immediate future," Rickert said. "Make yourselves comfortable. There's some food and drink in the fridge, and there's a crapper in the back. There's also a bed in one of those offices if anyone needs to lie down." He said this last part, staring at Finn. "But there's only one way in or out, so don't get any ideas about fleeing, Finn. Not this time."

Rickert fetched himself a soda from the fridge. Popped it open, then sat at a square card table set up near the door. He pulled out his phone and started scrolling, now in full babysitter mode.

Finn and I were on our own. Unfortunately, there wasn't much to explore.

The main room was empty. No TV. No bookshelf. No slick coffee table magazines, which made sense because there was no coffee table.

There were about ten mismatched chairs scattered around the room.

I reached for my phone, then realized it was probably still lying in the middle of Thorpe's back yard.

"Can I borrow your phone, Finn?"

"Don't have it. The prison warden took it." He tipped his head at Rickert.

I walked over to where he sat. "Can I have Finn's phone?"

He looked up at me. "It's in a drawer at Phil's house."

Figured. "May I borrow yours then?"

"No. Can't let you tell anyone your whereabouts."

"I don't even know where I am," I said.

He checked his phone. "Service is spotty anyway."

"Then how are we going to know what's going on?"

He shrugged. "If it's that important, someone will drive out and update us."

"That's crazy." And it was crazy. A bad feeling started to grow in my gut.

"That's the way it is." Rickert glared at me. "Anything else?"

"Who is this someone that's gonna drive out here?"

"The less you know, the better."

I felt like I was in a B-movie from the 70s. "I think I'm going to get some fresh air."

"I don't think that's a good idea."

"I don't care what you think." I started for the door, and Rickert jumped from his chair. He drew a gun from a holster on his hip and held it at his side.

Chapter Thirty-Seven

"Nobody's leaving until we get the all clear, okay? It's not safe." Rickert glared at me, gun in hand.

I glanced over at Finn, and he was transfixed by our interaction. "You think we're in danger, way out here? I thought this was a *safe* place."

"Protecting you two clowns is my job, and I'm going to do my job as I see fit. And if I have to shoot you to prevent you from getting killed, then I'll do it."

So Rickert did have a sense of humor.

"Now, sit down and shut up, okay? With a little luck, we'll all be home and snug in our beds real soon."

Rickert scooted his chair over about five feet so it blocked the door, then he returned to whatever game he was playing on his phone. I gestured to Finn to join me in one of the back offices. If Rickert minded that we'd left his sight, he didn't say a word.

A Spartan would have described the bedroom as spare. Rickert said there was a bed, but it was the kind of plastic chaise lounge you'd find at Walmart. A folding TV tray table stood next to the head of the bed. A battered metal desk had been pushed into one corner.

Finn plopped down on the chaise, and it almost buckled underneath him. I perched on the edge of the desk.

"Sorry about all this," I whispered. Someone had removed the door to the office, and Rickert could probably hear us if we spoke at normal volume.

"Not your fault," Finn whispered back. "I'm outstanding at getting into trouble on my own."

"Something doesn't smell right here," I said. "Do you think Rickert shot the guy on the back lawn?"

"I don't know. He said he shot the guy in the house, so maybe."

"Why would he shoot Thorpe, too?"

"Maybe he was aiming for the bad guy and missed."

Possibly. But Rickert had been awfully quick to clear us out of there. Maybe he didn't want to stick around for the EMTs and the cops because *he* was the mysterious shooter.

I lowered my voice as much as I could. "I'm not sure Rickert is on our side. When you were with him at your father's, did he do or say anything that seemed unusual?"

Finn paused so long I thought maybe he'd nodded off. "Seems sketchy, I'll give you that."

"I think we're best served by getting away from here. And from him. Take our chances elsewhere. We need to come up with a plan."

I stood and began searching through the desk, looking for something that might help us escape. Was it too much to ask for someone to have left behind a knife? Or at least a very sharp letter opener?

I pulled open a couple of the top drawers. Empty. I moved on to the lower, file-sized drawers. The first one was empty, too. The second one had a tangle of papers caught in the drawer roller mechanism. I pulled them out and scanned them.

Some old memos about permitting issues. Not important. But they were on Claypool Development letterhead. Was that important?

Was this a Claypool property? An old office, perhaps?

Why had Rickert brought us to a place owned by Claypool Development?

Could it be a coincidence? That firm owned a lot of area properties. It wouldn't be so unusual for them to have owned this warehouse building. Maybe they owned the entire industrial park and had plans to develop it. Would make perfect sense.

But...my mind started to spin conspiracy theories. My pulse raced as a crazy scenario gelled in my mind until it maybe wasn't so crazy.

Was Rickert working for Claypool Development? Had he been working with the two killers? He'd mentioned that they hadn't been operating on their own. Was Rickert the brains behind the murder? Had he directed those two goons to kill Claypool?

Had he killed Claypool to cover up some kind of gross corporate negligence that would bring the whole company down? Or maybe some kind of blackmail scheme gone bad? A dozen other reasons sprang to mind about why someone working for Claypool would want the CEO dead.

All those unsubstantiated guesses fell by the wayside as our predicament crystallized. If Rickert was indeed the man behind the curtain, and he killed his two heavies to keep them quiet, then I knew what was in store for me and Finn. I could worry about all the rest later.

I had no tangible evidence that Rickert was involved. Nothing solid. But I remembered Lia's passionate declaration that when she found herself needing to make a tough decision, she always went with her gut.

Right now, my gut was telling me that Rickert was a rat.

"We need to act, now." I moved closer to Finn and lowered my voice until I could barely hear it myself. "It's two against one. We need to try to overpower him." Difficult to tell what Finn was capable of. He'd probably been in more than his fair share of scrapes over the years, but he was in such a depressed state right now, who knew if he could even run, if we got the chance.

"He's got a gun," Finn said.

"We'll have to catch him by surprise." I examined Finn's face. "You think you're up to it?"

After a long moment, he nodded.

"How about this? One of us distracts him; the other gets the weapon. Once we have it, we tie him up at gunpoint. Get the car keys, and we're gone."

"How are we going to distract him?" Finn's voice wobbled.

When Finn and I played backyard football as kids, we used to draw up the plays on our chests in the huddle. I did that now. "Here's Rickert." I pointed to the middle of my chest. "And here we are." I tapped my stomach in two spots. "You go here, and I'll go this way." I diagrammed our movements on my shirt as I explained, then repeated it. "Understand?"

Finn nodded, and I hoped he grasped what we were trying to do better than he did some of the football plays, back in the day.

"Okay. Let's go in there. Wait until he's engrossed in his phone, and then we'll make our move."

We returned to the main room, trying to look as nonchalant as possible. Inside, my heart was banging a percussive rhythm against my rib cage, and I knew Finn must have felt the same, if not worse. I couldn't remember many times in my life when I was seriously worried about getting killed, and I hoped this would be the last—but not because I actually *got* killed, of course.

As we planned, Finn walked toward Rickert's right, and I drifted toward the mini-fridge on his left.

Rickert had glanced at us when we'd reentered the room, but then he'd returned to his phone. I'm sure he was tracking us out of the corner of his eyes. He seemed too smart to let us wander around without keeping some kind of tabs on us.

I wondered if he'd let Finn slip out from Uncle Phil's on purpose. Maybe he'd followed Finn somehow. But how, exactly? Then, a thought struck me. Maybe he'd followed *me*. I remembered Rickert leaning against my car at Phil's, weird expression on his face. Had he planted a GPS tracker on my car?

That would certainly explain how he knew we were at Thorpe's.

What's done was done. If we didn't get out of this alive, it wouldn't matter anyway.

I caught Finn's eyes from across the room and gave him a tiny nod. *Go time.*

I opened the mini-fridge and got a can of soda. Rickert looked over, and I held the can up in the air, as if I was toasting him. He didn't react, just frowned, and returned to his phone.

Finn started coughing. Rickert looked up again, and Finn kept coughing. Big, hacking coughs. He grabbed his chest, kept on coughing. Bent over at the waist, kept on coughing.

Rickert had his eyes locked on Finn. I inched closer to Rickert from behind.

Finn went down on one knee, coughing and gasping. William Shatner had nothing on him in the ham-it-up department.

I crept closer.

Now, Finn dropped to both knees. Suddenly, he stopped coughing and put his hands around his throat, signaling that he was choking. He must have really been holding his breath, because his face began to turn red.

Rickert stood. Tentatively. Probably trying to decide what to do. Save Finn, or just let him die? But if Rickert had wanted to kill us, he already would have.

Now or never. I sprang forward and bashed him on the back of the head with the soda. The can exploded in a fizzy shower of Coke. He whirled around, and I put my weight into it as I shoved him to the ground. Then I flipped the table over on top of him and kicked the chair in his direction. I didn't look to see if it connected.

"Run!" I yelled. Finn was already halfway out the door. I raced after him. Outside, Finn darted right, and I slanted left. We'd decided it would be wiser to split up once we got outside. Rickert might be able to catch one of us, but it would be much harder to get both of us.

Whoever made it out first would call for help.

Not a sophisticated plan, but we didn't have much experience escaping assassins.

I dashed along the long side of the warehouse, away from Rickert's car. I figured it was probably about half a mile to the nearest road and another half mile to a road with enough traffic so I could flag down a motorist quickly.

I glanced behind me. Finn was already out of sight; he'd sped around the near corner of the warehouse—the short side. But Rickert was coming out, and when he spotted me, he came tearing my way. "Stop, goddammit," he yelled. I noticed he hadn't yet pulled his weapon.

I turned and ran, rounding the far corner of the warehouse, looking for a place with some cover. Every building in the warehouse park looked similar. Blocky construction. One story. Industrial doors and loading docks and very few windows. These places were built for functionality, not aesthetics.

I sped across an access road and cut between two buildings. My quads hurt—I wasn't in terrible shape, but I certainly wasn't used to sprinting full-out. I'd gone about ten yards when I noticed it wasn't a road that I'd turned into. It was a dead end. Simply a driveway that terminated at a loading dock. Evidently, eighteen-wheelers would back up and unload here.

I was trapped. If Rickert caught me here, I was a dead man.

I reversed course and tore back the way I came, needing to get out of this dead-end before Rickert came along.

When I reached the end of the loading area, I stopped and peeked around the corner.

Rickert was about forty feet away and heading in my direction.

Shit!

If I ran, he'd be on me in no time. Either that, or he'd shoot me in the back.

I reversed course again and retreated to the loading dock. It was four or five feet off the ground. The adjacent metal staircase was bent and had twisted away from the platform—as if a truck had mauled it somehow, so there was only one way to go. Up.

Hopefully, I'd be able to gain access to the building somehow, although the rolltop door was closed. Was there another door?

I took a running start and leaped up, grabbing onto the edge of the loading dock and kicking my feet up. I managed to haul myself up onto the deck, suffering only a barked shin on the metal edge.

I ran over to the pedestrian door and tried the knob. Locked.

I glanced back at the mouth of the alley. No Rickert.

I bent over and yanked on the strap of the rolltop door. Didn't budge.

Out of time. I ducked behind a stack of pallets and other packing debris. I tugged an old tarp over my head. Not a very good hiding place, but I'd have to make do. Hopefully, Rickert would see this was a dead end and figure I wouldn't be stupid enough to get myself trapped here.

I didn't think Rickert could see me if he stood in the alley, but if he came closer, he might be able to hear my pulse pounding or me gasping for breath.

I strained to hear him approach, hoping I'd notice the crunch of gravel or the scuffing of a shoe on the asphalt. I examined my cramped hidey-hole for something I could use as a weapon. There was a strip of aluminum, but it was too flimsy. Behind it, though, was a length of wood. Part of a two-by-four?

It would make a decent club, if it came to that.

I prayed it wouldn't come to that.

A club was no match for a gun.

Chapter Thirty-Eight

Ten seconds passed. Then twenty. I considered peeking around the mound of trash I hid behind, but I didn't want to risk making a sound if something shifted, nor did I want to get spotted. So I waited, nerves jangling.

Finally, I heard something in the alley. It sounded like it was right below me. I got a better grasp on the piece of wood. In my mind, I choreographed my movements if he tried to look up here. Realistically, he'd have to do what I did—climb up onto the loading dock—if he wanted to see me. And if he did, he'd probably have to use both hands. Which meant he wouldn't be holding his gun.

I tried to calculate if I could smack him with my club before he realized what was happening. After surprising him with the can of soda, I didn't think I'd be able to get lucky again.

"Hopkins. I saw you run down this alley, and there's only one place to hide. So get your ass down here. I've already got your cousin, and if you don't cooperate, I might have to take it out on him." Rickert's disembodied voice floated up to me from below.

Finn had a head start and was running in the opposite direction, so I was reasonably sure Rickert was bluffing about catching him. But with Finn, you never really knew what the score was. Either way, Rickert had a gun and was less than ten feet away.

I kept quiet, hoping Rickert was bluffing about knowing I was up here.

"Maybe I should just fire into that pile of crap."

A stack of old decaying pallets wouldn't stop a bullet, that was for sure.

I hefted my wooden club. Swallowed. "Okay, okay. I'm here. Don't shoot. I'll come down."

Gunshots were loud, and even though we were isolated, you never knew who might hear them, especially with a loud echo off the warehouse walls. Acoustics were funny. If I had to bet, I'd say Rickert would rather kill me in a quieter, more discreet way.

Slowly, I stepped out from behind the stack of pallets, keeping the club at my side, hidden by my leg. Rickert stood about five feet away from the loading dock platform, gun aimed at me.

I noticed movement behind him, and my heart skipped a beat or three. Finn was hustling our way, running as quietly as he could.

He wielded some kind of weapon, too. A piece of metal pipe.

"Hands on top of your head, Hopkins," Rickert said.

I let go of the piece of wood, and it thumped hollowly on the loading dock platform. Then, I put my hands on my head, as instructed. "There's no need for that. I'll come willingly. You're supposed to be protecting us, remember?"

"Yeah, yeah. Just keep your hands where I can see them and get down here."

"How do I know you won't shoot me?" I stalled. Finn was almost within striking distance.

"I *will* shoot you, if you don't cooperate. And Finn, too."

"I wish I knew what this was all about," I said, trying not to look over Rickert's shoulder and give Finn away.

Finn was ready to pounce. He raised his length of pipe then brought it crashing down on Rickert, catching him in the side of the head. He went down, and his gun clattered to the ground. I leaped off the platform as Finn kept whacking him with the pipe. I scooped up Rickert's gun, but before I could say anything, the air filled with an ear-piercing scream, and Rickert grabbed his shin. "You broke my leg, goddamn it!"

His lower leg bent at a very weird angle.

Finn stepped back, still wielding the pipe. When he saw that I held the gun, he relaxed a bit. "Got him," Finn said, breathing hard. "We got him."

"Yeah, we did." I pointed the gun at Rickert. "Tell us what's going on."

"You idiots broke my leg, that's what. I was hired to protect you, and you went off and attacked me. Your uncle is not going to like that." He closed his eyes, grimacing.

So Rickert was sticking to the story. "I don't buy it. You're in on Claypool's murder. You shot Thorpe, and you killed both of those other guys. They were working for you, weren't they?"

He cracked one eye open. "You two are going to be sorry."

Finn and I exchanged glances. Now what? "Where's your phone?" I asked Rickert.

"Go to hell."

I considered our options. "Finn, check his pockets."

Finn bent over and patted Rickert down. "No phone, but I got these." He held up Rickert's car keys and a handful of industrial-strength zip ties.

"Planning on tying up somebody?" I asked.

Rickert stared a laser beam at me.

Without taking my eyes—and the gun—off Rickert, I spoke to Finn. "You were supposed to get help."

"I circled the warehouse, then saw you head down here. Rickert was following, so I figured you might need some help yourself," Finn said.

"Well, thanks." I nodded at Rickert on the ground. "We can't just leave him here. I need to call Ostervale."

"You could give me the gun, and I could stay with him while you go make the call. Maybe his phone is back at the safe house," Finn said.

It was now obvious Rickert wasn't the one calling the shots. If he had been, and he wanted us dead, he would have already killed us. Most likely, he was waiting on an order from somebody. But what if that somebody showed up here to give the order in person? If Rickert didn't check in sometime, that seemed a likely prospect.

Giving the gun to Finn didn't seem like a good option. I didn't want to put him in the position of having to shoot anyone. Of course, I didn't want to be in that position either, but I thought I could handle the situation better than Finn. Besides, people were after Finn, and leaving him alone didn't strike me as a good idea. "How about we zip-tie him to the metal staircase? He won't be able to escape, and even if he did, he's got a busted leg. Then both of us can stay together. If we can't find his phone, we can drive to get help."

Finn nodded, clearly relieved. "Sounds like a plan."

We zip-tied Rickert to the gnarled metal staircase, ignoring his impressively creative use of every cuss word in the book, in addition to a few I'd never heard before.

With Rickert neutralized, Finn and I jogged back toward the safe house. When we reached the parking lot, we spotted another car parked next to Rickert's, a big black Suburban. I grabbed Finn's arm and tugged him into an alcove by the entrance to another unit, out of sight. "Someone else is here. No doubt one of Rickert's cohorts." I hadn't explicitly told Finn about my theory, and I wondered how much he'd guessed on his own. "You do know that Rickert is associated with the guys who tried to kill you. And that Rickert would have killed us if given the order, right?"

Finn nodded. "I figured we were in deep shit. You think this new arrival is the man in charge?"

"I'd bet on it."

"What are we going to do?" Finn asked.

That was the question. Hopefully, the cops could get Rickert to flip on whoever was really in charge. If we stuck around here, trying to be heroes, things were bound to go south. I mean, Finn and I were not rough-and-tumble types, despite what we'd managed to do to Rickert. As tempting as it sounded to hang around and play cowboy, it would be a foolish decision. And possibly a deadly one. For us.

"We're going to get the hell out of here and notify the proper authorities."

"You mean, call the cops?" Finn asked.

"Exactly."

We bumped fists.

I peered around the corner. The car was still there. I couldn't tell if it was occupied, but I had to assume the big boss had already gone into the unit and found it empty. After he saw the overturned table and chair—along with the demolished can of soda on the floor—he probably assumed there had been some sort of struggle. What would I have done if I was in his shoes?

I'd try calling Rickert. If he did, and if Rickert's phone was still there, he'd have more evidence of an incident. Suppose the guy assumed what really had happened? Namely, that Finn and I had escaped, and Rickert had chased us. Then he'd probably search the entire area. Maybe he'd call for reinforcements first.

Which meant we didn't have much time.

Where had this guy gone? Was he still in the unit, waiting for more foot soldiers? Or was he out and about, scouring the industrial park?

The longer we waited, the more opportunity we gave him to spot us.

I told Finn what the plan was: Sprint to Rickert's car. Get out of there. Simple, yet harrowing. "One. Two. Three. Go!"

We took off as if we were launched from a bazooka. Straight for Rickert's car. I had the keys in one hand and Rickert's gun in the other. I ran as if my life depended on it, and it may have. Next to me, Finn kept pace.

Rickert had backed in, so the driver's side was closest to us. Ten yards from the car, I hit unlock on the key fob, and it beeped. Hit it again so the passenger side would unlock, too. I yanked Rickert's car door open and dove in. Seconds later, Finn threw open his door and clambered inside.

From behind, a yell. Had it come from somewhere within the unit?

I hit the Start button, but nothing happened. All the cars I'd owned still required a key in the ignition to start. It took me a moment to realize I needed to have my foot on the brake before I pressed the button.

Someone banged on the trunk. I glanced in the mirror and saw a guy standing behind the car, aiming a gun at the rear window. Gesturing at us. The bottom dropped out of my stomach.

"Duck!" I screamed at Finn, then ducked myself. Foot on the brake, I hit the Start button, and the engine roared to life. But I hesitated. If we took off, this guy could escape, and we may never know who killed Claypool. And Finn may never have peace, knowing people were out to kill him.

This had to end, now.

Keeping my head down, I jammed the gear selector into Reverse and stomped on the gas, turning the steering wheel slightly to aim where I'd last seen the guy with the gun.

Gunshots boomed, and glass shattered, followed by a disconcerting thud. I kept my foot mashed on the gas pedal until the car hit something solid. The warehouse wall.

There was screaming, lots of screaming, and it didn't all come from me and Finn.

Chapter Thirty-Nine

The impact snapped my neck back, but I was otherwise uninjured. A quick glance at Finn told me he was okay, too, if a bit shaken.

I leapt from the car, holding the gun I'd taken from Rickert. The mystery man was pinned against the warehouse wall, dazed, confused, and clearly injured in some fashion. He'd dropped his weapon, and I darted over to pick it up.

"How bad are you hurt?"

He grunted something, but he was barely conscious. I glanced around in case this guy had a buddy. Finn had gotten out, too, and I handed him the goon's gun. Then I jumped back into the car and eased it forward to release the guy. He slumped to the ground with another grunt. "Keep him covered. I'm going to see if there's anyone else inside."

Before I got the chance, someone came charging out of the doorway. Short. Long hair. Female. She feigned right, then bolted left. Trying to escape. Three quick steps, and I'd corralled her. I spun her around to face me.

I'd seen her before.

Danielle Sakai.

First, my mind went blank, completely blank. Then, the vacuum filled with a billion thoughts, some logical, some contradictory.

Danielle Sakai?

Danielle was the one who'd ordered Claypool's murder? I thought back to when I was in her office and mused about her murdering the boss to move up into the corner office. Had I picked up on some micro expression she'd displayed? Things now made sense. She'd had Long and Porter eliminate

Claypool; then she'd fed us misinformation to throw the suspicion onto Jimbo Young. She'd had her hired gun Rickert shoot the two guys who'd murdered Claypool, covering her tracks.

And now she'd come here to finish things off under her direct supervision. The control freak who had to be there for the grand finale to ensure it all went according to her wishes.

I held onto her, and she didn't struggle, just mumbled some kind of personal mantra, the same one, over and over. *Lord, give me strength.*

She was going to need it. You needed to be strong to survive in prison.

* * *

A week later, Lia and I sat in my Corolla parked in Izzy's driveway. We were there for a family dinner, but before we got out to face my often-overwhelming kin, I had something I needed to say. I faced Lia in the passenger seat and took her hands in mine.

"Lia. I owe you a big apology."

"You sure do." She smiled, and the scar on her chin winked at me. "What for?"

"For not giving your career the weight it deserves. I was dismissive that night, and—"

"What night?"

She was messing with me. Although we hadn't directly referenced that night since it happened, I was acutely aware of the fact it stood between us like some kind of gauzy divider. Thin, but present. "Funny. I'm trying to apologize here."

"Sorry." She waved her hand with a royal flourish. "Continue."

"Your job—your mission—is extremely important. To you, to society, to me. And you're really, really good at it." After Finn and I had exposed Danielle Sakai, Lia had written a series of articles detailing what had happened and why. Newspapers across the country had picked up the series, and she'd even gotten a couple of job offers from bigger papers in other cities.

"Thank you, Mess. I appreciate you saying so." She leaned over and kissed me.

"Well, it's the truth."

Lia arched one eyebrow. "You just want some make-up sex."

"Not *just*."

"We'll see. After this dinner with your family, I'm bound to be exhausted."

She had that right.

* * *

We went inside, and the entire family was already there. Russell and Izzy were busy putting the last touches on dinner. Emma and Olivia huddled on the floor in the corner, bent over something on a tablet. Uncle Phil, Aunt Vera, and Finn were in the living room having what seemed like a regular conversation. No yelling, no pouting, no histrionics.

Weird.

Lia already knew Finn, of course, and she'd met Uncle Phil once. I introduced her to the others, and pretty soon, everyone was having a grand ol' time.

The good feelings continued straight through dinner, and, honestly, I was having a bit of trouble reconciling tonight's dinner with every other family dinner over the years. This meal was actually pleasant. Lia was going to think I was crazy for spending fifteen minutes on the drive over, warning her about everyone's quirks and biases.

Before dessert got served, I caught Finn's eye and motioned him to join me away from the table, in the adjoining room. "Listen, man. I'm so happy things seem to be going well between you and your parents."

"Yeah, me too. I didn't really think we'd ever get to this point, and I'm feeling very optimistic."

"I'm glad Thorpe is recovering. Do you think you'll still...?"

"Naw, it's over between us. Still friends, though." Finn grabbed me in a tight hug. "You saved me, Mess. I want you to know that I wouldn't be standing here without you. I love you, always."

CHAPTER THIRTY-NINE

"I love you too, Finn."

Our mutual lovefest was interrupted by the clang of a knife tapping the side of a glass in the other room. Finn and I returned to the table as everyone quieted down. I grabbed Lia's hand under the table and squeezed. She squeezed back, and I was glad that we'd made up.

Uncle Phil stood at the head of the table, as if he was about to deliver a speech. Maybe I'd declared tonight's dinner a victory too early.

"I'd like to say a few words, if that's okay," he said.

Everyone nodded, of course. What else were we going to do?

"First, I'd like to thank Benjamin and his friend Lia for helping keep Finn safe. I can't tell you how much Vera and I owe you." Phil nodded graciously in our direction.

"Hear, hear," Izzy said.

Phil cleared his throat. "Vera and I also want to express how ecstatic we are that Finn has returned. And how proud we are of him for getting clean and on the right path. We've discussed some of our past issues, and while we may never be able to forget what has happened, we're hopeful we can move forward from a place of love and understanding." He looked over at Finn, and I couldn't remember the last time I'd seen Phil this happy.

I also couldn't remember feeling this happy myself in a long, long time.

Aunt Vera served dessert, and Uncle Phil sat, but he continued to natter on, about how great families were, about how hard his own parents worked, about striving to achieve one's legacy. Or some such crap meant to be motivational. I tuned him out, thoughts drifting back to the last several weeks.

After Danielle Sakai and Lanny Rickert were arrested, things came into focus. A bang-up investigation—spearheaded by Lia herself—uncovered a behind-the-scenes falling-out between Danielle Sakai and Webster Claypool. In response, Claypool was about to kick Danielle to the curb and replace her with his nephew, whose only business experience consisted of running a lawn-mowing service when he was in college.

Obviously, that didn't sit well with the uber-ambitious and uber-qualified Danielle, so she hired a couple of freelance security guys who'd done some work for Claypool in the past, Kyle Long and Nubs Porter. She figured they could get close to him without sending up any red flags, and she was right. But Claypool's murder left Finn as a witness, and Danielle couldn't abide any loose ends, so she ordered Long and Porter to eliminate him, too. Then, as I had correctly guessed, she gave Lia that bogus information to throw the blame on Jimbo Young.

One thing hadn't made sense to me. How had Danielle's fixer, Rickert, come to work for Uncle Phil? As part of her investigation, Lia figured it out. In what turned out to be a stroke of good fortune for Danielle, Phil had put out a request for bodyguard references on a local business executive listserv—one which she also belonged to. Danielle had seized the opportunity, giving a glowing recommendation to Rickert, and Phil had taken the bait.

Rickert flipped and spilled his guts. He'd killed the two assassins, Long and Porter, per Danielle's orders, making it all look legit in the skirmish at Thorpe's. Danielle wanted Rickert to kill me and Finn, too, but he was worried that he'd be implicated—after all, Vell had seen Rickert whisk me and Finn away from Thorpe's.

To put Rickert at ease, Danielle hired a hitman from Baltimore—the man with the gun I'd rammed with the car—and they were planning to stage an ambush at the safe house to make it look like Rickert was trying to protect us when we got killed in the crossfire.

Danielle and Rickert won't be hurting anyone again.

"Hey, Uncle Mess!" Olivia and Emma shouted together. They were both sitting on their knees in the same chair right across from me.

I snapped out of it. "Huh? What?"

They pointed at the slice of cake on my plate. "Are you going to eat that?" they asked in unison.

"Cake? Ooh, gross. Who likes cake?"

"We do!"

I slid my plate over to them. "Then will you eat mine?"

"Sure!"

I glanced over at Izzy, who frowned at me.

I shrugged. What were uncles for, anyway?

* * *

When Lia and I got back to the motel, I discovered I had a text from Cesar, about an hour old. *Please come to the office. There's an envelope for you.*

What now? If it wasn't important, Cesar would have waited until morning. "I'll be back in a few minutes. Got to check on something."

"Go ahead. I'll get comfortable." Lia's scar implored me to hurry up.

I left Lia in my room, then strode across the parking lot to the Inn's office. I opened the door, the bell jangled, and a man—actually a teen—popped up from behind the registration desk.

"May I help you?" he asked.

"Who the heck are you?" Had Cesar hired someone without my knowledge?

"I could ask you the same question," he replied, tone challenging.

"I'm Mess Hopkins. I own this place."

He snorted. "I don't think so."

"Well, technically, my parents still own it. But I run it."

"No, I don't think you're Mess Hopkins."

"Well, I am."

He eyed me. "Are you sure? Because according to Fareed, Mr. H is disorganized, disheveled, and barely able to function at times. You don't seem like that."

Um, thanks? "You know Fareed?"

He stood a little taller. "He's my older brother. He wasn't feeling well and didn't want to leave you in the lurch, so he asked me to fill in. I'm Bakir."

"Hello, Bakir." I took another look at him. Seemed kinda young. "How old are you, anyway?"

"How old do you have to be to work here?"

Never mind. "Did somebody train you on what to do?"

"Absolutely. Cesar spent, like, ten minutes going over everything."

"Well, then, I guess you know all there is to know about the hospitality industry," I said.

"And then some." He flashed another smile, and I could definitely see the resemblance to his brother.

Enough nonsense. "Is there an envelope with my name on it back there?"

He nodded. "Well, if you know about the envelope, then I guess you really are Mr. H. Please don't fire Fareed because of our tiny misunderstanding. Please? He really, really, really likes working here."

"Relax, I'm not firing anybody." I smiled back at him. "You love your brother, don't you?"

"Of course," he said. "I love my entire family."

Yeah, me too.

He handed me the envelope. "Here you go, Mr. H."

I stepped away from the registration desk and tore open the envelope. Inside were a handwritten note and a check. The note read:

> *To Mess,*
>
> *Thanks for everything you did to help Finn, and thanks for everything you're doing to help the community. You're a special guy. Please accept this donation to keep your place going for a while.*
>
> *And thanks for your discretion.*

It was signed *Tim T.*

I looked at the check from Thorpe and felt myself beaming.

So many zeroes!

* * *

When I got back to the room, Lia was sound asleep.

Acknowledgements

Many, many people contributed to this final product, directly and indirectly. Without them, this story would still be rattling around in my head. And nobody wants that.

My sincerest thanks go to:

The great folks (and good friends) at Level Best Books: my editor extraordinaire Verena Rose, uber-talented cover designer Shawn Reilly Simmons, and the super-efficient Deb Well.

The many readers and critique partners I've worked with through the years: Dan Phythyon and Ayesha Court. Dorothy Patton. Mark Skehan. Doug Bell. John Stevenson, Jill Balboni, Kim Stevenson, and Samantha Stevenson. Andy Heyman, Todd Hall. Lorraine Storms. Fred Rexroad. Tara Laskowski. Barb Goffman. John Betancourt, Carla Coupe, Bonner Menking, Adam Meyer, Megan Plyler. Ed Aymar. Eric Smith.

The Rumpi: Donna Andrews, Ellen Crosby, John Gilstrap, and Art Taylor. Amazing writers and friends.

Kenneth Creech for his astute sensitivity read.

My awesome crime fiction community: Mystery Writers of America, International Thriller Writers, and Sisters in Crime. My pals throughout cyberspace.

The P.J. Parrish sisters (Kris Montee and Kelly Nichols), Reed Farrel Coleman, Elaine Raco Chase, Jeff Deaver, Jim Grady, Hank Phillippi Ryan, Lori Rader-Day, Eli Cranor. Supportive teachers, mentors, and blurbers!

Booksellers, librarians, and, of course, my faithful readers.

My terrific, terrific agent, Michelle Richter, and the entire group at Fuse Literary.

My extended family.

My parents, for everything.

My children, Mark and Stuart, and my wife, Janet. My inspirations—in fiction and in life.

Thanks everyone!

Previously Published Works

Novels

Diamonds for the Dead, Midnight Ink 2010 (Agatha Award Finalist)

Killer Routine, Midnight Ink 2011

Deadly Campaign, Midnight Ink 2012

The Taste, 2011

First Time Killer, 2012

Ride-Along, 2013

Running From the Past, Kindle Press/Amazon Publishing, 2015

Pray for the Innocent, Kindle Press/Amazon Publishing, 2018 (ITW Thriller Award Winner)

I Know Where You Sleep, Down & Out Books, February 2020 (Shamus Award Finalist)

I Play One On TV, Down & Out Books, July 2021 (Agatha Award Winner, Anthony Award Winner)

Sanctuary Motel, Level Best Books, October 2023

Short Stories

(50+ including one in five consecutive *Best New England Crime Stories* anthologies).

Notable ones:

"Rule Number One" appeared in *Snowbound* and was selected for *Best American Mystery Stories 2018*.

"Dying in Dokesville" appeared in *Malice Presents: Mystery Most Geographical* and won a Derringer Award.

"Rent Due" appeared in *Mickey Finn: 21st Century Noir, Vol. 1* and won an ITW Thriller Award.

About the Author

Alan Orloff has published twelve novels and more than fifty short stories. His work has won an Anthony, an Agatha, a Derringer, and two ITW Thriller Awards. He's also been a finalist for the Shamus Award and has had a story selected for *The Best American Mystery Stories* anthology. He loves cake and arugula, but not together. Never together. He lives and writes in South Florida, where the examples of hijinks are endless. www.alanorloff.com

SOCIAL MEDIA HANDLES:
   https://www.facebook.com/alanorloff
   https://twitter.com/alanorloff
   https://www.instagram.com/alanorloff/
   https://www.threads.net/@alanorloff

AUTHOR WEBSITE:
   www.alanorloff.com